BALLBUSTER

A Playing Dirty Sports Romance
By Lane Hart

COPYRIGHT

This book is a work of fiction. The characters, incidents, and dialogue were created from the author's imagination and are not to be construed as real. Any resemblance to actual people or events is coincidental.

The author acknowledges the copyrighted and trademarked status of various products within this work of fiction.

Edited by Angela Snyder

Cover by Beetiful Book Covers

WARNING: THIS BOOK IS INTENDED FOR MATURE AUDIENCES 18+ ONLY. THE STORY CONTAINS ADULT LANGUAGE AND EXPLICIT SEX SCENES.

Chapter One

Kohen Hendricks

Forget days, hours, or even minutes. The defining moments of my life have always been measured in seconds. To most people, seconds are inconsequential, too small and insignificant to count. Yet, if you string a few together, it could be the difference in winning or losing, being the hero or a chump, finding a place in the history books or being completely forgotten.

Football stadiums aren't the only place where everything can change in a matter of seconds, but that's exactly where I was when my life was forever altered.

It was a scorching hot July morning, the first day of pre-season and a brand new year ahead of the Wilmington Wildcats. A clean slate. Time to forget last year when we went fourteen and two, all the way to the playoffs where we lost horribly in the first round. This is the time of year when all thirty-two teams in the league are pumped up, hopeful for a winning season. All of us are starting out with zero losses before going head-to-head for seventeen weeks to see who has what it takes to win the playoffs and ultimately lift the championship trophy in February.

"Now, listen closely, ladies," Coach Griffin, a small, yet powerful man of few words, says from where he paces in front of the gigantic PowerPoint screen in our stadium auditorium. As soon as he wraps up our first team meeting of the season, we'll all get in our cars and drive south down the highway to the campus of Pender University in South Carolina. The school will host seven grueling days of training camp. This is the part I dread most every year, the hours of standing around under the sweltering summer sun. As the team's starting placekicker, my conditioning drills are much easier than most of the guys, so I really shouldn't complain.

"There's one last important announcement to make before we hit the road," Coach continues. "We're adding a new player to the roster today; and by doing so, making history. Now, I want you to understand how important it is for each of you to maintain a high level of respect and dignity this season. Every media organization across the country will be watching and waiting to see how you handle yourselves. You will not, and I repeat, *you will not* disgrace this team in any way, shape or form or you will find yourself watching the action from the front row seat of your couch. Do you understand?"

The room of typically big, boisterous, obnoxious men falls silent since none of us know what the fuck Coach is going on about.

"I'm gonna reveal your new teammate on the screen behind me, and then you'll have fifty-nine seconds to get every single idiotic comment, whistle, or any other juvenile sounds out of your systems. This is your one and *only* chance to comment; because if you want to continue to play for this team, you'll sign the contract addendums Coach Bradley is handing out. You'll keep your trap shut and hands off for the rest of the season. Are you ready?" he asks.

A few murmurs of agreement rise from the crowd before Coach finally clicks the mouse in his hand. Instead of diagrams of circles and arrows, there's now a photo of a gorgeous blonde woman wearing nothing but a black sports bra and tiny matching shorts taking up the space of the entire wall.

"Holy fuck," I mutter aloud, but it's drowned out by the other catcalls and various curses being made by my teammates. I can't take my eyes away from the stunner before me. Her hair is so light it almost looks white in the bright sun perfectly contrasting with her smooth, tan skin. The fact that she has big, round, innocent green eyes with the tall, curvy body of a centerfold makes her even more intriguing. In fact, I realize that I'm no longer slouching in my seat but leaning forward with my elbows digging into my knees, trying to get a closer look to catalog every inch of this unknown woman.

"All right, time's up," Coach grumbles before the screen goes blank. A disgruntled masculine chorus fills the auditorium before Coach continues on. "Her name is Roxanne Benson, and she's gonna be Kohen's backup."

Hearing my name, I sit up straight, startled out of my hypnotic state of arousal. Wait, what did he just say?

"You'll all get a chance to meet Roxanne later tonight, and I want you to make her feel welcome. That means not uttering a single sexist comment. You will treat her like your sister and any other teammate, which means you *do not* lay a finger on her."

"*Kohen*," my best friend and the team's tight end, Lathan Savage, whispers from the seat to my right. When I glance over, I realize he's trying to hand me a stack of papers. I take one from the top and pass the rest down the row to my left.

"I'll read the important bits of the addendum aloud since I know some of you struggle with reading comprehension," Coach says before he pulls his bifocals down from the top of his head and goes through the list of cock-blocking rules. When he's finished, it's clear that not only will any inappropriate physical contact with Roxanne get you kicked off the team, but any offensive comments will also do the trick.

"Remember, this is history being made, gentlemen. Don't go down in the hall of shame as the dipshit who lost a contract worth millions of dollars because you decided to think with your dick instead of your brain," Coach warns us. "Send a copy to your agent, manager or mommy, whoever the fuck needs to approve it, and then sign it and turn it in when you check in this afternoon at Pender. See you then and have a safe drive."

"You lucky bastard," Lathan says with a punch to my shoulder as we get to our feet like the rest of our teammates. "If she can kick as good as she looks, you're in trouble, though."

"Whathefuckever," I mutter, folding the paper into quarters and then eighths until it fits into the pocket of my black nylon shorts. "I'm the third best kicker in the league, so there's no way she'll be better than me."

"You better hope not. Your contract's up for an extension renewal at the end of the season, right?" Lathan asks as we move down the stairs with the flow of big, beefy men leaving the auditorium.

"I'm not worried," I tell him, knowing my position as the starter is secure. "She's nothing more than a publicity stunt."

"We'll see," he says with a grin. "So you wanna carpool with Quinton and me up to Pender?"

"Sure," I agree. "Let me take the Audi home and get packed. Pick me up in an hour?"

"Make it thirty minutes. Quinton and I have a quick captain's meeting; then we want to try and get a head start on the road," Lathan says with a fist bump after I agree. Leaving him, I take off to the parking lot since I need to hurry home to pack.

On the way out of the stadium, all I can think about is that photo of the blonde bombshell. The woman was so goddamn mesmerizing that I worry the image of her has been branded into my brain and may never fade. And I'm not sure that I want it to. In fact, needing to see her face and her various other physical attributes again to determine if she's that hot or if the photo was an aberration, I pull out my phone and type Roxanne Benson into the search engine. I want to know more about this girl who's gonna be my backup. Is she gonna be a threat to my contract extension?

That's my last thought before my legs are suddenly knocked out from under me harder than a defensive lineman's chop block. After my back slams into something so hard the air is knocked out of my lungs, I go sailing through the air for several heartbeats before my palms fly out, bracing my fall and keeping my face from smashing into the abrasive pavement.

Pain radiates through my left knee that took the majority of the impact, and I definitely heard it make a god-awful popping noise. Fucking hell it hurts!

From my army crawl formation, I turn my head and make out what appears to be the fender of a black SUV, tires screeching it to a stop just inches away from my eyelashes. And with this unexpected accident, I know that after five years, the brakes were probably just slammed on my entire fucking football career.

Chapter Two

Roxanne Benson
Three hundred seconds earlier…

With every mile I put between Newtown, Tennessee and me, I'm feeling a little lighter. The bumps along the highway represent all the assholes who told me I couldn't hack it on our high school football team; that I would never score a point in college; that I should pick up a pair of pompoms and shake my ass if I wanted to step foot on a professional field. There's always been someone telling me I can't, which only made me want to work that much harder to prove them wrong.

The sign on the side of the road welcomes me to Wilmington, and I flip all the asshole naysayers behind me and ahead of me the proverbial middle finger because this is it. My lifelong dream is finally coming true! It hasn't always been easy, and there were several times I wanted to quit over the years. I thought for sure there was no chance I would ever make it on a professional team since I didn't get invited to the scouting combine in February. But giving up is exactly what all the haters wanted me to do, so I pushed through and kept practicing and working out even when it meant sacrificing my social life. My manager encouraged me to stay in top shape after my senior year of college ball ended while she continued hounding a few teams, and thank fuck I listened to her. Thinking of never being able to play the sport I love again was terrifying.

Growing up without a mother but with a football coach for a father, I've been a tomboy pretty much all my life. Watching football with my dad either on the sidelines or on television has always been one of my favorite pastimes. At least until I started playing flag football when I was six years old, and then in seventh grade when I got to put on a real jersey, actually getting to play for my junior high school team. Even though I wanted to be a wide receiver, the coaches wouldn't put me in at that position or any other contact position, for that matter. The best I could do was to be the extra point placekicker. Eventually in high school, as my leg strength improved, I was the team's starting placekicker for everything, including long distance field goals as well as the punter.

It hasn't always been easy being the only player on the football team without balls. The girls in school hated me for the attention the guys gave me, and the guys...well, they only saw me as a piece of ass, never as a serious competitor and definitely not as their equal.

College was pretty much more of the same but on a much bigger scale. Eventually, I learned to ignore the haters and let the sexist comments roll off my back. It helped that I started standing up for myself instead of slinking away like a coward, letting the hagglers think they were getting to me. I embraced the nickname "Ballbuster" instead of being embarrassed by the reason I earned it in my sophomore year of high school. I've also learned that proving myself on the field is the best strategy to make them shut their mouths.

So now I'm wondering what exactly the professional level has in store for me. My agent and manager, Winona Jones, will be meeting with the owner, manager and me today to finish negotiating my big, fat contract. I pray that the players here will be more mature than in high school and college. And, sure, some people will continue to dislike me, now on a national level, but I refuse to let them bring me down. I'm doing what no other woman has ever done before, not only for me but for the little girls out there who want to play any professional sport with the big boys. So, I'm going to kick ass; or, more specifically, I'm going to kick the hell out of some fucking balls.

The Wilmington Wildcats' stadium is even more enormous than I expected as I roll up to the front gate. I've played in a few professional stadiums while I was in college and traveled to plenty with my dad, but this one seems like Goliath compared to all of those.

"Name?" the thick, balding guard in matching black shirt and pants asks me as I pull up to the gatehouse and lower the Jeep's window, breathing in the warm, salty scent of the nearby ocean.

"Roxanne Benson!" I practically exclaim, bouncing in my seat. "I'm gonna play for the Wildcats!"

The corner of the man's lips quirk up from beneath his mustache before he looks down at the list in front of him.

"Here's your parking pass, Miss Benson. Welcome to the team," he says, offering me the plastic placard for my rearview mirror. My hand shakes so badly that it takes me two attempts to accept the official representation that I'm really part of the team and get it hung on my mirror.

"Thank you, sir," I say, flashing the guard the biggest grin of my life as he presses the button to lift the arm, allowing me to drive into the parking lot.

To say I'm nervous would be a drastic understatement. My best friend and my dad both offered to come with me, or more like begged, but I made them stay home since showing up with a buddy or parental escort is not exactly how the first woman signed by a professional football team should start her career with the big boys. Besides, my dad has his own season to worry about. Although the private college he coaches is small, the team depends on him to keep up the winning streak they've been on for three years now. The pay isn't all that great, so he doesn't have the extra cash to spend on plane tickets.

Thankfully I'm about to sign a two-year, million-dollar contract, which will not only provide me with enough money to live on but will ease my dad's financial stress. It's the least I can do for all that he's sacrificed for me over the years, including up and moving us to Newtown my sophomore year after what the high school team did to me in White Falls.

Accelerating forward and brushing aside the reason I refuse to ever think twice about dating another teammate, I ease closer to the towering structure that lurks in the distance. The enormous parking lot is nearly empty since it's the summer and only players and staff are probably milling about inside the facility. But in just a few weeks, thousands of fans will fill the stadium, and I'll be down there on the field in the center of it all.

Not that I'll ever actually get a chance to play, but this is still one small step for womankind and all that. What's important is that I've made it onto the team! I'll get to wear a jersey with my name on the back. And maybe someday, in a few years, after the first and second-string kickers retire or get traded, they'll sign me as the first-string kicker, and I'll have a shot to prove my worth. Until then, I'll just work my ass off to become the best damn kicker ever while happily riding the bench of one of the best football teams in the league. God, I can't wait!

Thump!

My excitement shatters right along with the glass of my front windshield when something massive lands on the hood of my Jeep. I slam my foot down on the brake to stop and try to figure out what the fuck just happened, causing the large object to bounce off the hood.

And then the realization hits me.

Oh dear God!

No, no, no!

Shoving the gearshift into park, I undo my seatbelt and throw my door open to run around the front of the fender. That's where I find a dark-haired man plastered face down on the pavement.

"Oh shit!" I shriek. "Did I hit you?"

"No," the man groans. "I do pushups...in the parking lot. Motherfucker! Yes, you hit me!"

"It was an accident! I didn't see you!" I tell him.

Jeez, he's grumpy, but okay, I guess he's entitled to a bit of snippiness since I just ran him over. His face is pinched with pain as he rolls to his side, holding his knee that's awkwardly bent. Despite the less than stellar circumstances, I can't help but notice that he's young and handsome, the dark scruff along his jaw the same color as his damp, wavy, chocolate hair that's in need of a cut. Wearing a white tank top and black athletic shorts, it's obvious his body is long and lean with cuts of muscle up and down his powerful arms and legs, not enough fat to pinch. Although, I would need to see all the covered bits to be sure. That seems highly unlikely at the moment since he's muttering a string of curses, each one making me feel even worse, if that's possible. There's also something about him that seems familiar...

"Oh my God! Kohen?" I ask, kneeling down next to him in my jeans, both of my shaking hands covering my mouth as I get a closer look. This *cannot* be him! Without my permission, my right hand shoots out and sweeps his hair back from his forehead for a better look at his face, making him flinch. "Ah, fuck!" I groan. "You're Kohen Hendricks!"

No, no, no! Of all the people in the world, please tell me that I didn't just run over Kohen fucking Hendricks, the Wildcats' starting kicker!

"What the hell? You a crazy stalker or something?" he grits out between groans before he finally pushes himself up into a sitting position. His palms and legs are scraped bloody and heavily dusted in dirt and tiny pieces of gravel.

Again, I lose control of my motor functions. My fingertips start swiping at the debris embedded in his knees and the thick, powerful thighs revealed just below the hem of his shorts.

"Whoa, whoa, whoa," he mutters, wrapping his strong hand over the top of mine and yanking it up and away from his thigh to halt my forward progress. At the sudden, harsh contact, a gasp parts my lips, and I nearly choke on the excess oxygen when I glance up, my green eyes meeting his fiery melted chocolate and caramel swirled ones only inches away from mine. "Whoa," he repeats softer, deeper than the others, and holding a completely different meaning. The first utterings of the word I'm pretty sure he meant for me to stop touching him, but the last one sounded more like...astonishment. "You're her, the girl from the screen."

"I'm so...so sorry," I stammer, not sure if he hit his head too since he's talking nonsense. *Why, God, did I have to hit* him *today of all days?* I didn't even step foot into the stadium, and now I probably never will because no one is *ever* gonna believe this was an accident. Fate is one cruel jackass.

"You drive like shit," he says before lowering my hand that's still in his tight grip back down to his muscular thigh. Of all places in the universe he could've put it, why did he choose there? He doesn't let go. Instead, he squeezes the top of my hand as if for comfort, right before his eyes widen like a light bulb is going off in his head. An instant later he suddenly shoves my hand away like it's burned him while those narrowed dark eyes thin even more, glaring at me. "You conniving little bitch!"

My breath catches in my throat at the harsh insult. I've been called plenty of horrible things over the years; but for some reason, this man's words are more brutal than all the rest combined. The burning sensation behind my eyes reminds me that I've stupidly let my guard down.

"It was an accident," I repeat, although I know it's useless. He's already decided that I intentionally ran him over and won't be convinced otherwise.

"You said my name! You knew *exactly* who I was --- your competition!"

"How stupid would I have to be to run you over on purpose in front of the stadium of all places?" I point out.

"Yeah, Tonya Harding. You probably should've hired someone else to do your fucking dirty work," he sneers.

My jaw drops as indignation spreads through me, hardening my skin like armor. "Fuck you. It was an accident. Why did you walk out in front of my car?" I ask indignantly. "You ever heard of looking both ways?"

"Pedestrians always have the right-of-way!"

"Bullshit!" I screech while poking him in the center of his chest with my finger. Damn, it's firmer than a brick wall. "This...this..." Shit, what was I saying? Oh yeah. "This isn't a crosswalk, mister, so *pedestrians* have to watch where they're going!"

"Get your hands off me, Tonya!" he exclaims, grabbing my wrist. He holds it tightly in his grip and pins it to the pavement on the outside of his thigh, leaving me hovering over top of the asshole, my long, blonde hair falling forward like a curtain around me.

"Let me go, jackass," I tell him through clenched teeth while using my left hand to brush my hair back from my face.

"Why?" he asks, squeezing my wrist tighter. "So you can run before they figure out what you did?"

"I didn't do anything!" I shriek.

"Might want to work on your story," he leans forward and whispers. "Because it's not very convincing."

"It doesn't have to be convincing; it's the truth!"

"My word against yours. Who do you think they'll believe, Tonya?" he asks, raising one of his dark eyebrows. And fuck if it isn't sexy as hell, despite what a jerk he's being to me.

"Stop calling me Tonya. My name's Roxy. And hopefully, they'll be smart enough to believe *the truth*."

"I bet you're used to always getting your way, right? Flaunting your tits and ass to make men cater to your every whim," he says before his dark eyes dip down to the V-neck of my navy blue tee. Thanks to him, the front has fallen open because of the way he's forced me to lean over him. After taking a good long look, his dark eyes finally meet my gaze again.

"If a man's weak enough to succumb to my whims based on nothing but my tits and ass, then he's an idiot," I reply, vaguely noticing that his thumb is now stroking along the skin of my wrist. "The owner of your team and coaches aren't idiots."

"I sure hope not," he says while stealing another glance at my lacy, sky blue bra. When his melted candy bar eyes land on mine again, there's no longer the hint of pain reflected in them. Instead, they're full of desire, and I can't tear my eyes away. It's like there's an invisible chain tethering us, holding our gazes hostage. And despite how much I wish I could deny it, and how long I've refused to give any man, especially football players, a second thought, there's no ignoring the honest to God truth.

I want this infuriating man.

Chapter Three

Kohen

Is there some sort of freaky ass, twisted version of Stockholm syndrome for accident victims that I don't know about?

That must be what this is, because deep down I know I should abhor this woman who I'm certain ran over me on purpose. And yet, I still want to strip the jeans and t-shirt off of her and fuck her right here in the middle of the stadium parking lot, even with my knee radiating pain like a son of a bitch. Which only makes me hate her more for causing this insane, instant physical reaction that I've never felt for another woman before. I like to fuck just as much as any other twenty-seven-year-old single guy, but she's making me feel like I'm a desperate horny teenager.

"Yo, Kohen, you okay?" one of my teammates calls out. I'm not even sure who it is since I can't seem to look away from the big, bright emerald eyes of the scheming woman in front of me. "Shit! Someone get the trainers," the same person yells.

Roxanne was beautiful in the photo Coach showed us. In person, she's…breathtakingly gorgeous. I've seen her type before, though, the stuck-up, high-maintenance diva that will make a man walk barefoot through glass shards scattered on hot coals to touch her, and then in bed turn out to be nothing more than a frigid bitch in a stunning package.

During my second year, straight out of a stellar rookie season and signing a three-year contract with more zeros than I had ever seen before, I fell into the trap hook, line and sinker for Lola Davis, one of the fresh-faced Lady Cats. That's every man's wet dream, right, to be with a professional cheerleader who's not only incredibly flexible but has the stunning face of a Hollywood movie star? Lola turned out to be one helluva actress before I found out she was only working her way through the Wildcats' roster to reel in the biggest fish she could find. As the team's newest kicker, that certainly wasn't me.

"Jesus, what happened?" the voice I recognize as Lathan's asks, and then Roxanne and I are suddenly surrounded by a group of big ass, grumbling men.

Someone pulls Roxanne to her feet, out of my grasp and away from me. Then, like a school of fish, the entire group of men shifts with her, asking her if she's hurt, does she need anything, pissing me off even more.

What the fuck?

"Is this what it looks like?" Lathan asks quietly, crouching down next to me, his gaze roaming from the busted windshield on the SUV to my bloody palms and the gravel still lodged in the skin of my knees and shins.

"Yeah, Tonya Harding the sequel," I tell him with a sigh.

Finding my cell phone face down on the pavement, Lathan picks it up and studies it for a moment before offering it to me with a raised blond eyebrow. Once it's in my hand, I see the photo of Roxanne on the screen and remember what I was doing when I got hit. *Fuck.*

"Are you hurt other than scrapes? Dave's gone to get the trainer," he says rather than comment on the phone discovery.

"Just bumps and bruises except for my left knee that got busted up," I admit, slipping my phone into my shorts pocket. "I think I felt it pop."

"Shit," he grumbles, well aware that a knee injury could be season ending, if not career ending, depending on how bad it is. And my fucking contract is up at the end of the season. That means that however bad this shit is, I've got to get back on the field ASAP, or I'm out of a job, assuming Dane, my backup, can hack it. There's no way in hell the blonde bombshell, who's currently being eye-fucked by half the team, will be the starter. Sure, she's pretty and a great pick to be the team's feminist movement poster girl, but it takes more than a pretty face to nail a ball through the uprights under pressure.

"A little physical therapy and I'm sure I'll be good as new," I tell Lathan, hoping I'm right.

"What are they gonna do with her?" he asks, nodding to the new fan club.

"No clue."

"What happened, Kohen?" Jon, one of the trainer's asks as he kneels down next to me.

"She fucking hit me," I tell him. "And something in my left knee snapped."

"Goddamn it," he grumbles as he gently prods my swollen knee with his fingers, making it hurt even worse. "How fucking fast was she going?"

"I dunno. Fast enough that my feet left the ground," I answer honestly. It's nice to have someone indignant on my behalf.

"Hey, Ben, why don't you go pull the surveillance footage? I know Coach and Robert are gonna wanna see it," he says to one of the security guards standing around us who nods and heads back inside. "Can you straighten your leg all the way out?" Jon asks me while untying my left shoe and removing it and my sock.

"That's as low as it goes," I tell him, gesturing to the slight incline.

"I'm gonna move your foot around, so tell me if this hurts or if it feels numb," Jon says before pressing my toes back and then shifting them forward.

"That doesn't make it worse," I tell him.

"Good. We'll need to get an x-ray to make sure there are no breaks in the bone and probably an ultrasound to check the blood flow and arteries, but the movement of your foot is a positive sign that it may only be a minor dislocation."

I nod, biting my tongue to avoid asking him the burning question on my mind, *when will I be able to play?* Until all the tests are done, I knew he won't be able to tell me shit.

Chapter Four

Roxy

Great, for the rest of my days on Earth I'll be forever known as the Tonya Harding of football instead of the first woman of football. Maybe other athletes in the future who harm their own teammates will become Roxanne Bensons. No one under the sun will ever believe this was a complete and total accident.

"Don't worry, Roxanne. It was clearly an accident," Quinton Dunn, the Wildcats' quarterback, assures me with a squeeze of his huge mitt to my shoulder.

Wow. Okay, so there's one person who can see reason, and I'm totally fangirling right now.

"Of course it was an accident," another player chimes in, followed by masculine sounds of agreement.

Maybe Kohen was right, and I've managed to use my tits and ass to sway the tide to the truth. At this point, I'll take whatever I can get.

"You need to come with me," one of the security guards says gruffly, jerking me forward by my elbow like I'm under arrest. Oh God, maybe I am! Did Harding do time? Shit, I can't remember. Not that this is the same situation, but still…

"Jeez, man. Let up on her," I hear Quinton mutter behind me as my head hangs and my shoulders slump forward with the weight of guilt for not paying better attention. I was too caught up in the moment, in the excitement that I looked away for one fucking life-altering second!

"Can I at least get my purse from the car?" I ask the security guard.

"Make it quick and leave the keys," he tells me before letting go of my arm so I can go over to the passenger side of the Jeep. Opening the door, I reach in to grab my quilted hipster bag covered in bright flowers and ladybugs. It was supposed to be another good luck charm from my dad. As a former football player and now coach, he's big on superstitions and charms. He's been buying me lucky ladybug presents ever since my sixth birthday. Right after my mom left us, he wasn't sure what to buy a little girl, but he knew I loved ladybugs. I still do, but mostly just because all the gifts from my dad remind me that wherever I am, he's thinking about me. Slipping the bag over my head, I'm starting to wonder if this latest gift of his may be cursed instead of good luck.

On the way back to the front of the stadium, I see Kohen still sitting on the ground while an older man carefully exams his leg.

Biting my bottom lip, I try to keep the tears at bay following the guard inside. That's Roxy's Rule Number Two, and I refuse to break it. I promised myself that I would never, under any circumstances, let someone see me cry like a little bitch. I'm a football player, dammit. Or I had been, until a few moments ago when I may have lost everything I've ever worked for.

Once we're inside the stadium, I'm ushered onto a glass elevator to the upper floors and shown into a nice, plush waiting area with navy blue leather seats where I'm left to await my fate. Thankfully, Winona shows up soon after, the sound of her clicking heels preceding her.

"Hey, girl. You ready?" my excited manager asks with a smile. Today she's dressed to the nines in an expensive looking white suit with black trim, her dark hair pulled back elegantly and her black-rimmed glasses looking more like a trendy accessory than a necessity. She looks so happy that I hate to pop her bubble.

"I fucked up," I tell her from where I'm slumped in my cushy seat, clutching my purse to my stomach.

"What do you mean? You haven't even started practice," she says, sitting down in the seat next to me.

"Did you miss the circus going on out front, or have they already cleaned it up?" I ask.

"Wait," she says when she grabs my forearm. "That was *your* Jeep?"

"Uh-huh."

"Pedestrian?"

"Yep."

"Oh God. Who did you hit?"

"Kohen Hendricks."

"Mother of fuck," she groans to the ceiling before facing me again, her voice lowering to a whisper even though we're the only people in sight. "Was it an accident?"

"Of course it was!" I exclaim. "The worst mistake of my fucking life."

"Good. That's good," Winona replies, taking a deep breath. "All hope isn't lost. Yet."

"They're gonna boot me, aren't they?" I ask, my heart pounding out of control in my chest.

"I don't know. How bad is it?"

"No clue yet. Kohen, of course, thinks I'm an evil, plotting bitch," I tell her.

"Well, put yourself in his place. I can't say I blame him. You were supposed to be his backup."

Shit. The way she phrased that in the past tense tells me just how optimistic she is about my chances.

"Ms. Benson, Ms. Jones, please come on in and have a seat," Coach Griffin says when he opens the door to the conference room. The one he's been in with the owner of the team and other coaches and staff coming and going for over two hours, while Winona and I have been left to agonize over my fate. Winona occasionally offered words of encouragement; but by the way she's chewed on her manicured nails, she's been just as anxious to hear the decision. Apparently, a verdict has finally been reached, so we get to our feet even though my legs feel wobbly, and follow him into the room.

Inside, there's a long, rectangular glass table with three other men, all standing in front of their chairs.

"Roxanne Benson, Winona Jones, I'm Mark Griffin, the team's head coach. Meet Robert Wright, the Wildcats' owner, Kyle Bradley, my assistant coach, and Rob Sigmon, our special teams and kickers' coach. Everyone, this is Ms. Benson and her agent, Ms. Jones."

"Nice to finally meet you," I say first to Mr. Wright, shaking his offered hand before Winona and I go around the room and do the same with coaches Bradley and Sigmon.

"Roxanne, Winona, please have a seat," Mr. Wright says, gesturing to the two empty chairs to his right, and everyone follows suit. I sit down, clutching my messenger bag in my lap, feeling like I probably should've dressed nicer than jeans for this meeting.

Picking up a remote control, Mr. Wright points it at a flat screen, and then there's an eagle eye view of my black Jeep outside the front of the stadium. You can't see me inside of it from this angle, but you can see Kohen walk out the stadium doors. His head is bent over the phone in his hand, and he doesn't look up or pause before his feet step off the curb. Two seconds later, based on the time stamp at the bottom of the screen, we collide.

"Tell us what happened," Mr. Wright says, pausing the video.

"God, if I could press rewind and go back…" I start, staring longingly at the remote while blinking back more tears that threaten to spill. "I was so excited to finally be here. The guard gave me my parking pass, and then I was…overwhelmed as I looked up at the stadium in the distance, representing everything I've worked so hard for, and then *boom!*"

"Did you know who you hit?" Coach Bradley asks.

"Not at first; but when I got out to check on him, I knew when I saw his face."

"I'm sure you can understand our initial hesitancy…" Mr. Wright starts.

"Of course," I tell them. "It looks awful, like I did it on purpose, but I never saw him. I-I should've been paying attention, but the parking lot was so empty…I never thought someone would walk out in front of my car."

"You stayed with Kohen until the trainers arrived?" Coach Griffin asks.

"Yes. How…how is he?" I ask. When my eyes flit around the room, and all the men stay silent while wearing the same grimace, I know it's not good.

"His left knee was dislocated," Robert tells me.

"Oh God," I mutter, slapping a palm over my mouth.

"He may need surgery to repair the ligament damage. We're still waiting on the orthopedist to finish up all the tests. Either way, he's looking at a lot of physical therapy."

"So he's…he's not gonna get to play for a few weeks?" I ask, knowing how devastating that will be to the team. They depend on Kohen almost as much as they do Quinton, the star quarterback. The kicker is crucial to scoring points and winning games.

"Roxanne, Kohen could very well be out for the rest of the season," Coach Griffin tells me.

And right there, on day fucking number one, I break my second stupid rule.

Even though I cover my face with both hands to hide it from them, they all had to know I was crying like the little girl I am with Winona's hand patting my back. I'd come to terms with the fact that I wasn't going to be playing professional football, but knowing Kohen is hurt so badly that he may miss an entire season is heartbreaking. Because of me, the entire team is gonna feel his loss.

Once I get myself mostly under control, I swipe away as much of the moisture from my cheeks as possible and push my chair back to get to my feet.

"Thank you all for being the first team to welcome a woman to the roster. I'm sorry I've…I've crippled your team, but I wish you the best for the season."

Quickly finding my way to the conference room door, I'm ready to escape this place and then have a meltdown in private before I have to break the news to my dad. I yank it open, thankful to be finally fleeing the scene.

"Roxanne?" Mr. Wright says, preventing my escape.

Shit. They probably need my driver's license and insurance information for the police report.

"Yes, sir?" I ask, steeling my spine, squaring my shoulders to look more put together than I am as I turn around to face him.

"Where do you think you're going?" he asks. "If you're gonna help this team win some games, we need to get the details of your contract hammered out and send you on down to camp."

"I'm sorry, what?" I ask, shaking my head to try and clear the fog.

"You do still want to play for my Wildcats, right?" he asks.

"Well, yes, of course, I still want to play, but –"

"No buts, except get yours to training camp," he replies with a grin. "Welcome to the team."

"Oh my God! You're kidding, right? I-I'm a fucking mess. I mean, freaking…" I slap a hand over my mouth to try and stop the word vomit.

"We've got faith in you. And while Kohen is irreplaceable, we think you've got a leg that will keep us moving forward until he recovers."

"Oh wow! Thank you so much!" I exclaim. "In that case, I'm ready to get to work, before you change your mind."

"Good," Mr. Wright says, standing up to shake my hand. "And I can assure you that we're going above and beyond the contract requirements you and Ms. Jones have asked for. I won't tolerate sexual harassment on my team, even if I have to let the entire first string go," he informs me, his face deadly serious. "I have two teenage daughters, so losing games isn't what keeps me up at night."

"I appreciate that, sir," I tell him, swallowing past the knot in my throat and pushing down the painful memories from high school. Those were stupid, juvenile boys, while these are grown, professional athletes. I survived college, so this should be a piece of cake.

"There's just one condition," Mr. Wright says, putting a damper on my celebration when his expression becomes even grimmer. "I don't want any bad blood between my players, and Kohen's given us five incredible years. He's not only dependable, but he's a good man and the coaches and I trust his judgment. Therefore, when the regular season starts, we're gonna let him make the final call on who'll be our starting kicker. If or when the doctors clear him, he'll be our man. Otherwise, it'll be his choice to play you or our punter, Dane Adams. Deal?"

"Deal," I reply, knowing I'm destined for the bench, but that's absolutely fine with me. I'm just happy to be a part of the team after being certain my dream had come to an end.

"And don't worry. Since this unfortunate accident thankfully happened on our property, we're gonna take care of the damage and try to keep it contained and out of the press. Only a few of the players saw anything, and we'll urge them to keep their mouths shut. We don't need the negative press surrounding us before the season starts," Mr. Wright says.

"Thank you, sir," I reply, appreciative that I won't be making my media debut as Tonya Harding.

"Just got an update," Coach Griffin says while looking down at the phone in his hands. "Kohen will *not* need surgery. Jon's gonna brace him up, and he'll start his rehab during training camp once the swelling goes down."

I exhale a sigh of relief since surgery would require a helluva lot longer recovery and could even be possibly career ending.

"That's good to hear," Mr. Wright responds before clapping me on the shoulder. "Roxy, since your vehicle is in need of repairs and Kohen's in no shape to drive, maybe you can give him a ride in his car to camp, try to mend fences and whatnot?"

"Sure," I agree, wondering how hard it will be to convince Kohen to ride in a car with me. Especially when he finds out I'll be driving his.

Chapter Five

Kohen

Two hours later, my leg is raised on a stack of towels on a table in one of the training rooms and my dislocated knee has been popped back into place. I feel as good as new, just a few scrapes and bruises, with only a little discomfort thanks to the pain reliever Jon gave me as soon as we came inside. Now I've got an ice pack on top of my knee to help with the swelling, and I'm waiting for him to give me the results of all the tests.

While I wait in the boring silence of the completely empty halls, I can't resist pulling out my phone, which is now sporting a crack down the middle of the screen, to continue my research on a certain female football player.

That's where Lathan Savage and Wildcats' star quarterback and pompous asshole, Quinton Dunn, find me.

"Dude, this seems a little extreme to avoid camp," Quinton says with his signature arrogant grin when he saunters into the room like he owns the place.

"Seriously, Kohen, how bad is it?" Lathan asks with a frown when he steps up beside the table in his gray tee that I just noticed says, *Show me your kitties*, with a wide-eyed feline in the center.

"I'll be back practicing with you all before the end of camp," I tell him.

"Really?" Lathan asks with an arched blond eyebrow. "You do realize your leg is doing an imitation of Mount Rushmore, right?"

"My knee popped out of place; the doctor put it back. It's a little swollen. No biggie," I tell them with a shrug.

"Well, at least you'll get a few more days of vacation," Lathan replies. "You still think she hit you with her car on purpose?"

"She ran me down! And in case you didn't notice, it wasn't a car, it was a fucking SUV."

"No way," Quinton perks up and interjects. "Roxanne looks too fucking sweet to do some fucked up shit like that."

Right, like me, he's already under her spell. As if he needs to add another woman to his roster. The man has fucked enough women for ten lifetimes. And what the hell? Why does the thought of him with this gorgeous girl, who drives like shit, make me want to punch him in his perfect fucking face? Maybe because I still hold a grudge from the Lola fallout. He claimed he had no idea we were together, but I called bullshit. Now he's trying to swoop in and nail Roxanne.

The memory of her grassy green eyes is one I can't seem to forget. I swear looking into her gorgeous gaze was like having a front row seat into a perfect, peaceful, never-ending football field. It's a shame she's a conniving bitch. Although, it doesn't feel right using the B word on her. There was nothing bitchy about her except for the fact she tried to kill me.

"What do you think, Lathan?" I ask, wanting an unbiased opinion. It feels like a gigantic knife is twisting my gut for thinking she did it on purpose and that I almost fell for her sweet, apologetic act.

"Cunning as fuck if she did," Lathan opines. "You talked to her, right? Did she seem like an evil bitch?"

"I don't know..."

"Fuck no," Quinton answers, and I shoot him a glare.

"And, I mean, come on, how would she know the exact moment when you would step into oncoming traffic?" Lathan asks.

"True," I mutter on an exhale.

"Well, I've got good news and bad news," Jon says when he comes into the room holding his electronic tablet. "You've escaped surgery, but now that it's been dislocated once, I can't promise you that it won't happen again. If it does, it'll probably be worse."

"When can he get back on the field?" Lathan asks.

"Kohen will need to wear a brace for support for several weeks and crutches for a few days to keep the swelling down. Once the inflammation decreases, we can try to start some rehab at training camp, and it's possible you'll be kicking again in about five or six weeks."

"So I'll definitely miss the preseason games but might be ready for the season opener?" I ask.

Jon cringes as he considers it. "Let's not rush it. How about we set our goal for week three of the regular season?"

"Okay," I agree. If I can play in week three, that'll give me the majority of the season to earn a contract extension. I hate missing any games, but I can handle that.

"Oh, and management wants you and the rest of the team to keep a lid on what happened," Jon explains. "Since tomorrow's the first day of training camp, we're gonna hold off and tell the press you dislocated your knee in an early morning run."

Great, so now I'll sound like a klutz who can't put one foot in front of the other.

"The PR team thinks it's critical that we don't have any public rifts in the team before the season starts," Jon adds when he notices my hesitation.

"Fine," I agree.

"Great. Now you two better get on the road and head to camp," Jon turns and tells Lathan and Quinton.

"Do you need a ride?" Lathan asks me, but Jon interrupts before I can answer in the affirmative.

"Kohen's transportation has already been arranged," he tells us just as a tall, beautiful blonde fills the doorway, nervously clutching her shoulder bag to her stomach. "Ah, here she is now."

"Wait a fucking second," I grumble, moving the ice pack from my knee to throw my legs over the side of the table so that I'm sitting up. "What the hell is she still doing here?"

"Looks like you're stuck with me as your backup and temporary chauffeur," she says with a stunning grin.

Great. Her magical tits and ass power has already done a number on the team's owner and manager. Now she's using her feminine wiles on my teammates, who quickly rush over to congratulate her with hugs, welcoming her to the team. Even Jon, who previously seemed immune, gravitates to her.

"Hi, Roxanne, right? I'm Jon Young, the head trainer. If you ever need anything, just let me know," he tells her, practically bowing when he offers her his hand to shake.

"Nice to meet you, Jon, and I appreciate that," she replies. "Thank you all for being so welcoming."

"No problem. It's gonna be a great season," Quinton says with his chest puffed out like a fucking peacock.

"Glad to have you on the team," Lathan tells her. *Traitor.* "Guess we'll see you at camp."

"Yeah, see you there," she tells the three men as they reluctantly leave the room, but not without final once-overs from her head to toe. Meanwhile, I'm completely forgotten.

"You're a maneater," I tell her once they're out of earshot.

"No, I'm not," she scoffs, crossing her arms over her ample chest. "It's not my fault that men only see one thing when they look at me."

"A manipulative bitch?" I offer with a smirk, earning a glare so powerful it's a wonder I don't turn to stone.

"Everyone upstairs saw the surveillance video. You were on your phone, tweeting, texting, or playing Pokémon Go. Whatever it was, you were distracted and stepped out right in front of me. There was no time for me to stop!"

"First of all, I don't play Pokémon Go. And second of all, bullshit!" I shout.

"You are the most stubborn man I've ever met, and that's really saying something since Joe Benson is my father!" she replies, coming up to the table to start poking me in the chest with her index finger again.

"What is with you and the damn poking?" I ask, snatching her hand and yanking her forward until she's standing between the V of my spread thighs. And, damn, she's really fucking tall. From my seat on the table, she now hovers over me a few inches.

"I-I don't know," she replies to my question, and then I watch her anger deflate right before my eyes. It shows in the slump of her shoulders and exhale of breath that escapes so close to my face that I can practically taste the sweet, refreshing watermelon scent on my tongue. Fuck that, I *need* to taste it.

Reaching for the nape of her neck, I bring Roxanne's mouth down to mine, and she comes willingly, without putting up an ounce of resistance. Her lips part, allowing my tongue to slip inside and stroke hers. Then I'm drowning in her mouthwatering watermelon flavor, my dick bobbing up between us, trying hard to breach the surface of cloth suffocating it.

Thoughts like I'm not supposed to be touching her, much less kissing her, swirl around in the back of my lust hazed mind. The forbidden only makes it that much hotter, and just like when I was a teenager, telling me I can't do something just makes me want to do it even more.

And fucking hell.

It's not just me who's turned on. Roxanne's definitely an eager participant in the most erotic kiss of my life. Her hands are gripping both sides of my face to keep it tilted and angled to the side for optimum tongue penetration. And since I'm sitting, when she steps forward, the gap between her thighs meets the tip of my cock, causing us to both moan simultaneously. I need more of that incredible friction, so I slip my hand over her hip bone and lower it until I have a handful of her tight ass, using it to grind her pelvis closer, harder.

"*Uhh*," Roxanne cries out while spearing her fingers up through my hair and giving it a tug that unfortunately pulls her lips away from mine. "What are we doing?" she asks, still panting, her now cloudy green eyes reminding me of the early morning fog covering the football field.

"You were poking me," I remind her, thrusting my hips up against her and trying to ignore the jolt of pain it sends to my knee. "Now I'm poking you back."

"We should stop," she says, and then immediately contradicts her words when she shoves her tongue back into my mouth and presses her full breasts to my chest. Just as my fingertips skim underneath her shirt, the sound of footsteps approaching echo from the linoleum hallway.

"Fuck," I mutter, shoving Roxanne away with one hand while reaching down to adjust the tepee in my shorts with the other.

Her eyes widen in surprise a second before they narrow in apparent indignation for either stopping or for starting the kiss. I'm not sure which, but I hope it's the former.

"All right, I've got your brace and crutches," Jon says when he steps into the room. Roxanne startles at his words before taking a few more steps away from me while subtly reaching up to wipe off her damp mouth, which only makes me want to rewet those plump red lips of hers.

"Great, thanks, Jon," I say, trying not to be obvious about the rapid breaths I'm taking. Jon's intelligent eyes flick quickly up to my mahogany hair that's longer on top and likely has a just fucked look before darting away. If he suspects Roxanne and I were just mauling each other, he thankfully doesn't comment as he fastens the big, black brace on my knee.

"You're good to go," he tells me, positioning the crutches on either side of me so I can lean on them as I ease my feet to the floor. "See you both at camp. Tomorrow, we'll figure out if your knee's up for a little rehab. Tonight, I want you icing it for thirty minutes every three or four hours. Got it?"

"Sure. See ya," I say, and Roxanne forces a smile in his direction that falls as soon as he leaves.

"If you tell anyone about…*that*, I'll render you infertile with my foot," Roxanne warns me.

"Well, if you tell anyone, I'll…" Shit, what can I threaten her with? Now that the lust is clearing, I realize how reckless what I did was. But I haven't signed that sheet of paper folded in my pocket yet, so I'm in the clear.

"You'll what?" she asks, shoving the floral shoulder bag she's wearing back so she can brace her hands on her hips. "Get pats on the back congratulating you for being the first of your teammates to try and get in my panties?"

"Wait, the *first* to get in your panties? Are you planning on letting any other teammates in your panties?" I ask her with a frown, hating that thought right away. I'm not finished trying to get in her panties, so I sure as fuck don't want anyone else finding their way inside there either. Although, in a few hours, the contract addendum has to be signed and turned in, and all bets are off. There's no way I can get my fill of her over the next few hours, even if she agreed and we wouldn't be driving down the road for the majority of it.

"No one, especially you, is getting in my panties," she declares, pointing her index finger at me again like she wants to poke me with it, causing a smug smile to stretch across my face.

"You sure seemed to like how I poked your panties," I tell her. "In fact, if Jon hadn't interrupted, I think you would've gotten off with all your clothes still on."

"You are so full of yourself, aren't you?" she scoffs, looking away, but not before I see the blazing red color spreading across her cheeks.

"I don't think you would mind being *full of me*," I reply. "And I mean, you did run me over, so easing the ache in my cock is really the least you could do."

As soon as the stupid words leave my mouth, I know I've gone too far. Roxanne squares her shoulders before she turns back to me again, her face a calm, cool mask as she saunters over. I know I'm in trouble before she touches me but I can't seem to make myself move.

Roxanne goes up on her toes to brush her lips over my ear while her palms sneak their way up underneath my shirt. A shameless shudder runs through me when she strokes her fingernails over the contours of my abdomen, outlining each and every muscle.

"How would you want me to ease the ache?" she asks, letting the tip of her tongue swipe over my earlobe. I barely refrain from trembling with need as my cock re-inflates to capacity in my nylon shorts. If I was ready to explode before, I'm nearly bursting now. Roxanne's so close to me that she's bound to have noticed the pressure against her stomach before she continues teasing me with her sultry voice.

"What if I wanted to get on my knees and use my mouth? Would you let me swirl my wet tongue up and down your dick to ease the ache?"

Goddamn her words are hot. Several drops of pre-cum coat the head of my shaft as soon as she said the word *dick* with a heavy emphasis on the k. Even when she's not speaking to me, her warm, watermelon breath is ghosting over my ear, sexy as fuck. I want to touch her again; but if I let go of the crutches, I'll topple over, so I resist and let her keep teasing me.

"I could suck you really good too, Kohen," she says, demonstrating on my earlobe and causing me to groan a curse. The weight of my body sags even harder on the crutches. Her fingernails drag down my abs and then tease just inside the elastic waistband of my shorts. "I wouldn't stop until I took every long, thick inch of your cock."

Roxanne slowly rakes her fingernails up and down the length of my shaft through the thin nylon, causing all of my stomach muscles to tense violently. My cock jerks in warning right before I embarrass the fuck out of myself, coming with the force of a rocket blasting off in my shorts. The intensity of the orgasm nearly sends me and the crutches crashing to the floor before the waves of pleasure eventually ebb.

Fuck.

I haven't been laid in weeks since my brother's been staying with me during his summer break. That's my excuse, and I'm sticking to it.

"Now if you tell anyone what we did, I'll tell them that you came quicker than a virgin without a single stroke of my fist," Roxanne whispers into my ear before she steps away, smiling at me in triumph.

"You play dirty," I tell her while trying to gather what's left of my composure. "But don't think you've won. In fact, this game is just getting started."

Chapter Six

Roxy

Did I bust my head on the windshield earlier today when I hit Kohen?

While I wait in the hallway of the training center for the infuriating man to clean himself up, I run my fingers over my forehead and scalp, checking for knots before tying my long hair back in a ponytail. Clearly, I must have a concussion or some type of brain damage. That's the only explanation for why in the world I let him kiss me. Although kiss seems too innocent of a word to describe what just went down between us. Kohen thoroughly tongue fucked me, and I not only let him, but I encouraged it! Then the jerk had to go and, well, act like a big jerk by saying I owed him sex for injuring him. Fuck that. I got my revenge and have now vowed to never again even think of straying from Roxy Rule Number One again – *Thou shall not screw around with teammates.* Even if a teammate happens to be the sexiest man I've ever seen. Or kissed. Or touched. Wow, was his stomach ripped and his cock massive...

Enough, Roxy! Get your shit together before you end up being named the floozy of football.

When Kohen finally hobbles out of the training room and starts down the hall, he's sporting a goofy ass grin that would be ridiculous on anyone else, but he's so damn pretty that it only makes him more endearing. It's also unnerving, like he's plotting on how to get me back for causing a mess in his shorts. I have a feeling Kohen is just as competitive as I am, and that's bad news for me.

"Ready?" he asks when he's a foot away.

"Did I mention I'm driving your car?" I ask.

He shrugs with indifference. "I'm so relaxed after that wordjob that I'm not even freaking out about you wrecking my ride."

"Wordjob?" I repeat.

"Even if I'm the first grown man in history to get off on words, I'm owning that shit."

Here I was thinking I had shamed him into backing off; and instead he's able to laugh at himself, making me want him even more. There's nothing sexier than a man with a sense of humor. Except for a hot as fuck man with a sense of humor.

"Keys?" I ask to change the subject, holding out my palm. "What will I be driving, by the way?" I'm not sure what the higher-ups will do with my old Jeep; but until the kaleidoscope windshield is fixed, there's no way to drive it.

Kohen's grin broadens before we start toward the exit. "You'll see."

"It's expensive, isn't it? And you're gonna kill me if I put a ding in it, right?"

He chuckles, proving he's in a much better mood now that he came in his shorts. "You think I would be more upset about you wrecking my car than dislocating my knee that's my moneymaker?" he asks.

"Well, um, I guess not if you put it that way," I answer as the guilt creeps back up on me with every *clomp* of the bottom of his crutches hitting the linoleum floor.

It's not just the team who suffers from Kohen being injured. This is his career, how he pays his bills. And while I may have only been partially responsible for hitting him, it sucks to know what's at stake.

The stadium is empty except for a few guards in black outfits, and the sun is still up when we walk out into the nearly empty parking lot. Someone has already moved my Jeep from the curb. Out of the few remaining choices, there's only one possible car that could fit this gorgeous man – the sleek and sexy blue sports car.

"The Audi R8?" I ask him, already smiling at the thought of driving such a beauty, even knowing it probably cost more than my father's house.

"That's my girl," he says proudly before reaching into his pocket and pulling out a set of keys. He clicks the button to unlock the doors before offering the keyring to me. "Go easy on her and try not to run over anyone...again."

"It was an accident!" I tell him as I take the keys from his hand.

"Yeah, a bizarre accident that just so happened to benefit you," he replies while trying to get the passenger door open. I reach and lift the handle for him, and then he hops backward to try and maneuver the crutches inside.

Pulling the door all the way open, I tell him, "Here, hold on to the door, and I'll slide the crutches between the seats."

Kohen does as asked, his forehead creased with displeasure, likely because he doesn't seem like the type of man who's ever needed help before and clearly doesn't like being in this position.

Once I wedge the crutches between the leather seats, Kohen holds up his injured left leg while bending over to slide the seat back as far as it will go, until he can sit down, gently placing his leg wrapped up in the big brace in first.

"You good?" I ask him.

"Yeah," he mumbles, his handsome face pinched with pain before I shut the door to walk around and climb in behind the wheel. I heft my purse up and over behind my seat so that it's out of the way. And, great, now I realize that I don't have any of my clothes or toiletries. They were all in my Jeep, and I have no idea where it is. Nothing I can do about it now. Maybe there will be a few stores near the training camp campus.

Taking a deep breath of brand new leather, I try not to worry about where my things are. And, damn, if I'm not nervous because this car is so nice and so much newer than my old ride. With all the buttons and gadgets in random places, I swear it feels like I'm trying to launch a space shuttle. I can't even figure out where to put the damn key!

"Put your foot on the brake," Kohen says after fastening his seatbelt. I'm already buckled in; safety first and all that. After I do as he ordered, he reaches over and pushes the circular red "Start" button in front of me. The car purrs to life.

"Nice," I tell him. "What do I do with this?" I ask, holding up the keyring. He takes it and tosses it in the console between us.

"Does this fancy thing drive itself too?"

"No," he chuckles. "Put it in drive, foot on the gas, and we're good to go."

Oh, Lord. Please don't let me wreck this beautiful car.

I pull the gear stick between us back into "D" and then ease my foot down on the gas since there are no cars parked in front of us. And, damn, this is a really smooth ride.

"I think I'm in love," I tell Kohen as I guide us toward the stadium exit. Immediately I want to press rewind on a remote again and take the words back. For whatever reason, my cheeks warm.

"Turn right when we get to the street," Kohen says, thankfully ignoring my comment. "I need to grab my bag from my house, so we'll stop there on the way."

"Okay," I agree. "Just give me directions."

For a moment, I almost consider asking him to borrow some tees and shorts, maybe even some body wash and a toothbrush, but I think I've imposed on him enough as it is.

I realize as soon as we hit the highway that we're, unfortunately, running right into rush-hour traffic. This trip is gonna take a while. The thought of being trapped in a small space with Kohen for a long period of time makes me nervous. He obviously hates me and still thinks I hit him on purpose; but for some reason, neither of us were able to fight the weird, lustful pull between us earlier. That can't happen again, no matter how much I may want him. We're teammates, and I refuse to be nothing more than a conquest again.

"Is it always like this?" I ask him when we come to a standstill on the highway.

"Pretty much. Welcome to Wilmington during tourist season," Kohen says, his head bowed over the cell phone in his hands.

Sighing since there's nothing to do but wait, I relax a little in the driver's seat, figuring it's gonna be awhile before we move again so I might as well get comfortable.

Kohen chuckles to himself, and when I look over, he explains. "Apparently Lathan and Quinton made a bet with some wide receivers to see who could get to the campus first. They've already lost."

"What were the stakes?" I ask.

"New hairdos."

"Wow. Big stakes," I tease, but I know money, of course, can't ever be exchanged.

"Actually, it is pretty big," Kohen says. "Tomorrow everyone in the media will come out to see how the Wildcats are looking on the first day of camp. There will be press conferences like crazy, and those two unfortunate bastards will have to do all that with fucked up heads. The photos will probably be shared a million times on social media."

"Okay, so that's sort of evil," I admit.

"How about we place our own bet?" Kohen asks.

"Sure," I say without hesitation. Competitiveness runs in my blood, inherited from my stubborn father, so I'm always up for a chance to prove I can win at something.

"All right, since you've got the whole ten and two grip going on with my steering wheel, I bet you can't keep both of your hands on the wheel from now until we get to my house."

"Is this a trick?" I ask skeptically. "I mean, what if I need to shift into reverse?"

"No shifting required since we're only going forward, an inch at a time. You won't need reverse; and if for some reason you do, I'll do it for you."

I glance over at his face that's too pretty to be real, trying to judge whether or not he's up to something. His neutral expression shows nothing.

"What are the stakes?" I ask.

"The winner picks the loser's outfit for the first pre-season away game. Loser has to wear the designated outfit to the airport, on the plane and until we get to the hotel."

That doesn't sound so bad. I can already picture putting Kohen in a few ridiculous costumes.

"Okay, fine. I accept," I tell him with a shrug.

"You can remove a hand to shake on it," he says, sticking his palm out toward me; and I accept it, knowing my dad always said no bet is final unless you shake hands.

Returning my hand to the wheel, Kohen smirks while reaching over to turn up the radio, filling the car with the loud feminine moans at the beginning of White Zombie's "More Human Than Human" as we crawl forward through traffic.

"Kind of loud," I shout to tell him over the electric guitar and angry words. "I didn't take you as a fan of heavy metal."

"Growing up it annoyed my parents the most, and then it sort of grew on me," he answers, still grinning. I'm trying to figure out what Kohen looks so smug about when he finally speaks loud enough for me to hear over the radio. "You know, it's not really fair that I got off earlier, but you didn't."

What the fuck?

"Huh?" I ask, forcing my eyes to stay on the "Save the sea turtles" license plate of the red Beemer in front of me.

"I mean, you look really tense. You could probably use a release too, right?"

"What?" I ask, wondering if he's actually referring to an orgasm. "If you think you're gonna lay a finger on me again, you're out of your mind," I warn him.

"Nope, not a finger. But if I did, you can't do much about it right now unless you want to lose our bet."

"You asshole," I tell him when I finally understand where this is going. "Don't you dare –"

"I think I deserve a little payback, don't you?" he asks.

"No!"

"When was the last time someone made your toes curl and your legs shake?"

"That-that is none of your business," I tell him, the warmth in my cheeks rising. Since my hair is now pulled back, I know he can see me blushing, which makes me hate him even more. The truth is, the orgasms I've had for the past few months have been self-induced. Sure, I dated a few non-teammates in college, but nothing serious; and I only went out with a certain type of guy. You know, the quiet but cute bookworm types who aren't popular. Those guys never ran their mouth about sleeping with me because they were smart enough to know it wouldn't happen again if they did.

Taking advantage of my moment of distraction, Kohen leans over the console and sticks his phone in between the gap of my thighs.

"What the –" My words die out when I realize the device is vibrating. Constantly. Right up against the center seam of my jeans. I tighten my grip on the steering wheel as I debate using my hands to shove the phone down Kohen's throat, which would mean losing the bet or letting it stay where it is.

Losing is not an option.

There has to be some way to get rid of the phone without my hands. Lifting my hips with my foot steadily on the brake, I try to wiggle away from the vibrating device, but that only ends up with the edge of the phone tilting, increasing the pressure on my most sensitive flesh. And I hate to admit that it feels good.

"Move your fucking phone, or I'm gonna wreck your car," I threaten Kohen.

"It would probably be worth it," he replies, followed by a chuckle when I squirm again in my seat. "I wish I had a camera to record this, but it's...otherwise occupied at the moment."

"You're a pervy bastard," I tell him, trying to keep my voice steady. There's already a noticeable tremble in my voice with those few words as my body starts to heat up despite the air conditioning blowing from the vents. My heart is not only racing around in my chest, but it obviously thinks it's at the raceway trying to qualify for Daytona.

"You'll consider me a pervy bastard as a compliment in about, oh, ninety seconds or so. Besides, you seemed tense, probably wound up tight from all that maneating you do."

"Fuck you," I tell him, the two words little more than breathless exhales. My vision starts blurring around the edges, the red Beemer and rest of traffic hazy as the phones vibrations causes the pulse between my legs to throb erratically against the seam of my jeans. My nipples are tingling almost painfully.

"Deny it all you want, but you need this. You may not know me or even like me, but no one kisses the way you did with me earlier unless you're expecting the two of us to end up naked and sweaty with a headboard banging against the wall."

A gasp escapes my parted lips, and my head falls back against the leather seat hearing his naughty but true words. As insane as it is, I've wanted Kohen since I first saw him lying on the ground. And back at the stadium, if the trainer hadn't interrupted us, I'm not sure how things would've ended. I know how I wanted it to end – just as he said, with the two of us naked, sweaty and me sitting on his brick size dick. The muscles in my lower belly tense at the memory. I know I'm close to a release unless I move the stupid phone, but I refuse to give in and take my hands off the wheel. Besides, I'm too far gone.

"I hate you," I tell Kohen.

"Well, honey, I can't say I'm real fond of you either," he replies with a slight southern drawl.

"*Honey?*" I repeat in disbelief. Of course, I'm used to the assholes in high school and college calling me *babe* or *sweet cheeks* as insults, taunts to remind me I don't belong on the field with them because I wasn't born with balls. I'm just not used to hearing a man other than my father say one of those words and make it sound like Kohen's term of endearment.

"Honey," he says again before he reaches over to grind the phone into my pelvis. His lips and the tip of his tongue tease the right side of my ear like I did to him earlier before he speaks. "Because you're about to make a hot, sticky mess in your panties."

"Ugh, God," I moan as a shiver runs down my spine. My hips lift on their own when the muscles in my thighs and ass tense before the pleasurable waves of bliss erupt in an explosion of heat from the clenching of my core. My hands tighten on the wheel but never let go even as my eyelids grow so heavy I can't hold them open any longer.

As soon as my body relaxes again, I remember where I am and who I'm with. My eyes flutter open, but thankfully Kohen has shifted his car into park, and there's no more than half a car length between it and the Beemer in front of us. The phone is also absent from between my legs, and I'm not sure if I'm relieved or disappointed. A scorching flush of arousal now covers my face and chest like a spotlight emitting my embarrassment. On the bright side, at least I didn't lose the bet.

I try to avoid the man sitting inches away from me at all costs until his movement catches my eye. His hand grips his cock that's jutting out from his athletic shorts and adjusts it.

"You're welcome," he says, causing me to scoff.

"I didn't say thank you."

Kohen chuckles. "Maybe I should be the one thanking you," he says. "That was so fucking hot. But now I've got a craving for honey."

"Will you put the car back into drive?" I ask, avoiding his compliment and innuendo.

"Are you still uptight? Because that was supposed to loosen you up," he says as he does as I asked and shifts the car into drive so I can inch up behind the Beemer.

"How much further?" I ask, ignoring that jab as well.

"Only about ten minutes."

"Good."

"If we were actually moving."

"Fuck."

"Do you want the phone back?" he asks, followed by a snicker when I glare at him. "Fine. I have to say, though, I'm surprised you didn't forfeit the bet to move it. I was almost certain you would give up."

"I'm not a quitter. I've worked my ass off to be a great football player, just like you," I tell him, reminding myself why I can't let anything like that happen again between Kohen and me, or any other player.

Chapter Seven

Kohen

God, I can't wait to make Roxanne come for me again. Only next time, I'll be using my hands, tongue or dick to make it happen.

I can tell by the way she's clenching her jaw and avoiding my eyes that she's gonna put up a fight before she caves again to this crazy attraction between us. That only makes me want to break her even more. I like a challenge, and for some reason, she's the equivalent to the Super Bowl of fucking. The lethal combination of forbidden and feisty makes my cock swell with a desperate need to succeed in getting inside her. Never before have I thought that I needed to fuck a woman or risk my balls bursting from the pressure. Forget blue balls, this here is a horse of a different color.

The fact that we're on the way to my house means we'll have easy access to a bed. Not that a mattress is needed for the type of fucking I want to do to her, but it would be preferable since my knee's fucked up. Time's running out too. Soon I have to hand over the signed document promising to stay away from Roxanne. While I may have a long record of bending the rules and stretching laws to the fullest extent, I never actually break them. Especially not ones that involve my much needed paycheck.

We finally start moving at more than two miles an hour, and eventually my exit ramp can be seen in the distance.

"The next exit and then a left," I tell her, the words coming out in a rush thanks to the urgency of the situation, mainly my log of a cock that's currently siphoning all my blood supply away from my brain. Even on my best day, I'm not the brightest bulb in the box, but at this moment in time, I couldn't add two plus two. All I know for sure is one plus one equals hell yes squared to the ninth power.

"Take this right at the light, and we're there," I tell Roxanne, already removing my seatbelt. It felt too tight across my chest. My loose fitting cotton wife-beater and nylon shorts are now snug and suffocating me as well. I need them off. First, I need to figure out how to get Roxanne out of her clothes.

Shit, I can't think of a plan. Nothing's coming to me. The phone between her legs was my one ingenious move of the day. All that's left is for me to try and use my looks and charm. Maybe that's all it will take thanks to the magnetism that's been simultaneously pulling us together and repelling us since we met.

"You can park anywhere along the second dock," I instruct her before we come to a stop.

"Where's your house?" she asks with her forehead creased in confusion.

"Right there," I answer, pointing to the *Wet Dream*, my houseboat. While money may not buy happiness, it does buy a four bedroom, seventy-five foot, million-dollar houseboat, which makes me pretty fucking ecstatic. Not all kickers are probably paid as well as me, but yours truly is the third best placekicker in the entire fucking league, baby.

Do you know how many games come down to a field goal for the big win? A shitload. When there's three seconds on the clock and the score is tied, I'm the person who has saved the Wildcats more times than I can count from crunching it out on the field in overtime simply by booting a pigskin straight through the uprights to seal the deal.

And, yeah, I maybe splurged a little too much thanks to an unfortunate influence at the time I purchased the boat, but I love life out on the ocean and hope to earn and save enough money to retire here in my thirties.

"Hold on. You *live* on a boat?" Roxanne asks, appalled or astonished. I'm not sure which.

"Yeah. Come on, and I'll show you around," I suggest to get her inside.

"I'll wait here," she replies with a shrug.

No, no, no. If she doesn't come in, I can't *get* it in.

"Fine, but I've gotta take the keys," I tell her, grabbing them out of the console and shoving them in my pocket with my phone. "And once I'm halfway down that dock right there, the car will cut off, and you'll be sitting in the heat until I get back. Probably close to a hundred degrees today, and it may take me a while since I haven't even packed yet."

All true statements.

Roxanne works her bottom lip between her front teeth for several silent seconds like she wants to say something but is trying to refrain. Finally, she speaks. "Do you, um, do you think I could borrow some clothes and maybe some bathroom travel supplies if you have them? My bag and the rest of my things are in my Jeep that's now gone to who knows where –"

"Hell yeah," I say eagerly, cutting her off since that means she'll have to get out and come in. "You can try on a few things, see what you like."

"Thanks," she says, obviously unaware of my ulterior motives.

"My pleasure," I reply before trying to get the door open. It soon becomes obvious that the car is so low, that getting out without the crutches may be a problem. "A little help?" I ask, not feeling bad about asking for assistance since it's her fault my knee is messed up anyway. And who knows, a little sympathy might be the key ingredient to getting into those panties of hers. Wonder if they're light blue ones that match the bra I saw a flash of earlier, and if they're now soaked with her honey. "Fuck," I groan at the thought, craving a taste.

"Hold your horses," Roxanne says before getting out. Grabbing the crutches, she walks around the car. She thinks I was cursing because of the pain. Yeah, there's a pain that's just a little higher than my knee.

Once she's in front of me, holding up the sticks, I pull myself up, putting my weight on the crutches and keeping my left foot off the ground. God, this sucks.

"Are you gonna change your shorts?" Roxanne asks with a grin when I'm standing in front of her, lowering her eyes to the crotch.

"Yeah, thanks to you, they're sticky," I tell her. Taking a few steps away from the car, I shut the door and start down the wooden dock.

"Won't the guys notice?" she asks, and it takes me a second to figure out what she's talking about since I'm too busy trying to stay upright on the uneven surface.

"No one will notice I changed my shorts," I assure her, leading the way to the *Wet Dream*.

"It's beautiful out here," she says, glancing around the marina.

"Yeah, even more beautiful away from civilization."

Thankfully, I keep a ramp down for my boat; because otherwise, jumping over to the deck on one leg would suck.

"Can you get my keys out of my pocket?" I ask Roxanne instead of leaning one of the crutches against the sliding glass door just because I want her hand in my pants.

She huffs, but then her small hand is fishing in my pocket, pulling out not only my keyring but my phone.

"Shit. I fucked up your phone," she says, looking down at the broken screen.

"Don't worry. Your pussy didn't crack it; it was your SUV," I tease her.

"I'll, um, get you another one," she tells me, dropping it into my pocket and then unlocking my door without me asking.

"I'm sort of partial to this one after where it's been," I joke.

"Oh my gosh. Could you please not ever mention that again?" she asks. "Besides, you lost. I won the bet despite how much you tried to screw me over."

"Right, you get to pick my outfit on the first away game," I reply. "Small price to pay for seeing a beautiful woman come apart."

Roxanne doesn't respond to my compliment. Instead, she slides the door open and steps inside.

"Wow. Your place is...wow," she mutters as she spins in a circle in the center of the main salon. And I admit I'm filled with pride knowing that she's impressed with my home that I love. She looks damn good standing in it too.

"Thanks," I tell her, following behind.

"I had no idea a boat could be this big or have this much space," she remarks.

"Yeah, well, I wanted a yacht, and the ones I looked at cost as much if not more than most houses, so I said fuck it and went with a two-in-one." Lola actually picked this model with a ton of upgrades and shit I didn't need, but the luxury is really fucking nice even if it did put a huge drain on my bank account.

"Generators keep the power and everything on at sea?" Roxanne asks.

"Yeah. My brother and I spend the summers traveling up and down the east coast."

"Sounds fun," she says.

"Yeah, it was pretty cool to relax out in the Atlantic for a few weeks while he was on summer break, but he just graduated from college, so…"

"So no more summer vacations?" she finishes.

"Right. Now Chase has done the unthinkable and gone to work for our dad," I tell her, and then wonder why the hell I'm oversharing.

"Family business?" she asks.

"Uh-huh. Law enforcement."

"Oh, so they're cops?"

I nod. "My dad's the sheriff in Summerville, our small hometown near the Virginia border."

"Nice. So I guess you grew up pretty straight-laced, huh?"

"Nope. I was a troublemaker. A perfect angel while my parents or teachers were watching; but as soon as they turned around, I raised hell. Drove them crazy because they couldn't ever catch me in the act. Actually, I'm surprised they decided to have another kid after the shit I pulled."

"And now you're a professional football player living on a boat. You didn't turn out so bad."

"I'm sure my parents are just as surprised as I am. If or when I retire or quit, they expect me to move back home and join the force. I mean, Summerville has six deputies, so you would think seven would be pushing it, but I'm sure Dad can rearrange the budget to make room for me."

"You sound excited about the prospect," Roxanne jokes.

"Never gonna happen. I'll figure something else out when the time comes."

As soon as I say the words, I realize that the time could be coming sooner rather than later thanks to the woman in front of me. I'll do whatever it takes to get back on the field and stay there, but Jon's words remind me that now that the damage to my knee has been done it can happen again. Next time could be worse.

Roxy

Kohen's houseboat is a freaking floating mansion. Back home, the few friends I had in high school were all from one-level brick houses like ours. And in college, most of the students were living on scholarships and student loans too. Never before have I ever seen this sort of extravagance before.

The cherry wood floors and matching tables glisten throughout the place, and the white curvy leather sofas in front of a wall-mounted flat screen look comfy and inviting for taking a load off after a long, hard day. I think my favorite place, though, would be the seating area on the deck, looking out over the water.

"You want to take a tour and come grab some clothes?" Kohen asks.

"Nah, can you just throw a few tees and shorts in a bag? I want to go check out the deck."

Kohen's shoulder's slump, and his dark eyes lower either in annoyance or disappointment, I'm not sure.

"Ah, sure," he says before hobbling off down a hallway.

I would love to see the bedrooms, but I'm afraid I would fall even more in love with this place than I already am. It's beautiful, and I can't imagine how fun it must be to sail out onto the ocean, to watch the sunrise or sunset over the water. I'm seriously jealous of this place because, while I love the water, there are not many large bodies of it in Tennessee. There's also guilt gnawing on my gut after what Kohen said about his family. If he loses his career in football because of my Jeep crashing into his knee, then what will he do?

I'm not delusional. Careers in professional football are short, and the most I can probably expect is ten years if I'm lucky. After that, it would be nice if I would be able to save enough money to live off of, but that's doubtful. I want to get married and have kids, so a steady income is sort of important for the future.

My bachelor's degree is in communications, pretty much like every other athlete in college, but I really would like to be a sports reporter once it all ends. I don't mind speaking in front of crowds or being on camera except for when I'm being badmouthed. As the preseason progresses, I should toughen my skin, because everyone will be waiting for the first woman to play professional football to fail. Or to screw all my teammates.

Leaning my forearms against the rail and looking out over the Atlantic, I remind myself that I have to do whatever it takes to avoid either of those options. I'll succeed, and I won't let there be even a hint of a rumor that I'm having any sort of physical relationship with one of the players. Or their vibrating cell phones. I made it all this way, and now it's time to get serious. This is my dream come true. So why is there a nagging doubt in my chest when I think about staying away from Kohen?

It's more than his handsome face and muscular physique. He's also funny and nice to be around when he isn't calling me a manipulative bitch. More than that, the way he looks at me and talks to me sets my soul on fire, which is pretty damn hard to ignore. Maybe I'm just emotional. It has been a crazy, hectic, whirlwind of a day. One of the most important days of my life. Doing this all alone is scary. At college, I was one freshman among thousands, a new player among hundreds trying out for the football team.

Here, I'm a one woman island. Literally. There's only gonna be a handful of rookies joining the Wildcats this season, all men, who will have it easy fitting in. Sure, some of my teammates will become my friends, but to most, if not all of the guys, I'll never really earn their respect. Physically, although I'm tall for a woman, I'm nowhere near as strong as the other kickers in the league. I'll never set any records for longest field goals or anything else other than being the first woman to step out onto the field in a team's jersey. And if I suck or mess this chance up by becoming the floozy of football, I'll be solely responsible for holding back other women from getting signed.

Sometimes I wonder if I'm in over my head, but then I remember the reason I play football in the first place.

I love it.

The rivalries, the excitement in never knowing what will happen in a game, the best, most athletic players in the world…Yeah, I want to be a part of that, and Lord have mercy on anyone who tries to get in my way.

Chapter Eight

Kohen

Roxanne barely spoke a word after we got on the road heading for PU. Yeah, that's an unfortunate abbreviation for Pender University. I eventually gave up trying to talk to her. Between the ache in my balls and the throbbing pain in my knee, I wasn't in the best mood myself. My leg felt tight and swollen, so I knew it would be time to ice it as soon as we got to campus.

The campus parking lot is packed full since all of our teammates had a few hours head start. Also present is Roxanne's Jeep, the glass on the windshield already repaired, which improved Roxanne's mood since she was able to grab her bag out of it. I was sort of disappointed that she wouldn't be wearing my clothes or sleeping in them this week.

When we walk into the main residence hall, everyone is gathered in the lobby, lounging on one of the blue or brown university colored sofas or ottomans, shooting pool or playing air hockey. It's a lot of huge men crammed into one room, but thankfully it's a massive space with a big open ceiling showing the balconies on each of the three stories. Oh, and there's only one woman in attendance, and everyone's eyes are on her.

Roxanne and I check in at the registration desk to get our room assignments, keys and schedules for the next week, my duffle bag hanging over my shoulder as I maneuver around on the crutches. Based on the agenda, it looks like everyone's been here waiting in the lobby for an hour to meet her before finally getting dismissed by Coach for the night. As soon as she's finished registering, Coach Griffin greets Roxanne and leads her by the elbow to the center of the room. Roxanne seems to handle the attention well, not even a hint of red on her cheeks. But really, what does she have to hide? She's gorgeous, even in a pair of jeans and plain blue tee.

"You're all set, Mr. Hendricks. I just need to get your signed contract addendum," the young guy manning the registration desk tells me. I reach into the pocket of my shorts and then realize all I have are my keys and phone. "Shit," I mutter, remembering the form is in the jizz-stained shorts that I took off at home. "I left my copy back in Wilmington. You got another one?" I ask the kid.

He scratches his dark, floppy head of hair while looking through a file organizer in front of him and pulling out an empty blue folder. "I did have a few extras, but they've all been used."

Son of a bitch. Luck is on my side.

"I'll make a note to get one to you later this week," he says, pencil poised over a sheet of paper.

"Kohen, good to see you made it here safely under Ms. Benson's care," Jon says when he appears next to me. "Ryan, now that everyone's here, can you go grab my training bag from my truck?" Jon hands over his keys to the kid at the registration table before he has a chance to answer. Guess the young guy is an intern and does whatever grunt work is required.

"S-sure, Dr. Young," the boy says, jumping to his feet and heading outside.

I feel like I've won the lottery, since he didn't get a chance to write down my name and will probably be busy with other chores the rest of the night. Of course, I know it's only a matter of time before management comes up with more copies and requires my John Hancock on it.

"Come on and have a seat," Jon tells me, walking me over to one of the sofas where he runs off a rotund third string linebacker so I can sit. "I don't want you on your feet more than a few hours a day. It'll keep the swelling down."

"Okay," I agree, flopping back into the seat and tossing the duffle back to the floor beside my feet.

"Did you change your shorts?" Jon asks me with a raised eyebrow, eyeing the navy blue nylon.

"What? No," I lie.

"I could've sworn you were wearing black ones earlier."

"Some people think navy blue looks black," I say, and then thankfully Coach begins talking to the group.

"Everyone meet Roxanne Benson, our team's new placekicker," he says with a grin as he gestures to Roxanne standing on his right. I frown since he said *placekicker* and not *backup placekicker*. "Make her feel welcome, introduce yourselves over the next few days. Tonight, you should all get to your rooms by ten and get a good night's sleep. I want you refreshed and ready to bust your asses tomorrow morning on the field at nine sharp. If you're late, well, believe me when I say that you *do not* want to be late. The media and fans will be here at sunrise waiting to watch you from the stands; and if you make them wait, you'll regret it."

A moment later the Ryan kid comes back in with Jon's bag. Jon takes out a travel ice pack, then snaps it and shakes it. "This will do until you get to your room and we find some real ice," he says, wrapping an ace bandage around the knee brace to hold the pack on the opening at the center. "Tomorrow I'll come get you a little before nine once I get a therapy room set up somewhere on campus. I'll find you a golf cart to ride around in too while you're here. You may not be able to drive a car, but you can maneuver one of those, right?" he asks.

"Yeah, sure."

"Good," he says, taking out a bottle of pills. "Here are some pain relievers. Take one before bed and one as soon as you wake up tomorrow before we put your knee through the ringer." He slips the bottle into my duffle.

"Thanks, Jon," I say before he walks away.

Everyone else begins to disperse too, or more like flock to Roxanne, all the guys eager to talk to her.

"You finally made it," Lathan says when he approaches and takes the now vacant seat on the sofa next to me. "Did you change your shorts?" he asks.

"What the fuck?" I mutter. "Who notices that sort of shit?"

"You did change. Why? Potty accident?" he asks with a smirk.

"No."

"So?" he prompts, staring me down, waiting for an answer.

No excuses come to mind, as hard as I try to think of one.

"Don't tell me that you and her..." Lathan draws his own fairly accurate conclusion.

"Can we talk about this later?" I ask him.

"You dirty dog," he says with a grin and punch to my shoulder. "Should've known you would find a way around the no contact agreement."

"Would you please shut your mouth?" I ask him.

"I want details –"

"No," I cut him off. "So when's Cameron and Nixon gonna get you and Quinton to pay up for your bet?" I ask to change the subject.

It works. Lathan groans and shoves his fingers through his blond locks. "In about half an hour," he says with a grimace. "How bad do you think it will be?" he asks, his pleading silver eyes wanting me to sugarcoat it for him.

"Knowing those two, I would say pretty damn bad."

"Fuck," he grumbles. "This is all your fault. If you hadn't gotten hit, then Quinton and I wouldn't have been late."

"Hey, it's not my fault I got mowed down by Evel Knievel."

"She doesn't look evil," Lathan replies, finding Roxanne in the crowd. Although, you can only see a tiny bit of her whitish-gold ponytail since there are so many men still surrounding her. "She looks more angelic than demonic."

"Looks can be deceiving," I tell him, even though it's a lie. Roxanne has been nothing but nice to me. But maybe that's because her goal has already been accomplished. She took me, her competition, out.

"Looks like Dane is smitten," Lathan points out. He's right. Our team's punter and my backup before Roxanne joined the team is staring her down, practically drooling.

"Who isn't? She's a maneater."

"Ballbuster," Lathan corrects.

"Huh?" I ask him in confusion.

"Her nickname from college is Roxanne 'The Ballbuster' Benson," Lathan explains.

"How do you know that?"

"Google," he answers with a shrug. Guess if I had read more words instead of ogling her pictures I would've seen that too.

Ballbuster.

That's a pretty fucking accurate description.

I'm not sure what it is about the woman, but I can't seem to get her off my mind, especially later that night when I head to the small, cramped dorm room I'm sharing with Lathan. Lying in bed, my knee's stiff and so is my cock. And the strangest thing is, I'm not just thinking about what Roxanne looks like naked. I'm actually worried about her too.

Is Roxanne nervous about her first practice tomorrow? Will she be able to hack it in this man's world where even the smallest kickers probably weigh thirty pounds more than her and have stronger legs?

That's the sort of shit that keeps me up half the night.

I also can't help but wonder if she's in her tiny twin bed somewhere in this building thinking about me and the hot as fuck kiss we shared.

Chapter Nine

Roxy

So sleeping in a dorm room without air conditioning sucks. If that had been the case at Rockford, I never would've made it through all four years. You would think a team that pays millions for players and billions for a stadium could provide us with the minimum comforts, but nope.

This morning I'm grumpy and tired from sleeping in a shitty twin bed, and today is only the first day of camp. It also doesn't help that while I was tossing and turning, while not just alone in my room, but the entire third floor, I couldn't stop thinking about Kohen. How incredible that kiss had been, or how much I still want him even though I know I shouldn't.

"Okay, ladies, listen up," Coach Griffin says to the fifty or so sweaty men spread out before us on the bleachers while I stand next to him. I long for air conditioning because the scorching Carolina sun already feels like it's melting me into a puddle. The small relief is that we're only required to wear shoulder pads and shorts, not the entire bulky getup for most of these camp practices. I doubt I'll even need my helmet since this week is about conditioning. Besides, kickers rarely take hits.

I try to avoid eye contact with any individual player on the bleachers; and instead, I keep my eyes moving. Locking eyes with one of them is like waving a red flag in front of the bull. They'll charge, and I'll end up trying to run out of the practice field by throwing myself over the fence.

Jeez, calm down, Roxy. They're not gonna attack you. Most of the guys I met last night seemed really nice. And I'm not so much worried about the physical abuse as I am the verbal. Has Kohen run his mouth about me to anyone? All it takes is telling one teammate, and they'll all know. I swear football players are nothing but a bunch of gossiping hens. The thought makes me think of my best friend, Paxton, missing him. He was another reason I survived college relatively unscathed. As a wide receiver, he may not have been the biggest guy on the team, but he threw the best parties at his townhouse. Therefore, no one wanted to piss him off by causing problems for me and risk getting banned from the debauchery only he offered.

"Yesterday most of you got a chance to meet Roxanne. Now let me tell you a little bit about her career and why she deserves a spot on this team," Coach goes on to say. "She's proven herself all four years of college ball at Rockford. Ninety field goals with eighty-five percent accuracy; her longest kick made from the fifty-nine-yard line." Coach pauses to let the impressed whistles die down. "Not to mention two hundred extra-point kicks with one-hundred percent accuracy. She's earned this spot on your team, and you *will* treat her with dignity and respect, or you'll find yourself on the other end of a sexual harassment lawsuit and out of a job. Got it?" he threatens. They all mumble words of agreement, and then Coach says, "All right, now get your pudgy asses to work. Some of you didn't leave the sofa this off-season, did you?"

I'm standing there, waiting for my next instructions when a guy with a hot pink Mohawk walks up to me.

Son of a bitch.

"Quinton?" I ask and cover my mouth with my hand to hide my smile. Quinton Dunn, all six feet and six inches of him, is standing inches away from me in white shorts and white number eighteen jersey, sapphire eyes sparkling, a stunning smile on his perfect face despite the horrific hairstyle while he offers me his enormous mitt to shake. Yesterday his hair was jet black, and today it's…pink. *Very* pink.

"We didn't really get to officially meet yesterday with all the chaos. I'm one of the team captains and quarterback –"

"Quinton Dunn," I finish for him while shaking his offered hand. "You didn't have to introduce yourself. You're the second best quarterback in the league."

"Hey now, that was *last* season. We'll see who's first in a few weeks," he replies, grinning even wider to show both rows of his white, perfect teeth.

"I've been a huge fan since your rookie year," I tell him honestly. "It's a shame you guys lost the Super Bowl year before last. Your throw was on the money, if only Jefferson had hung on to it."

"Damn right," he says with a nod, making his pink rooster hairstyle bob. "He was wide open, the ball smacked him in the chest, and the fucker still juggled it. Good riddance."

"I heard he was just cut from the Sharks who didn't want to renew his contract either."

"Of course not. He's got butter fingers."

"Yeah, and with him gone, your tight end, Lathan Savage, has been killing it. Since he sometimes blocks, the D forgets all about him. I don't know how, but that man catches everything you throw at him!" I say in awe, finding Lathan on the field. And, yep, he's sporting the exact same pink Mohawk.

"Don't let Lathan hear you say that; it'll go to his head," Quinton leans forward and whispers, making me laugh since that's coming from what rumors say is the most arrogant man on the team. Not that he doesn't live up to it, but still.

"So, um, speaking of heads...this the punishment for losing the bet?" I ask.

"Ugh," he groans while patting his hair with his palm. "We have a bit of a gambling problem."

"Well, maybe you shouldn't put your locks up on the chopping block next time," I suggest.

"Good advice."

"So, about the whole thing with Kohen..." he starts, making every muscle in my body tense with anxiety. Goddamn it! Why did Kohen have to run his mouth about our romps to the team captain, of all people? "Don't worry about that shit," Quinton finishes. "The coaches said the video showed he was distracted and walked right in front of you. It was a horrible accident."

"Yeah, thanks," I say on a sigh of relief when I realize he's referring to me running over the kicker and not the groping. "How is Kohen doing this morning? I haven't seen him since last night." I can't help but ask about him, which is so stupid I could facepalm myself.

"I think he started rehab with Jon this morning," he answers.

"Good," I tell him.

"If you need anything or have any problems with anyone, just let me know, okay?" Quinton offers, his blue eyes sincere.

"I appreciate that," I tell him as we start to walk further onto the practice field.

"So," Quinton says. "Let's see what that leg of yours can do. Although, you might want to reconsider your attire for tomorrow," he adds, eyeing my loose black pants.

"What? Why?" I ask.

"Because it's gonna be almost a hundred degrees today. That's why we all wear white jerseys and white shorts," he explains.

"Right," I say. "I'm just more comfortable in pants." The truth is, I don't want to draw more attention to myself or my feminine form. That's why I always try to dress conservatively at practices.

"Fine, but don't say I didn't warn you," Quinton remarks before he jogs off.

Wow. If the rest of the team is half as nice as their quarterback, I won't have anything to worry about here. Except for Kohen.

"Hi, Roxanne," a tall, thick player with a shaved head wearing the number two jersey says when he jogs up to me. "I'm Dane. Dane Adams, the team's punter."

"Nice to meet you," I say, offering my hand, but he pulls me into a hug instead. Alrighty then. He doesn't let go right away, but sniffs my hair so loudly I can hear it. At the same time, his hands are gripping my lower back, inches away from my ass. My what-the-hell alarms go off like crazy, but then just as quickly he lets me go and steps away smiling at me. So, maybe he's just a hugger.

"Let's warm up with a quick mile jog around campus and then stretch out before we set up some kicks," he suggests, taking off toward the stadium exit while my feet remain firmly planted in place. "Come on," he says, turning around to jog backward. "Coach Sigmon's orders." He nods to the tank of a man I met yesterday, huddled with some of the other coaches. Coach Sigmon looks up and waves me off toward Dane.

Exhaling a breath, I do as I'm told and sprint over to the punter. Today's my first day and I don't want to look like a slacker, so I keep up the brisk pace that Dane sets as we make our way through the university buildings. There's barely a soul in sight since it's summer break. Once we get to the entrance sign, Dane turns around, and I'm relieved to be getting back to the rest of the team.

"Good job. Keep it up, rookie," Dane says with a swat to my ass. I glance over, but he's focused on the road in front of him again, feet pounding on the pavement. Maybe I imagined it, or maybe it was nothing more than how the guys slap each other's asses as often as they high five. I guess I'm just not used to that same treatment. If one of my college teammates had tried that, I would've snapped their wrist; and then Paxton would've made them bleed. But Pax isn't here; and if I want to stay on the team, I've got to be on my best behavior and learn to ignore the minor things. I have a feeling there will be more pressing concerns later on, so there's no use in making waves until I absolutely have to.

Kohen

Hobbling on crutches sucks so bad especially when you have to wander around somewhere as big as a fucking gated football field where golf carts aren't allowed. All morning I endured rehab with Jon that hurt like a bitch. Now I'll have to risk heatstroke.

After I make it to the practice field, I sink down onto one of the benches to catch my breath. Sweat is streaming down like a river between my shoulder blades because it's hot as Hades out here. But then, when I see *her*…I swear the temperature goes up at least ten more degrees.

The bottom of her white jersey, with a blue number three, is tucked up underneath the front of her shoulder pads, flashing her flat stomach. And unlike all the guys wearing white, knee length nylon shorts, hers are more like white…panties showcasing her long, beautiful, toned legs. Damn, she looks even taller with her legs on display. She's at least six feet, give or take an inch since she's standing shoulder to shoulder with Dane Adams, our team's punter.

"Jesus fucking Christ," I mutter aloud when I realize that she's setting up for a field goal…from fifty-five yards out. Those legs of hers might be fine as fuck, but there's no way they can launch a football through the uprights from that distance, especially kicking against the coastal winds.

Roxanne walks three big steps away from the tripod metal football holder, sighting the goal with her raised right arm and then takes two giant steps to the left, just like I've done a million times before. She goes for it at full speed and...

Whoosh.

The ball sails right through the center of the goal posts with plenty of ass on it. She could've made it from fifty-eight yards out or, hell, maybe even sixty.

Some of the guys standing around watching hoot and holler, either because she actually made the kick or because of Roxanne's sexy celebratory dance. Both of her arms are raised straight up in the air as she does this little swiveling hip shake that causes all dicks within a ten-mile radius to stir in interest, including my own.

"Well, if nothing else, she'll be one helluva distraction," Lathan declares when he takes a seat on the bench next to me, pink haired, drenched in sweat, and guzzling from the water bottle clutched in his hand.

"A distraction for the other team or us?" I ask with a snort as we hear Coach Griffin yell, "Okay, ladies and Roxy, get back to work!"

"Hopefully we'll all be immune by game time. Or not," my best friend croaks right about the time Roxanne looks over her shoulder, still smiling triumphantly from her kick, and makes eye contact with me for the first time since we got to campus last night.

Like a rerun of *Baywatch*, Roxanne comes running over towards us in slow motion, her ponytail swishing, hair so light it looks white like a halo in the bright, summer sun.

"Oh God. I can't be this close to her yet," Lathan groans as if in pain before he slides down the length of the metal bench and heads for the other end of the field.

"Hey, Kohen. How are you feeling?" Roxy asks when she comes to a stop in front of me. Since I'm still sitting down, that puts me right at navel level with the scantily dressed woman. There's a drop of sweat that's hanging suspended right above her bellybutton, and my mouth waters, my tongue desperate to lick it up before it falls.

Fuck.

Clearly, I'm in serious need of some self-love. I hate that it's all her fault for leaving me so horny, and now she's flaunting her hotness inches away from my fucking face. I'm sure this is nothing more than part of her maneating, ball-busting scheme. Annoyed even more than I was thanks to the heat, the corners of my lips tug down hard in a scowl.

"I'm just great," I answer her question sarcastically. "My armpits hurt from having to shuffle along on fucking crutches everywhere I go, and my knee is aching like a son of a bitch after my first rehab session. But enough about me. How are *you*, Roxy? And why are dressed like a slut? Looking for your next wordjob victim, or have you already progressed to handjobs and blowjobs?"

"Fuck you," she replies. "In case you haven't noticed, it's hot as hell out here. And are you always such a dick to women, or should I feel flattered to be the only beneficiary of your sexist insults?"

Son of a bitch. Is she threatening to report me? No way I'm gonna tell her that I haven't actually signed the goddamn addendum.

"Hendricks! Good to see you back on the field." Coach Sigmon says when he walks up next to us. "Roxy, you and Dane get stretched out, and we'll call it quits for the afternoon. I've gotta work on receiving with special teams the rest of the day."

"Thanks, Coach," Roxanne replies before jogging back over to Dane in the end zone. The two talk, standing closer than necessary before Roxanne lies down on her back in the grass. One leg on the ground, she lifts the other straight up in the air. Dane grips her leg with both of his hands, pressing it down, guiding her thigh to her chest, leaning over her in what looks just like a sexual position. That's when I start seeing red.

Getting to my feet, my fingers clench around the hand grips on the crutches as I watch him manhandle her. I want to storm over there and beat him with one of my sticks while warning him to back the fuck off; but before I can hobble two steps, they've switched positions. Now Dane's on the ground with Roxanne stretching him out. She presses his legs to his body and then leans down to whisper something in his ear. Whatever it is makes him smile and makes me fucking furious. Yesterday she was acting like she wanted me, like she could barely keep her hands off me despite the fact that she hated me, and now she's flirting and shit with another teammate.

The sun's bearing down on me, heating me up and making me swear I'm in hell, especially when I watch Quinton jog over to them, eating her up with his eyes and glaring at Dane like...well, like I'm doing. But for some reason, my team captain's response to her makes me want to shove my foot up his ass. Roxanne gets to her feet and walks up to Quinton. She doesn't seem bothered by his cotton candy head either as they talk and grin at each other like they're both smitten.

Goddamn it. It looks like overcoming my suspicions of her ulterior motives was premature. Roxanne's a maneater, no different than Lola. I made the mistake of trusting a woman once, and she made a fool out of me. That shit won't happen again.

In the preseason of my second year, I met Lola Davis. She was a gorgeous, outgoing Lady Cat who could flash a smile while tossing her long, raven hair over her shoulder, making even the strongest men crumble. We started dating exclusively within weeks, and she practically lived in my apartment by Christmas. During the off season, we were so serious that I asked her to marry me. And when she agreed, I bought her the gigantic rock she picked out that cost more like six months' salary instead of the standard two. Then, I let her help me choose the houseboat because I thought *we* were going to be sharing it together. She wanted the one with extra bedrooms I didn't think we needed and all sorts of other fancy upgrades, stretching my budget more than I should have. But I wanted her to be happy with our home because I loved her.

Apparently, she couldn't wait to christen our new houseboat. The week after I bought it we threw a party, inviting half the team, including our new rookie quarterback. Quinton had just signed a fat four-year contract worth five times that of my own. Chasing those dollars, my fiancée gave Quinton the grand tour of our new home, ending in our master bedroom where she fucked him.

How did I find out? Well, Quinton was kind enough to apologize to me for screwing in my bedroom, but couldn't resist telling Lathan and me about how limber his recent conquest was before kindly sharing her name with us. I lost my shit and got in a few punches on the asshole's perfect face before Lathan and some of the other guys broke it up.

Quinton swore he didn't know Lola and I were together and promised he was done with her for good. He kept to his word, so I eventually gave him the benefit of the doubt, especially after Lola moved up the chain to her new conquest --- our defensive coordinator. Seems she decided to focus on a long-term investment. Coach Powers was only in his early forties, making a decent earning with the potential to coach professionally for many more years to come, perhaps even moving up to head coach for a team someday.

The two were married before the end of the year and just had their first child together. That means I still, unfortunately, have to see the whore at all the group functions. Lola never wastes an opportunity to find me and say hello, reminding me how stupid I was and how easily she manipulated me. The bitch didn't even give me back the engagement ring I spent a fucking fortune on.

So, for the past several years, thanks to Lola, I've lived by an entirely new dating playbook. For starters, I never see the same woman more than three times. I never take her anywhere but out to dinner. If we have sex, I refuse to ever spend the night sleeping in the same bed. No uses of pet names, not even the generic "baby" or "sweetheart." And last, but certainly not least, I never, under any circumstances let a date meet my friends, family or teammates. Without these rules in place, things can become complicated with women. Shit gets serious and then hearts get broken.

I've learned my lesson, so despite how gorgeous Roxanne might be, I refuse to get played by any woman again on or off the field.

Chapter Ten

Roxy

"Tell me I'm wrong, but it sure looked like Dane was getting a little too touchy-feely with you," Quinton says after he jogged over to the end zone.

"It's fine," I tell him with a smile, trying to appear as though my heart isn't racing in my chest and I want to throw up on his shoelaces. "I was just telling Dane that I would stomp my cleat into his balls so hard it would leave permanent imprints if he touched me like that again."

"Good," Quinton replies with a smirk in the asshole's direction. "And then you'll have to answer to me and Coach Griffin. Got it dickhead?" he asks Dane, who is still sitting on the ground.

"We were just stretching. What's the big fucking deal?" Dane replies, getting to his feet and trudging back to campus.

"I'll talk to Coach about getting you some security or some shit," Quinton says, reaching up to run his fingers through his hair and then pausing and wincing when he remembers it's now a pink Mohawk. "Hard for me to be threatening with pink hair," he grumbles.

"Don't worry about it. I can take care of myself. Dane's not the first jerk to mess with me and won't be the last. I don't want to cause problems any more than I already am being the first woman and all," I tell him with a shrug, swiping away the sweat dripping from my forehead. Quinton was right about the blistering heat, so during the lunch break, I said fuck it, trading my black pants in for white shorts.

"It doesn't matter if you're the first or the five hundredth woman to play in this league. You shouldn't have to put up with that shit," Quinton says, gesturing with his thumb over his shoulder into the direction of Dane's retreating back.

"It's fine, really," I assure him. "Let me handle it."

"Okay, but you tell me if Dane crosses the line again," he says.

"I will, or more likely, you'll hear him screaming when I remove his testicles."

"Is that how you got the Ballbuster nickname?" Quinton asks, arching a dark eyebrow and smirking.

"Mostly it's for kicking balls through the goal posts; but once, when I was in high school, there was an incident," I tell him honestly. I'm not sure why, but I feel like I can trust Quinton not to run his mouth and to actually have my back. Maybe even be a friend. He sort of reminds me of Paxton, who I miss like crazy.

"An incident?" Quinton repeats.

"Let's just say the asshole now only has a fifty percent chance of having biological children," I explain, unable to prevent my smile when I remember badass Tommy Wilson falling to his knees and shrieking like a little girl.

"Ouch," Quinton mutters, shifting his hips away from me. "Guess he deserved it?"

"Yeah, he did. See ya later," I say with a wave before lumbering off the field, back to the dorms to get a cold shower and get ready for my first press conference.

Thinking back to my sophomore year in high school on the way, I was so damn young and naïve. When I made the varsity team, suddenly I was the most popular girl in school. My teammates were giving me flowers and other gifts and asking me out like crazy. I was flattered but ignored them all until Tommy, the senior star running back on the team, started flirting with me. He was funny, charismatic and the hottest guy in the school, if not the whole town. Every girl wanted him, and I felt special that, out of all of his available choices, he wanted me.

On our first date, we just kissed goodnight, but then things got hot and heavy real fast. Tommy had serious skills in foreplay that, to a girl like me with zero prior experience, were almost overwhelming. I got wrapped up in his compliments and blame it partially on my raging hormones that liked how easily he could have me begging him for more. Before long, things with Tommy progressed to his hand in my panties. And then during the homecoming party at his house, he convinced me to take my panties off for him. That night I lost my virginity in Tommy's bed. It was like ripping off a Band-Aid, quick and painful. When it was suddenly over, I was still lying there stunned, frozen while Tommy wasted no time going back out to the party with all our teammates. The asshole actually waved around my white panties, a symbol of my innocence he carelessly stole, before collecting his winnings. That's right. Most, if not all of the varsity players had placed bets on who could pop my cherry first. What should have been special and meant something was nothing more than a prize to be won, along with the bragging rights. Tommy was paid his winnings, and then he spent the rest of the night in the hospital after I found him and kneed him between his legs so hard and so many times that his right testicle ruptured. Whoops.

His parents actually wanted him to press charges against me, the sixteen-year-old girl who lost her virginity to the inconsiderate asshole. My dad stood up for me, but the rest of the team gave me hell after that. They slashed the tires on my first POS car, peed a miniature lake in my locker, ruining all of my books, and told everyone I took part in a gang bang with the offensive line, including disgusting, explicit details that never happened.

It was obvious that in White Falls I would never be more than a joke to everyone in that school. All the girls already hated me before any of that happened. So, my dad quit his job as a history teacher and coach at a middle school and moved us to a new town a few hours away where he got a job coaching at a small, private university. Some of the kids there had heard the stories from White Falls, but the coaches stuck up for me, shutting down the bullies. They actually worked with me to help me improve on the field. The one good thing from the whole ordeal was that I learned an important lesson about not sleeping with teammates. What stuck with me the most was that men, especially football players, are assholes who can't be trusted.

While I love my father like crazy and know he would do anything for me, he didn't instill in me much hope for the opposite sex either. My mom up and left us right before my sixth birthday to be with her high school sweetheart she had been cheating on my dad with for months. My dad was obviously crushed by her betrayal and abandonment. A few years later, he seemed to rebound, though, and started dating again. Only, my dad rarely saw a woman for more than a handful of dates. As I grew older, I realized that the women in our house on weekend mornings didn't actually come over to cook us breakfast. No, they had spent the night. After my dad grew tired of them, they would never come around again.

My mother, my father, Tommy Wilson, the White Falls football team --- these are all the reasons that I've never put much faith in relationships. They've all taught me that everyone is selfish, and the best thing to do is look out for myself because no one else will. Love is a sham. Being intimate with a man is fun and feels great for a few wonderful seconds, but then it's back to reality. One where feelings are bound to get hurt, so what's the point?

"How was your first day of practice as a Wildcat?" one of the men with a recorder asks me.

Winona was allowed to come to campus this afternoon to help guide me through the press conference. An hour before it started, we practiced several question and answers that I would likely be asked, including this easy one.

"I think my first practice went well. There's still a lot for me to learn as a rookie in the league, but I'm surrounded by a great group of players and couldn't ask for a better coaching staff."

"Speaking of your teammates," a reporter with a pixie cut starts, her nose wrinkled like she smells shit. My gut clenches in a knot, expecting the worst. "How unfortunate is it that Kohen Hendricks, the team's starting kicker for the past five years, has been injured on the first day of the season? A dislocated knee is not only uncommon but unheard of outside of a brutal hit during a game, isn't it?"

"We all wish Kohen a speedy recovery. He's not only a veteran but one of the best kickers in the league, so I know I can learn a lot from him this season once he's able to get back on the field."

I hate lying, but management is right. There's enough heat on me as it is. Throw in a Tonya Harding scandal, and I'll be forever screwed. The fans would automatically hate me for injuring their starting kicker, even if was an accident, and the press would eat me alive. Hopefully, the rest of the team will keep their mouth shut about what really happened.

Winona lets me field a few more questions before she calls a stop and thanks everyone, ushering me out of the conference room.

"You did good," she whispers as we make our escape. "Thank fuck the story is still buried, or all hell would be breaking loose."

"Yeah really," I agree.

"Oh my God," she mutters, her high heels freezing in the middle of the hallway. "Who knew pink hair could be so hot on a man?"

Following her line of sight, I see she's referring to Lathan and Quinton standing across the lobby with Kohen, all three dressed in expensive looking suits, looking every bit like the million bucks each of them is earning on their paychecks.

"Yeah, those two pull off pink Mohawks pretty well," I admit, even though my eyes are on Kohen.

Every time I see him it's like someone lights a match and tosses it into my belly that's more flammable than gasoline. Heat with an intensity that could rival a wildfire rages through my soul, especially when his dark eyes meet and hold mine from across the room. The crutches are propped under the arms of his dark suit jacket, but they don't distract from his gorgeousness. His longer on top dark hair looks like waves of melted chocolate, styled to stand up in the front, giving him a fresh-from-a-roll-around-the-hay look. There's a dusting of dark scruff along his chiseled jawline, making him look even more masculine and sexy. Knowing exactly the type of muscle definition he's hiding underneath the well-fitting suit, Kohen belongs on billboards modeling boxer briefs rather than on a football field.

"Will you introduce me?" Winona asks, snapping me out of the staring contest with Kohen. But the memory of running my fingernails over the curves and valleys of his sculpted stomach lingers, keeping me off balance.

"S-sure," I tell Winona, leading the way over to the group of handsome men, not as insecure about talking to them now that I've got an excuse to approach them.

"Hey, guys," I say when Winona and I step up between Lathan and Quinton.

"Looking gorgeous, Roxy," Quinton says with a grin and a wink.

"Hey, I mean, um, hi, Roxanne," Lathan stutters and blushes before flashing me a shy smile.

Kohen on the other hand simply glares at me or, more specifically, my sleeveless, knee-length navy blue dress and bright yellow heels that I picked out because they're the team colors.

"You guys look great," I tell the three men while looking only at Kohen.

An elbow rams into the left side of my ribs, making me jump when I remember Winona's next to me. "Oh, right. Quinton, Lathan and Kohen, this is Winona Jones, my manager."

"Nice to meet you," she says, reaching out to shake all of their hands, Kohen's awkwardly since he's propped up on the crutches, and Quinton's last since he's standing to her left.

"Where were you a few years ago when I needed a manager?" Quinton asks Winona. His sapphire eyes give her a slow once-over of her black dress before he wets his bottom lip with his tongue, all while still holding her hand in his. "I ended up making a fat, grumpy, bald man rich when I would've much rather preferred to have a beautiful woman like you by my side."

Whoa, he's not wasting any time putting on the moves. I've, of course, heard about Quinton Dunn's player abilities off the field, but it's shocking to see them in person, especially since he hasn't been anything but purely platonic with me.

I glance over at Winona's face that looks stunned. Finally, she recovers, pushing her glasses up her nose before she says, "That's very sweet of you. I guess the rumors about you are true."

"Maybe a few, but the rest are embellishments," Quinton answers with a wink. "I would love to play a private game of truth or dare so you can try to guess which ones."

Ugh, who falls for that load of crap? I wonder, rolling my eyes.

"I'm free the rest of the night," Winona says, and then the two are strolling away from us.

"What the hell just happened?" I ask Kohen and Lathan, my gaping mouth still open in shock as I watch the two disappear down the hall.

"I've heard worse. That was actually one of his better spiels," Lathan says.

"You're kidding," I say.

"Sadly, no. The worse his lines are, the faster they fall into bed," Lathan explains with a shrug. "I thought for sure he would have to double his efforts to counter the pink Mohawk, but I guess I was wrong."

"Unbelievable," I mutter, crossing my arms over my chest. I thought Quinton was a nice, decent guy, not a sleazy player.

"What? Are you jealous?" Kohen asks with a scowl that oddly enough I want to kiss off of his infuriating face.

"Ah, no. I'm appalled. Winona's always so...and then she just...with him..." I wave in the direction they went, unable to explain why a woman so tough and together could become putty in a man's hands so quickly. Although, that's sort of what happened to me thanks to Kohen...

"It's not just her. Even knowing how he is, women can't seem to help themselves," Lathan tells me.

"That's unfortunate," I reply. "What about you? Are you the type to love 'em and leave 'em?" I ask Lathan, because I don't want to know if Kohen is that type of man.

Lathan's blush deepens. It's such an oddity to see a big, handsome man looking so embarrassed.

"Lathan's a victim of the ugly duckling syndrome," Kohen remarks with a teasing grin at his friend. His panty-dropping grin isn't even being directed at me, but yet it's so powerful that I can feel the dainty strings of my thong starting to slip down my hips.

"Ugly duckling syndrome?" I repeat once I recover.

"Shut your face, Kohen," Lathan snaps before turning back to me, running a palm over the back of his neck. "I was...I had issues in high school," he tells me.

"Didn't we all?" I reply in sympathy.

"Nice try, but someone like you has no idea what it was like to be me."

"Ha!" I bark out a non-humorous laugh. "You can't imagine what high school was like for me. Everyone hated the only girl on the football team."

"At least you were," Lathan starts and pauses, gesturing with his hands up and down my form. "Pretty. I, on the other hand, was the fat kid that everyone picked on and girls avoided like the plague."

"Seriously?" I ask, looking at his tall, massive frame in disbelief.

"Shit. All this emotional baggage upheaval is making me want a Twinkie," Lathan grumbles before wandering off, leaving me standing alone with Kohen.

"Quite a set of friends you've got there," I tell him.

"Looks like you've been making your own friends," Kohen remarks, and I follow his gaze to the man seated at the lobby's entrance, staring at me.

"Who? Dane?" I ask. "He's an idiot."

"You're not worried about him beating you to get the starting spot while I'm out?" Kohen asks.

"Heck no. You have seen him try to kick field goals, right? I think I could do better blindfolded. Actually, I'm certain I could. He may be able to punt the ball across the field, but his accuracy through the uprights is shit."

"True," Kohen agrees with a chuckle that fans the flames of the wildfire inside me that had started to simmer down. Now the fire is raging once more, and my thong is trying to slip down my thighs.

Gah! Why does my body have to have such a dramatic reaction to this aggravating man? *He's off limits! Off. Limits!* I remind my hormones.

"Well, I hate to leave this titillating conversation, but it's time for me to go lie to everyone about how my knee got fucked up," Kohen says, water bombing the wildfire, causing it to fizzle out.

"I'm sorry you have to be dishonest, but that wasn't my decision," I tell him. "I don't like lying either, but management is right. There's no reason to give the media ammo to blow it out of proportion."

"True, but if it gets out, and I'm almost certain it will eventually, they're gonna give you even more hell for it," Kohen says before hobbling off.

Chapter Eleven

Kohen

Of all the stadiums in the world, why did the first woman to play professional football have to plow through mine?

Don't get me wrong. I'm all for women competing in professional football. But what I'm not for is Roxanne taking over my position and turning my life upside down in the process. Just seeing her enter the same room takes my breath away. And, no, I'm not stupid enough to think I'm the only one affected by her in such a dramatic way.

Ballbuster. Maneater. Call her what you want, but she uses the whole wide-eyed, innocent maiden look to get everything she wants from men. She's a cocktease of the highest level. A manipulative temptress. An all-around pain in my fucking ass.

And I want her.

I want her so much that I was a second away from getting on my knees and begging for a night with her before I made my escape. Which is fucked up considering my dislocated knee still doesn't bend correctly thanks to her running me over in her goddamn SUV.

So now I have to go tell lies thanks to the she-devil. I'll lie for her. Because however much I want to hate her, I don't want to do anything to hurt her. Ironic, I know.

If management thinks they can hide the whole accident by repairing her car in hours and blaming my injury on being a klutz, then so be it. The problem is I worry that they're wrong. And when it blows up, the fallout will be on Roxanne, not me or the team. She'll be the one that suffers, and that bothers me for some reason I don't even understand.

At least Roxanne has got to see firsthand what a manwhore Quinton is. I seriously doubt she'll want to hop in the sack with him now, knowing her manager has already been there, done that, along with half the world's female population.

I don't understand why, but I really don't like to think about her with anyone else.

The next day, I'm getting around much better on the crutches, and physical therapy wasn't nearly as painful since the swelling is going down in my knee.

"You made it just in time," Lathan says when I slump down onto the practice field bench.

"Why?" I ask, still out of breath from trudging across the entire field.

"Roxanne and Dane have a bet going that almost everyone else is in on too," he says, nodding to the two in the center of the field. He's right, everyone, including the coaches, have stopped practicing to turn and watch.

"What's going on?" I ask.

"Roxanne and Dane are going best out of three field goals from the twenty-five, then thirty-five and finally forty-five. If there's a tie, they keep moving back five yards from there until someone wins."

"What are the stakes? Can't be hair since Dane's head is shaved."

"Get this, the loser has to put on the Wildcat mascot costume, head and all, and then carry all of the team's equipment back to campus at the end of practice."

"Damn," I mutter, not wanting any part of that shit even if my knee wasn't fucked up. Today's the hottest day yet, a hundred and two damn degrees on the thermometer. Inside of a big, fuzzy cat, it'll be more like a hundred and twenty.

Dane's up first. He makes his kick from the twenty-five, but misses the second two longer field goals.

The football is placed underneath the metal tripod holder, and then Coach Sigmon starts tying something black on Roxanne's face.

"What the hell is he doing?" I ask Lathan.

"Oh, did I forget to mention what the real kicker is?" He chuckles. "Roxanne is doing hers blindfolded."

"That's suicidal," I tell him.

"Guess we'll see," Lathan answers with a shrug.

Once the blindfold is in place, Roxanne does the usual steps backward and to the left before she runs at it and…

"Holy shit, she made it," I mutter in shock. When Coach tells Roxanne she made it, she does her cute little victory dance.

"Yep," Lathan laughs. "Now just one more to go."

Coach walks Roxanne backward to the thirty-five-yard line without her taking off the blindfold. Once the ball is set up under the holder, she counts her steps back and to the side. This time, when she goes for it, her timing is off, and only her toe hits the pigskin causing it to wobble awkwardly before hitting the bottom of the upright and bouncing off. No good.

"Shit," Lathan says. "Gotta make this one."

Again they set up the holder, ten yards further away. Roxanne takes bigger steps to compensate, and the side of her foot hits the ball perfectly, sending it through the uprights.

Everyone is already cheering when Roxanne removes the blindfold with a grin.

"She did it. She actually fucking beat him blindfolded," I say aloud in astonishment, talking to myself or Lathan, I'm not sure which.

"Looks like Dane will be sticking to punts from now on," Lathan replies, followed by another chuckle when Roxanne runs to the sideline and grabs the yellow and blue Wildcat costume and jogs over to hand it to Dane with a smile. "Well, if he survives this afternoon in that suit," Lathan finishes before heading over with the rest of the team to congratulate Roxanne.

I sit there, alone on the bench, watching her in awe. There's a seed of doubt starting to plant itself in my confidence, wondering if Roxanne is a better kicker than I am. Once I'm back on the field, could she beat me blindfolded too? I'm not sure if I want to find out, especially not if I end up embarrassing myself like Dane in front of the entire fucking team.

Chapter Twelve

Roxy

This week has gone by so fast. Thank God.

I'm grumpy, sore and tired, but today is finally the last day of training camp, and no pads have to be worn today. Thank fuck. This afternoon I'll be allowed to go home, well, get a hotel room since I haven't had a chance to look for a place to live around here yet. All my belongings are still in boxes in my Jeep. In a way, I'm sort of feeling superstitious about unpacking, afraid I'll jinx everything and lose out on this fantasy come true. Well, not the hot dorm room or grueling training camp. Overall, the practices haven't been much different from college. I'm holding my own; and after the last few days, I think I'm slowly earning the respect of the other players.

Too deep in my thoughts is how I manage to get caught off-guard, finding Dane coming toward me in the hallway as I was leaving my room to hit the field for the last practice. The guys are all bunking on the first and second floors, so I've had the third to myself. There's no reason for him to be up here. For the last few days, he's been quiet in practice. Almost too quiet ever since I beat him in the blindfolded bet he was so confident he would win.

"What's up, Dane?" I ask, trying to keep my voice from sounding panicked by his presence in the otherwise empty corridor.

Dane laughs like I just told him a joke before he comes closer. "My dick," he says when he's just a few feet away.

With all the warning bells sounding off in my mind, it takes me a second to figure out what the hell he's talking about. I asked what was up, and he was telling me. Right. *Stupid question, Roxy.*

"Good thing today's the last day of camp," I say as I start walking past him toward the stairwell. Although that doesn't seem like the best idea, to be alone with this two-hundred and twenty-pound man in the small space, neither does being alone on an entire floor with him.

Fuck.

If I hurry, I can get down to the second floor where some of the other guys are probably still lurking around.

"Oh, come on, darlin'," Dane says when he follows me down the stairs, my heart beating faster as my feet increase their pace. "What's the rush? We've got twenty minutes until we have to be on the field, and you and I need to have a little talk."

"I like to be early," I say over my shoulder when I make it to the second-floor landing. "And we can talk on the way."

Just a few more stairs to go and I'll be with other teammates.

I don't make it down those steps.

The asshole pushes me face first into the wall, and then his heavy body is pinning me. My cheek is pressed against the coarse bricks, and his palms are covering my flattened palms.

Shit. If I were facing him, I could knee his balls. If I could get my hands free, I could try to gouge his eyeballs. But in this position, my options are limited.

"I'll make this quick," Dane says when he pushes his hardness into my ass. "Here's the bottom line. You need to ease the hell up. Stop making me look bad. I want the starting kicker spot, and you're gonna give it to me along with whatever else I decide I want from you." Releasing my hands, one of his forearms moves to press against the back of my neck, while his other hand starts jerking down my panties and shorts.

Fuck this. I refuse to be a victim without putting up a fight. It's why I started taking self-defense classes during the off-season in high school. My mind races, trying to figure out a way out of this, while my body remains scared and frozen.

"You're gonna keep your fucking mouth shut too," he says, squeezing my right ass cheek in his palm. "Or I'll tell the world about how you ran down your own teammate, *on purpose,* then lied to everyone about it."

Dane telling me to keep my mouth shut brings up a memory from my classes. Since he thankfully wasn't smart enough to cover my mouth, thinking his stupid threat would be enough to keep me quiet, I yell as loud as I can.

"QUINTON!"

Why did I scream his name? I'm not sure. His is just the second name that came to mind, someone the entire team looks up to and someone I've grown to trust in the short time I've known him. I trust Kohen too, but he can't exactly race up two flights of stairs on crutches. Since my yell for help caught Dane off guard, he relaxes his hold on my neck and moves back a few inches, giving me enough room to move. I haul back and ram my elbow into his ribs so hard that his breath rushes out of his mouth in a loud *humph*.

"You fucking bitch!" he groans, slamming me against the wall again. "Oh shit!"

That's all he manages to get out of his mouth before his body is thankfully yanked away from mine. Turning around, I flatten my back to the wall while quickly dragging my panties and shorts back up. I try to catch my breath as I watch Quinton and two other players wrestle with the bastard before he's manhandled and slammed down on the ground.

"You okay?" one of the guys ask.

I nod in response, unable to speak a word or lift my eyes to theirs. All I know is that my worst nightmare could have just happened because I let down my guard for one second. How stupid am I for thinking that I was safe here? No matter how far up I go in this sport, there will always be someone lurking nearby, waiting in the wings to remind me why women aren't welcome on their team because they feel threatened or only see me as just a piece of ass.

Jogging back up the steps to my room with wetness coating my cheeks, I start throwing my things into my duffle bag.

"Roxy, wait. I mean, we're leaving later anyway, so I hope that's the only reason you're packing," Quinton says softly from the doorway, but I keep my back to him so he won't witness the tears on my face. "Look, I saw…we saw what he was doing. Cameron and Tim are taking him straight to Coach Griffin."

I nod and continue flitting around the room to see if there's anything else left.

"I need you to come with me, though, tell them exactly what happened. They'll can Dane, toss him out on his ass for that shit."

I shake my head since it's not that easy. "If they kick him off the team, the story will come out; and then not only am I Tonya Harding, but I'm a lying bitch for not telling the truth about the accident when they all asked at the press conference. It's better if I just go now –"

"Yeah, it's gonna suck if Dane runs his mouth, but he's gonna be gone, and we need you on the team, especially with Kohen out," Quinton says.

"I started playing football because I loved it, but all the…bullshit I have to put up with is just not worth it," I tell him before flopping down on the end of the mattress and using the heels of my hands to wipe the wetness from my face.

"It is worth it. Think about all the women, all the little girls looking up to you. No, you shouldn't have to deal with the sexist crap, but you're right, it's not gonna ever disappear. If we take precautions to keep it from happening again, though, and if you stand up to it, you're standing up for them too, not just yourself."

"Ugh," I groan. "Why do you have to be all reasonable and shit too? Isn't it enough that you're pretty?"

Quinton chuckles before coming around and squatting down in front of me, forcing me to look at him without touching me.

"Are you really gonna let that jerk win?" he asks, his blue eyes searching mine. "Where's the Ballbuster? She would've kicked him in the nuts and told him to go fuck himself, right?"

"Yeah, she would've," I admit, thinking back to when I was just sixteen, standing up to the guy who slept with me for a stupid bet. "But aren't you a bit of a hypocrite?" I ask him.

"What do you mean?"

"Well, you sleep with women like it's an addiction and then send them on their way."

He gives me a *humph* followed by several seconds of silence before answering. "Maybe I'm just waiting to settle down until I find the one woman who tells me to kiss her ass and tries to castrate me instead of letting me touch her. Excuse me for wanting a challenge, but is it my fault I haven't found that one, lone woman yet?" he asks.

"So you sleep with all the rest, including my manager, as, what? Consolation prizes?" I ask with a raised eyebrow.

"That's more fun than being celibate until I find this mythical creature. It could take me decades to find a woman who refuses to sleep with me," he says with a smile.

"You're so full of shit," I tell him, unable to help my grin.

"Come on," he says, getting to his feet and holding his palm out to me. "Quit trying to change the subject. Let's go bust that asshole's balls. Figuratively speaking. Maybe."

Trying to think of giving up football after coming so far makes me sad. I made it here because of all my hard work and dedication, so it would be stupid to let some little prick try to ruin it.

"Fine," I agree, taking Quinton's hand. While most women might faint at the prospect of touching the team's star quarterback, there's nothing more than a comradery of mutual respect between us. "You're a good captain," I tell him on the way down the stairs, letting his hand go now that I have the confidence to do what needs to be done.

"Thanks," Quinton says, flashing me a grin. "I was an only child, but if I had a sister or, God forbid, one day have a daughter, I would want someone to look out for her, you know?"

"I appreciate that, and my dad would too," I tell him, understanding exactly where he's coming from. He reminds me of how Paxton was always protective of me without asking for anything in return or having any ulterior motives.

"No problem," Quinton says. "Now let's try and sort this all out so we can go home."

Chapter Thirteen

Kohen

"How's therapy going?" Coach Griffin asks on Friday afternoon, the last day of our training camp, when he walks into the weight room.

"Great," Jon answers. "We're going slowly, but Kohen's tough, ready to get back on the field as soon as he can."

"Good to hear it. Looks like I'm gonna need him back sooner than expected."

"What do you mean?" I ask, pausing on the leg press machine.

"Dane's out."

"What the fuck?" I ask. "Why? Did he get hurt today in practice?"

"There was a…situation with Roxanne. He violated his contract addendum," he adds quickly before swiping his hand through the air. "Doesn't matter. The asshole is gone, and we've already got a free agent punter on a plane that will start practice Monday."

Situation with Roxanne? He violated the no touching/no sexist comments agreement? What does that mean?

Wow.

Has Roxanne figured out a way to get rid of more competition? How can Coach and the higher-ups not see what the fuck she's doing so damn deliberately?

"You're gonna get a new punter ready to play in the first preseason game within three days?" Jon asks.

"Pretty much. Coach Sigmon will be spending time with the new punter, so I need Kohen on the field, mentoring Roxanne."

"I'm sorry, but did you just say that you want me to *mentor* the girl who ran over me, cost Dane his job and train her to take over *mine?*" I sit up straighter on the machine to ask in complete shock.

While Dane and I weren't best buddies or whatever, he was a good guy and came to most of my houseboat parties. He was dependable and reliable for the team.

"Ran you over? That was clearly an accident," Coach Griffin says with another wave of his hand like he's a magician, making it all disappear. "The surveillance video showed that you weren't paying attention. Believe me, we went over it from every angle for hours. Roxy was driving pretty slowly, but you walked out in front of her, Kohen. You know this!"

I grumble and fall backward against the seat since I can't exactly argue with that. What still pisses me off is that she was the reason I was distracted, why I was on my phone.

"And you won't be training Roxy to take your job," Coach tells me. "When you're up for it, you will play; no ifs, ands or buts about it. Until then, she's our best chance of winning games, even if they're just preseason matchups. That girl's got a leg like you wouldn't believe!"

"Yeah, cause she's got a lead foot," I mutter sarcastically, although it's bullshit. I've watched Roxanne kick several times this week from my golf cart. Not to mention the blindfolded ones. She's damn good.

"There's no free agent kicker better, and Robert and the PR team refuse to trade her, wanting all the publicity she's gonna get this season as the first woman to play pro. That is, if you can take her under your wing and help her reach the next level by showing her how to do what you do..."

"How am I supposed to show her shit when I'll be in rehab for weeks?" I huff.

"You can talk to her, watch her at practice, give her advice. Look, your contract is coming up for renewal, and now your ass is on the injured reserve list. So even if you can't play, you can still be an asset to the team while you recover. Just think about letting her have the spotlight for a few weeks during the preseason to get some experience; and then, once you've recovered, we'll bench her. The guys upstairs will appreciate and remember it if we can win games while you're out. Which will also be good for your contract negotiations in spring."

I get his message loud and clear. The money men want to show her off for a few weeks while they can use the excuse that she's playing because of my injury. And if she sucks, which she no doubt will as a rookie, they'll have a reason to bench her when I'm healthy. That way feminists won't be able to bitch, and we'll win games. Everyone wins. Except for Roxy. Why do I even give a shit?

"Fine," I grumble.

"Great. Whenever you're finished up in here, pack it up and head on home. We're out of time today, but we can pick things up Monday when we're all back on the practice field."

Chapter Fourteen

Roxy

My duffle bag is thrown over my shoulder, along with my purse as I walk down the stairs of the dorm for the second time today.

I was only able to get on the field for thirty minutes this afternoon after all the meetings about Dane we had to have. The manager and PR team were called to the campus, along with several lawyers and Winona, who just left. Quinton hung around with me, not that he was needed other than to give a witness statement. It was more of just a show of support, which I appreciated.

It's been a long day, and I'm more than ready to say goodbye to training camp. Now, I just have to find a hotel to stay in for a few days while I start apartment hunting. It's doubtful that I'll be able to look for a place this weekend without being hounded by paparazzi.

The team's PR people decided that they're going to release the video of when I hit Kohen tonight, along with all the details, to try to cover their asses after releasing Dane from the team. Winona agreed releasing the video was in my best interest, despite having to own up to lying about it for a week. Management is gonna say that Kohen and I didn't want to worry the team, so we hid it from them, and they just figured it out.

I'm worried about the bad press, of course, but what other options do we have at this point?

Seeing Kohen in the lobby, I want to run over and throw my arms around his neck and ask him to help me lose myself the way only he can accomplish. Stupid, I know. It's been a shitty day, and I guess I'm just desperate for a distraction. Having someone to hold me and comfort me for a few hours wouldn't be the worst thing either. Not that I've ever actually had that with a guy. I've never spent the night with anyone, figuring there was no point in getting too comfortable before things ultimately end.

Knowing I'm being unrealistic, I still walk over to Kohen since I'm not sure if he knows the video is about to be released or not. He wasn't present at any of the meetings today, so he probably hasn't heard, and I don't want him blindsided.

"Hey, Kohen," I say in greeting. He maneuvers around on his crutches to face me. It seems like he's getting around on them easier and much quicker after a week of practicing.

"Shouldn't you look happier?" he asks me tersely, and for the first time, I notice the scowl on his face. Initially, I think it's just from the heat since his sleeveless tee is drenched with sweat, or that he's grumpy because he's uncomfortable on the crutches. But no, his anger seems to be directed solely at me.

"What do you mean? Because today's the last day of camp?" I ask, since happy is the furthest emotion from my mind at the moment. Even if I am relieved to be getting back to Wilmington and settling in, it's not like I actually have a place to go.

"No, I mean your manipulation worked. Congratulations on getting rid of more competition."

"What?" I ask in confusion.

"Don't even give me that innocent act like you don't know *exactly* what I'm talking about. I have to give it to you, though, you sure are determined to get what you want," Kohen accuses. "How did you get rid of Dane? Lie and say he called you a bitch or a slut? Did he look at your ass the wrong way?"

"Oh my God," I mutter in shock at his cold words. "You-you don't know what the fuck you're talking about!" I tightly grip the straps of my purse at my hip, because I really want to slap Kohen or poke him in his broad chest for being a dick. I'm also aware that all the players coming in and out of the lobby are looking at us thanks to my shouting.

"I think I know better than anyone what you're capable of, seeing as how I'm the one with the fucked up knee thanks to you!" Kohen hisses.

My throat and eyes begin to burn, but I refuse to let him see me cry.

"Stay the hell away from me," I warn him quietly before I turn to leave.

"No such luck!" he calls out before I can get out the door, loud enough for everyone in the building to hear. "Looks like you're stuck with me since the coaches have their hands full with our new teammate. Bet you wished you hadn't gotten rid of Dane now, right?"

"You're a fucking asshole," I tell him before I make my escape, climbing into my SUV but unable to leave the parking lot because I'm shaking so badly with anger and hurt.

I don't know why I let his words get to me. Kohen's a jerk, just like all the others I've dealt with over the years; but for some reason, I don't want him to think the worst of me. Now the entire team will know what happened with Dane. It'll be like high school all over again, everyone hating me for hurting the team even more.

My body feels like it weighs as much as a herd of elephants. I'm so…exhausted. Tired of the obnoxious players, the drama, the worry. It's been weighing down on me for six years, and I'm just not sure it's worth the headache anymore.

Hearing a group of masculine chuckles, I realize the other players are all packing up to leave and starting toward the parking lot. I need to go. Not sure where I'm headed, home to Tennessee to wallow, or if I'll just keep driving and never look back, I decide to ride along the coast until I run low on gas and have to pull over to fill up.

Finally, in the parking lot of a run-down gas station in the middle of nowhere is where I let myself crumble.

After I cry until there are no more tears, I pull out my cell phone and call the one man who's always been there for me and believed in me.

"Hey, Ladybug," my dad answers right away.

"Hey, Daddy," I say between sniffles.

"What's wrong, Roxanne? Are you okay?" he asks, hearing the tears in my voice.

"No," I tell him. "I'm not sure if I can do this anymore."

Kohen

"You guys seen Roxy?" Quinton asks with a wrinkled forehead when he walks up to where Lathan and I are sitting in the lobby. We've been waiting for his slow ass so we can hit the road and go home.

Hearing her name, especially from him, the way he said it so familiarly, has me sulking even more.

"She left," I tell him. "Why do you care? Was she supposed to kiss your ass before leaving?"

Quinton's jaw ticks as he glares at me. The pink coloring may have faded from his dark hair, but he still looks ridiculous with a fucking Mohawk.

"How can you say that shit after what happened?" Quinton asks me, lowering his voice as he glances around to see who is within earshot.

"You might want to watch out. I mean, if she decides she wants to try her hand at quarterback, you'll be fucked too," I tell him.

He looks away for a second, long enough for me to see the muscle in his jaw tick again before he responds. "You better be glad she's already crippled you, or I would kick your ass."

"Whoa," Lathan chimes in, getting to his feet and inserting himself into the space between Quinton and me. "What's going on with you two?"

"Kohen's mouth is gonna meet my fist if he doesn't shut the hell up!" Quinton says to Lathan.

"He's so fucking blinded by her tits and ass that he can't see the manipulative shady shit she's doing to this team!" I exclaim.

Quinton shoves Lathan out of the way, and then he's in my face with a hand full of my shirt collar in his fist. "You don't know what the fuck you're talking about, so you need to shut your mouth or I'll shut it for you," he threatens me. It's not the fact that he's a heartbeat away from hitting me that gets my attention but the words he used. Ones similar to Roxanne's, saying I didn't know what I'm talking about.

"Enlighten me," I tell him, wanting to know what the hell I'm missing.

"Quinton, man, back off," Lathan urges, trying to pull him away by his upper arm. Quinton eventually lets my shirt go and straightens to his full height.

"We're not gonna talk about it here," he says before storming off, grabbing his bag from the floor and shoving the front door open.

"I'm starting to think there's more to the story about why Dane got the axe," Lathan says once he's gone. "Come on. Let's get on the road and try to figure out what happened."

Getting to my feet, I hobble out on my crutches with Lathan carrying my things to his SUV. Quinton's already sitting in the passenger's seat with the door open, which sucks because I wanted the front to stretch my leg out. Guess I'll have to take the back.

Once we're loaded up, Lathan pulls away from the campus. It takes Quinton fifteen minutes of silently stewing before he finally speaks.

"Why the fuck do you think Dane's gone?" he practically snarls at us like it's obvious.

"I dunno. Why is he gone?" Lathan asks calmly.

Quinton sighs and looks out the window. "He threatened her, and, um, was in the process of sexually assaulting her this morning in the stairwell."

Son of a bitch.

My heart plummets to my stomach, and my lungs stop functioning, refusing to provide me with any oxygen after hearing the words *sexually assaulting.*

"We pulled him off her before he got very far, but still..." Quinton adds.

"Jesus Christ!" I exclaim when my body remembers how to breathe.

So this is why Roxanne looked so upset when I saw her. He touched her. That asshole fucking touched her and tried to do no telling what else to her!

And I was a complete asshole to her when she came to talk to me.

"The lawyers and everyone else had to come down to campus. We spent the whole day in meetings. Dane threatened to tell the media that Roxanne hit you if she didn't make him look better on the field and do...whatever else he wanted."

I will murder that stupid fucker!

"Thanks to the contract addendum we signed, the team had all they needed to legally get rid of Dane. They asked Roxy if she wanted to press charges, but she said no, that she didn't want to have to deal with the media any more than she had to. The video of the accident is gonna be released tonight before Dane can get the story out."

"God, that sucks," Lathan grumbles. "How's Roxanne handling everything?"

"I don't fucking know. That's why I was looking for her. She had a rough day and probably shouldn't be alone. Roxy was already talking about quitting this morning. I convinced her to stay. This afternoon, once that video is out, and the media goes apeshit...I don't know if she'll change her mind. I don't want the team to lose her, but she left before I could talk to her or see how she's holding up."

"It's my fault," I admit, swallowing around the lump of regret lodged in my throat. "I ran my mouth to her. I didn't know..."

"Fuck," Quinton grumbles.

Dammit. Looks like I owe Roxanne one hell of an apology, although that doesn't seem like enough to repair the damage I've done. I have a feeling that she may never forgive me for the shit I said after all she had been through today. And that thought is more agonizing than getting run over by her Jeep.

Chapter Fifteen

Roxy

After talking to my dad for almost an hour, he convinced me to stay in town for a few more days to calm down and see how everything will play out. I can spend some time at the beach this weekend and try to relax on my two days off.

While I'm talking to him, he even gets on his computer and makes reservations for me at an oceanfront hotel in Wilmington. So, that's where my ass is dragging to at the moment. My dad is right. I'm in no shape to drive all the way back to Tennessee or anywhere else tonight. I'll try to get some rest, think things through, and then decide what I'm gonna do about everything tomorrow.

Parking at the hotel, I leave all the boxes of my belongings in the car and just grab my duffle bag with pajamas, a change of clothes and toiletries before heading inside to check-in.

As soon as I step through the automatic doors, my tired, shuffling feet come to a stop, and my bag falls from my shoulder when I see him – the tall, gorgeous man with his auburn hair combed perfectly to the side, wearing an immaculate, pinstriped suit.

"Paxton!" I exclaim as my best friend rushes over and sweeps me into his arms.

"Thought you could use a friend after surviving camp," he says with a kiss to my cheek.

His words, his kindness of coming all the way here causes me to collapse into his arms, the weight of the day catching up to me.

"Aw, what's wrong, Rox? Rough week?" he asks while I sob into the collar of his dress shirt. I'm not a crier, and Paxton knows it.

"You have…no idea," I tell him.

"Let's get you up to the room. Hope you don't mind me crashing with you," he says as he lets me go and grabs my hand, stopping long enough to pick up my bag from the floor. "Your dad booked the room with two queen beds in my name since he knew I would probably beat you here."

"Thanks for coming," I tell him, leaning my weight against his shoulder while we wait for the elevator. "I could definitely use a friend tonight."

"Oh shit," Pax mutters before yanking me against his chest and stepping in front of me. "Paparazzi alert."

"Paparazzi?" I ask, stupidly looking around his shoulder before I see them, two guys with cameras, snapping away pictures of Paxton and me.

"Shit," I grumble, using Pax as a human shield. Thankfully, the elevator doors open, and we step inside, Paxton pushing the close button and number four before anyone gets on with us. "They were persistent," I turn to say to him.

Paxton's tan cheeks reddening in anger. "I take it you haven't had access to a computer or internet this week?" he asks as the elevator begins to ascend.

"Ah, not really. I've had my phone, but we weren't supposed to use it unless it's an emergency."

"Oh, well, that's good. But just so you know, you're a hot topic – the first woman to play with the pros. This afternoon a video of you in an accident came out, so a few are dissing you. But that was totally not your fault. I've seen it."

"How bad are they coming down on me?" I ask.

"Some are saying nasty shit, but there's a lot of positive too, people rooting for you."

"Rooting for me to fail," I mutter, relieved when the elevator doors open and we're soon inside the privacy of our room. "I'm thinking about quitting," I tell Paxton after we flop down next to each other on one of the beds.

"Quitting?" he repeats, rolling to his side to face me. "You can't be serious, Roxy. This is the chance of a lifetime. I would love to be in your shoes."

"One of the players attacked me today," I admit to him.

Paxton comes off the bed like it's on fire, straightening to all six feet, two inches of his lean height. "Tell me who and I'll go kill that motherfucker!" he growls.

"You're not gonna kill anyone," I tell him, reaching for his hand and pulling him back down on the bed.

"What happened, Roxy?" he asks, pushing the hair that's fallen loose from my ponytail and tucking it behind my ear.

I go through the details of the event that lasted only a few seconds but managed to shake the foundation underneath me. The foundation that took me years to rebuild after it was jerked out from underneath me in high school.

"I can't imagine how hard that was for you, but you can't let one asshole take this monumental opportunity away from you," Pax says after he listens to the whole story quietly.

"It's not just one asshole," I tell him, thinking about Kohen and the harsh words he said to me. "They'll all think I'm a bitch for ruining the team. None of them will take me seriously, just like in college. Just like high school."

"Look, Rox, I get that you're upset about what happened, but are you sure you're not just trying to find a way out because you're scared of failing?"

"That was a low blow," I tell Paxton, poking him in the chest with my index finger, which of course reminds me of Kohen.

The sound of my phone ringing brings our conversation to a halt, so I get up to dig the device from my purse that's still on the floor. I figure it's my dad, making sure I got checked in okay, but the number on the screen is an unknown one.

"Answer it or I will," Pax threatens when it continues to ring in my hand.

"Fine," I grumble, hitting the green button. "Hello?"

"Roxanne, hi, it's Robert," the masculine voice replies. My jaw drops and I mouth "Oh shit" to Paxton, who's now sitting on the edge of the mattress, when I realize it's the Wildcats' owner.

"Hi, Mr. Wright," I say when I'm finally able to recover from the shock. It was one thing to speak to the Wildcats' owner the day I was signed, but I figured that would be the only time I would ever talk directly to the man in charge.

"I just wanted to call and apologize for what happened earlier," he says. "Even though I wasn't there, I take full responsibility. It was my job to make sure that you're safe. And honestly, I didn't think one of my players would ever...I'm sorry, Roxanne, but I can assure you that Mr. Adams has been released and won't play professional ball ever again. I'll inform the other teams of his transgression, so they won't touch him with a ten-foot pole."

"I-I'm not sure what to say," I tell him honestly following the silence after his statement.

"Give me another chance, Roxanne. Let us show you that our team is more than one bad apple. We're a family, and I promise I won't let you down again. My daughters, Joselyn and Amber, are already clambering to meet you. The whole world wants to see you succeed."

I blink to try and hold off the tears. Otherwise, I'll be incapable of having a conversation.

"I don't want to cause more problems for the team, and I feel like I already have with everything that happened with Kohen and now Dane," I tell him.

"After releasing the video, I'm sure you'll start hearing some of the knuckleheads in the media beating the whole accident to death, but we've moved past that, and I hope you have too. If we keep pushing forward, show them that you're a true football player, a damn good one at that, I'm sure they'll get back to talking about games instead of the other nonsense. So, what do you say? Are you gonna help us win some games this season, or let my daughters and me down?"

"Whoa, that's a cheap shot there, Mr. Wright," I tell him even though a smile stretches across my face. Glancing over at Paxton, he's giving me a thumbs up.

"There's a lot more on the line than winning, and I would hate to see you throw it away."

"Okay, you've convinced me," I say with a sigh, hoping I'm not making a mistake.

Chapter Sixteen

Kohen

All weekend I sulked, feeling so damn guilty about the shit I said to Roxanne. I didn't even take the boat out. For two days I sacked out on my sofa, alone, and flipped channels.

It didn't help that all the entertainment news, even the sports networks, were all showing the video of Roxanne hitting me, and then stalking her during our weekend off. She apparently spent a lot of time at the beach, and she definitely wasn't alone. Some copper-haired douchebag was by her side every second, and the articles said they were rumored to be sharing a fucking hotel room. Now, I can't help but wonder who the hell the bastard is.

Does Roxanne have a boyfriend? If so, what the fuck was she doing kissing me and doing…other things with me? Those are the questions that were hammering into my skull over and over again all weekend.

Today, we're on the practice field for the first time this season. I watch from the bench in awe for half an hour as Roxanne kicks ball after ball, my dick getting heavier with each one that sails through the air. Who knew that seeing a woman do what's as routine as breathing for me would be so fucking hot? And why the fuck haven't I gone out there to apologize? Probably because I know she'll never forgive me, and I don't want to see the hurt I've caused on her face.

"Roxy, bring it in," Coach Griffin calls out as he takes a seat on the bench beside me.

"Yeah, Coach?" Roxanne asks after jogging over, standing in front of us in her shoulder pads covered by a navy blue jersey with her yellow number three and white shorts, sweat dripping down her gorgeous face. She doesn't even glance in my direction, pretending I don't exist.

Instead of answering her, Coach suddenly turns to me and starts firing off questions like a machine gun. "How are you getting around, Kohen? I know Jon said you shouldn't be on your feet more than a few hours a day, right? You got friends or family staying with you to help out?"

"Ah, I'm getting around pretty well, and I did okay on my own this weekend," I answer.

Coach rubs the dark stubble on his chin as if in thought. "Roxy, Kohen here is gonna be your coach, trainer, and mentor for the rest of the season," he says before patting me on the shoulder.

"Yes, sir, I've heard," Roxanne answers, sounding like she would rather be skinned alive than suffer through a season with me.

"So, how's the apartment search going, by the way? Still looking for a permanent place in Wilmington?" Coach asks her.

"Oh, well, I've just been staying in a hotel room until I can check out a few places…" *With some douchebag*, I silently add to her response.

"Well, then this is perfect. Kohen is gonna need help getting around and has plenty of extra bedrooms. Ain't that right, Kohen?"

"Ah, what?" I ask, glancing between my head coach and the girl who looks like she walked out of a naughty magazine, a football fan's wet dream.

"Your house. How many bedrooms does it have?" Coach repeats.

"Bedrooms? My bedrooms?" I ask him in confusion. Am I high on painkillers or suffering from heatstroke? I'm pretty sure I only had one over-the-counter pain reliever this morning before I went to PT, and I haven't been sitting out under the sun but thirty minutes or so.

"You've got several spare rooms, right?" Coach prompts.

"Yeah, there's two spare bedrooms."

"Roxy's looking for a place…" he starts, but she interrupts.

"No, sir, that's okay. I appreciate the thought, but I really can't impose on Kohen like that."

"But you're partially responsible for why he's on crutches," Coach guilt trips her while I sit there with my jaw hanging open, stunned at the turn of this conversation. "And since he's gonna be helping you out, don't you think it's the least you can do?"

Roxanne opens and closes her mouth like a fish out of water as if she's trying to formulate an adequate response and is coming up empty. It would probably be funny if I weren't in the same boat with her. Apparently literally.

"Kohen?" Roxanne asks, her grassy green eyes pleading when they finally meet mine for the first time, hoping I'll save her because she thinks I hate her after I put my foot in my stupid mouth, calling her out on her manipulative bitch antics. The problem is, if I speak up and say *hell fucking no, I don't want to share the same space with her*, I'll look like an asshole to my Coach. But then, if I say yes, can I really endure this woman prancing half-naked around my house even if she pretends I don't exist and will never forgive me for the shit I said?

Fuck yes. Having an angry Roxanne around is better than no Roxanne.

"Sure, I mean, why not?" I say. There's also the benefit of having her practically waiting on my every beck and call. I'm almost enjoying the thought of this arrangement except for the look of sheer terror on her pale face. She hates me so fucking much that she can't stand the thought of staying with me.

"But...but what about the media? Won't they think that we're...you know...wouldn't they get the wrong idea?" Roxanne asks Coach, grasping at straws. Or maybe she's worried about what her boyfriend will say about her living with another man.

"Nah. Kohen's boat is the only place that's off the radar, with no actual address, which is perfect. No one will be able to find you there. Even if the media was to eventually track you down, we could easily spin it, showing that despite what happened on the first day, you two have made amends and are not only roommates but friends," Coach says. "Well, I'm glad that's all worked out." Getting to his feet, he places a slap on Roxanne's shoulder pads, unaware or uncaring that she looks like a scared colt about to make a run for the hills. "I'll let you two work out the details after practice. Roxy, get back over there to the left hash mark and keep backing up from the forty yard line a yard at a time until you miss," he tells her. After a stunned moment, Roxanne finally jogs away.

"There's another reason I need you to be her roommate and shadow, besides trying to hide her from the press hounds," Coach says quietly to me once Roxanne's out of earshot. His tone is more serious as he takes off his ball cap and rubs his sweaty head while pacing in front of the bench.

"Her shadow?" I repeat. Isn't it enough that I'll be spending my days with her on the field and nights with her in my home?

"You're a good guy, Kohen. One of the best on the team. I've never questioned your moral compass."

"Huh? My moral compass?" I ask, not sure where he's going with this. Especially since Roxanne's so goddamn sexy on the field that I'm gonna be throwing wood in a hurry if I don't think about dead fish or something else equally revolting very soon.

"Roxy has a bullseye on her. This is between you and me only, you hear?" he asks, eyes narrowed.

"Sure," I assure him.

"The lawyers are terrified of a harassment or assault lawsuit. If another player says the wrong thing or touches her…well, that would be a nightmare."

"And what exactly do you expect me to do on crutches?" I ask, trying not to think about the times I've touched her inappropriately so my cock doesn't get any harder. Thinking about her being touched by that asshole Dane or another player without her permission douses the heat quickly, though.

"Your presence should be enough to keep the bastards away from her. The rest of the guys will be busy on the field, but you won't have anything to worry about except her. Making sure she's the best damn kicker she can be and that no one else lays a finger on her."

Crutches or not, I would kill any fucker who tries to paw at her without her permission. Oddly enough, I sort of want to do the same to any of the ones she *does* give permission, like the dickhead who spent the whole weekend on the beach with her.

What the fuck is my deal with Roxanne? I barely know her, she ran me over, and yet I've somehow ended up wanting to protect her.

Roxy

Oh my freaking God!

Of all the players on the team, Coach wants me to live with *Kohen*? Seriously? That's like my worst PR nightmare. I can already see the tabloid heading, "*Football floozy sleeping with Hendricks to steal his starting position since running him over didn't work.*"

But it wasn't like I could tell my head coach no without looking like a bitch. He's right. It is partially my fault that Kohen's hobbling around on crutches. It can't be easy for him to do the regular everyday things like cooking and cleaning, and it didn't sound like he had anyone to help him.

Besides, Kohen has signed the same no contact agreement as Dane and all the other players. Not that he kept his hands off me the first day we met, but he's never set off my perv alert. No, he's one of the first men I've met who sets off my holy-hell-he's-hot alarm. And what did I do? Run him over, hurting him and our team.

If I had to be attracted to one of my teammates, why couldn't it at least be Quinton? He's been chatting with me every chance he gets; and while he definitely hasn't been lewd or sleazy about it, I think he's been subtly flirting with me. Like right now, standing in the middle of the practice field, Quinton's telling me about a restaurant downtown that has the hottest wings and a million television sets with every sport imaginable. In fact, he sounds like he's seconds away from asking me if I want to join him one night, either with a group of friends or just him and me.

While I'm certainly flattered, because I've been fangirling over him for the past few years watching him play on television, there's not even an ounce of desire flaring, nothing like the searing heat that I feel in my panties watching the lean, dark-haired hottie limping over to us on his crutches. But then I remember Kohen's asshole comments from Friday when I was down in the dumps. And the sexist ones before that, asking if I was giving handjobs and blowjobs to the other guys. The bastard has no idea what it's like to be the only woman on a football team. I'm sure he's always been Mr. Popular with the guys on the field and with plenty of ladies off of it.

"Do you plan on…kicking some more balls…or are you just gonna…stand around for the next two hours?" Kohen asks when he comes to a stop beside me, out of breath.

"I better get back to work, too," Quinton says. "See ya, Kohen," he says before jogging over to the quarterback coach.

"See you," Kohen calls out to his retreating back.

"Do you plan on always being a dick to me?" I ask him with my hands on my hips.

"I guess you can consider me your very own personal dick from now until February," he tells me with a smug smile.

"In that case, I think I'll call you Coach Dildo, because all I have to say to you is go fuck yourself," I reply. The smile on Kohen's face vanishes, and he blows out a breath while looking at the grass.

"Look, I'm sorry about the shit I said…if I had known what really happened…"

"That's right, you didn't know! You assumed the worst of me, just like you've been doing since the moment we met."

"I said I'm sorry, okay? Just put yourself in my shoes for a second. This is the only job I've ever had. It's the difference in being stuck in a small town and making it on my own. When it was threatened, I lashed out at you because you were the reason I was distracted."

"What?" I ask, my anger diffusing slightly with his apology and the reminder that I'm partially responsible for almost ending his livelihood.

Kohen glances away, avoiding my eyes before he finally responds, mumbling something so quietly I can't catch it between the wind noise and whistles being blown as practice goes on around us.

"Can you repeat that?" I ask. "I couldn't hear you.'

He grumbles and finally locks his melted chocolate and caramel swirled eyes with mine. "I was looking you up on the Internet. That's why I wasn't paying attention and stepped out into the road."

"Me?" I shriek, surprised and…flattered that I was the reason he was so distracted that he never saw my big ass Jeep barreling toward him. "Why were you looking me up?"

"It doesn't matter," he says, the sun or embarrassment causing a reddish hue to spread over his tan cheeks. "I'm sorry about what happened with that dipshit Dane. I never thought he would've done something so stupid, but Quinton said he saw him..."

"Yeah, he did. If not, would you still call me a liar?" I snap at him defensively.

"I was an asshole, and I spent the whole weekend feeling like shit, okay?"

"So did I," I reply honestly. "I never meant to cause problems for the team with you or him. Believe me, I wish I could just play football without all the drama."

"I know that. So can we agree to try and put all that shit behind us? Not only will we be working together for the next few weeks, but it looks like we'll be living together too..."

"Yes," I agree on a heavy exhale. "But, I mean, we don't have to live together. I can find somewhere else to stay," I assure him.

"Uh-uh. Coach's orders," he says while shaking his head. "And neither of us wants to be on his shit list."

"Guess not," I agree, feeling equal parts nervous about living with Kohen and excited. His houseboat is freakin' amazing. The prospect of living there, even for a few weeks until we can figure something else out should be fun. If we don't kill each other.

"So I guess we should get to work. Looks like you may need me punting too. The new guy, Warren, isn't getting any better."

We both look over and watch as our rookie punter's practice kickoff only makes it twenty feet before going out of bounds.

God, he sucks.

"How are you on punting?" Kohen asks me.

"Well, Coach Dildo, shouldn't you have, I dunno, maybe looked up your player's stats?" I tease him with a small smile.

"Since I've had shit to worry about after getting mowed down, why don't you give me the CliffsNotes version," he replies with his own grin.

"Fine. Last year I had thirty-three punts in ten games, eleven-hundred and twenty-one yards, and averaging thirty-five yards per punt. Not a single one went out of bounds upfield, and twelve of them were corner coffin punts, thank you very much."

"Damnnnn. At least your kicking is better than your driving," he mutters, actually sounding impressed.

"Ha-ha."

While punting may look easier than making a field goal, it's not. Not only do you have to put a lot of ass into it, but there's also various strategies on each one. Sometimes, if you're facing a punt returner with a history of running back kickoff touchdowns, the special team's coach will instruct you to kick the ball all the way through the back of the end zone, so that there's no chance of a runback. If time needs to be run off the clock, there's the ground kick that will bounce several times before a player can pick it up. Getting a punted ball to stay right around the five-yard line or less without going into the end zone could be critical for helping pin the other team's offense to their own side of the field, giving our defense the chance to score a fumble and recovery for a touchdown or get a safety. And finally, and the most tricky, is the onside kick. Not only does the ball have to go at least ten yards forward, but it needs to have enough hang time to give our special teams' players the opportunity to get up underneath it to try and catch it before the other team. It's a gamble, and most teams only use it when they're losing and desperate; because if it fails, the other team gets to have the ball at midfield, almost guaranteeing a field goal, if not a touchdown.

"What should we start with, Coach?" I ask Kohen.

"Let's see you punt a few balls. If you look better than Warren, I'll go talk to Coach Sigmon and see what he thinks."

For the next two hours, Kohen pretty much tells me everything I do wrong, but he agrees that we may have a better shot with me punting than the new guy. Coach Sigmon said he would consider it after giving Warren a shot in the first preseason game. Which is fine with me. That means in the first game all I have to worry about is extra points and field goals.

Finally, Coach Griffin calls us all in for the huddle to bring practice to an end. We get a quick pep talk before he dismisses us until tomorrow morning.

Pulling out his cell phone on the way to the parking lot, Kohen asks me, "What's your number so I can text you my address?"

I recite the digits and tell him I'll be over once I get checked out of the hotel.

Smiling, I make my way to my Jeep, coveting a cold shower right about now. I'll have to wait to take one when I get back to my room since the practice field doesn't have any women's locker rooms. While I shower, I'll have Paxton pack up my things for me. He's been hanging out all weekend, despite my assurances that I'm fine and he should be home doing...whatever it is he's gonna do now that we've graduated and he wasn't one of the lucky ones able to go pro.

I wonder what Paxton will say when he finds out where I'll be living for the next few weeks or months. I may normally tell my best friend everything, but I haven't told him about kissing Kohen or how much I want him. I know what Pax would say – that it's stupid and history repeating itself, etcetera. He's right, but sometimes at night, before I drift off to sleep, I can't help but think about the hot kiss Kohen and I shared, pretending it goes a little further. Even when I was angry with him, there was no disputing the fact that Kohen is sexy as fuck, and now I'll be sharing a houseboat with him.

Chapter Seventeen

Kohen

I'm expecting Roxanne when I hear the car door shutting on the dock; but when I hear the second one, I wonder who the hell could be with her. Did she seriously bring that douchebag from this weekend?

Hobbling over to the sliding glass door, I pull it open and watch with my jaw hanging open as the asshole in an expensive looking gray suit grabs boxes out of the back of Roxanne's SUV and follows her to my boat.

"I really love this place. Are you sure this is okay? Me staying here?" Roxanne asks when she glances up and sees me waiting at the door for them.

"Yeah, but I didn't know you had...someone coming with you," I remark. "Is he moving in too?" The words come out snarkier than I intended. Wait, no, I'm pretty sure I meant them to be snarky.

"No, he's not moving in. This is Paxton Price. Paxton, meet Kohen Hendricks, my victim and now roommate," Roxanne says, making introductions.

"I would shake your hand, but mine is kind of full," the too-cool-for-school dude says when he approaches, his dark shades hiding his eyes.

"Right," I say. "So, there are two spare bedrooms. Pick whichever one you want."

"Isn't this place amazing?" Roxanne mutters to the prick.

She looks fucking amazing in her black cotton shorts and skintight blue tank top. Not that it matters what she looks like. She's off limits, my responsibility to Coach and nothing else from now on.

"Could you pick a room already?" the douche behind her huffs, readjusting his hold on the boxes in his arms.

Roxanne laughs, but then the two disappear down the hall. I resume my seat on the white leather sofa watching a soccer game with my leg propped up on the ottoman.

"If you lay a finger on her, you'll have two bad knees," the dickhead says to me quietly when he walks back in the living room alone, empty handed.

"Oh, will she run me over again?" I ask once I recover from his unexpected threat.

"No, I'll break it," he tells me on the way out the door.

Jackass. What sort of name is Paxton anyway?

Once everything has been brought in, Roxanne walks the prick to the door. I try to ignore watching their goodbye from my seat on the sofa but can't help myself. The two hug for several long seconds, and then Roxy kisses him quickly on the lips before he finally slips out the door.

"So, thanks for letting me stay here," Roxy says, sitting her ass down on the arm of the sofa.

"No problem," I remark.

"Do you need anything? Have you had dinner? I can make something."

"No thanks, I'm good," I tell her. "But help yourself to whatever's in the kitchen."

"What do I owe you for rent and utilities?" she asks.

"Nothing," I say without hesitation. "It's not like I need the money."

"Well, I have to pay you something. I can't just live here mooching off of you."

"I guess you can help out with buying groceries," I suggest since I can't drive yet or hobble around on crutches trying to push a buggy. "And, I mean, if you want to cook and clean that'd be cool since I hate doing both."

"Sure, I don't mind. Back at home, I did all of the housework since my dad worked so much," she explains.

"What about your mom?" I ask her before my brain can filter the question.

"She left when I was five, so it's just been my dad and me since," Roxy tells me with a shrug like having her mother up and leave, never coming back is no big deal.

"I'm sorry," I say sincerely. "That sucks. Although, our house would've been more peaceful without our mom."

"You don't get along with her?" Roxy asks as she slides down from the armrest onto the sofa cushion, tucking her legs underneath her.

"Hell no. Not with her or my dad. It's a wonder my brother and I weren't born with the genetic condition of our heads already lodged up our asses."

"Ouch," she mutters. "My dad's like my best friend, so I couldn't imagine us not getting along," she admits while her fingers fidget with the charm on her bracelet, one that looks like a ladybug.

"You're lucky then," I tell her honestly, my eyes going back to the television.

"So…soccer?" she asks, noticing the game.

"Yeah, didn't you play in college or high school?" I ask since that's the path most kickers take to end up on a football field.

"God, no. Didn't your Internet search tell you? I'm a football girl through and through. Soccer's…boring," she says with a wrinkled nose.

"Boring?" I reply indignantly.

"Yep. And it's a wimpy sport," she teases with a grin. "Now, rugby? *That* is a badass sport."

"Whatever. We can't be friends if you disrespect my sport," I tell her.

Roxanne laughs, and I realize it's the first time I've ever heard such a sweet sound, not just out of her mouth but in all my twenty-seven years on Earth. It's one that I already crave to hear again, wanting the happy sound to originate because of something I say or do, even if it costs me my dignity or respect.

But then I remember that Roxanne just said goodbye to her boyfriend, so it's stupid of me to want her laughs to belong solely to me.

And that thought is depressing as fuck.

Chapter Eighteen

Roxy

The gentle rocking of the boat actually calms my nerves enough for me to relax and drift off to sleep Monday and Tuesday night, despite being in a strange place.

When I wake up Wednesday morning, it's way too early. The sun's not even up yet, but trying to go back to sleep is a lost cause. Now, the pesky worries feel like they're being battered into my brain by a persistent woodpecker.

Today's the last practice before the team travels to New Orleans for our first preseason game. My first game as a professional football player. The first time a woman has ever put on a jersey and stepped foot in a stadium.

David Bowie's "Under Pressure" is currently playing on repeat in my mind as if it's my new theme song. I don't want to let anyone down, my dad, the team, the young girls looking up to me as a role model. The worst thing I could do is say, "Sure, girls, you can do anything you want if you work hard enough" and then go and make a fool of myself, proving that I'm not cut out for professional football.

There's this nagging doubt I can't shrug off that maybe all the naysayers I've dealt with over the years are right – women can't physically compete on the professional level in this male-dominated sport. These are not just average men either, but humongous giants that seem to get bigger every year. Unlike college where, at six feet tall, I was pretty much head level with all the guys, I feel like a shrimp out on the field with my Wildcats teammates.

Now that I'm antsy, I've kicked off all the sheets and am unable to fall back to sleep. Since I can't sit still, watching television is obviously out. I may as well do some work around Kohen's boathouse, doing what I always do when I have nervous energy to burn --- clean. Not that his place is dirty and needs it. He's not messy like most guys, keeping the place nice and tidy. Although for the last two days, we haven't spent much time here. Instead, we've spent most of our time with the team, practicing and even eating dinner as a group before coming home to crash from the heat and exhaustion.

I climb out of bed and pad barefoot down the hall. In the kitchen I rummage around in the cabinets under the sink, looking for cleaning products. Since Kohen's still asleep, I decide to start with dusting from the front of the boat and making my way to the back because it's a quiet activity. There's a lot of dark wooden surfaces, tables, an entertainment center, and bookcases that I go to work dusting with paper towels and furniture cleaner. The darkening of my white towels is not a testament to Kohen's cleanliness. It's just what happens if you don't swipe a rag over everything about once a week. Dust will no doubt collect, and this morning I'm a dust eliminator.

Once all the furniture smells fresh like lemons, I head back to the kitchen to wash up the few dishes in the sink. Noticing that Kohen has a dishwasher, I rinse the dirty plates, cups, and silverware, then load it up. Dad and I have never had anything but the sink for dishes, but I get the gist of how it works and fill up the opening with detergent. Shutting the front of the washer, I turn the dial until the machine kicks on and goes to work.

Now that I've worked up a sweat, I decide to head back to my room and get a shower before practice, thankful that I have my own private bathroom. Even though the facilities are compact, the space is still bigger than either of the bathrooms at the two houses my dad and I have lived in, and it's so much newer and nicer. This place is dripping with elegance and...money. There's no doubt that Kohen has made quite a bit during his time as a starting kicker, yet I'm not the least bit upset that I'm paid way less. I have to work my way up and prove myself during clutch times to make the big dollars. Let's hope that I can actually do that.

Once my hair is dried, I pull it back into a ponytail and get dressed in a blue team tee and yellow shorts. I'm about to step out of my room to search for something to make for breakfast when I hear Kohen shout, *"What the fuck?"*

I rush out to see what he's yelling about and find him standing in the kitchen in nothing but a pair of black shorts. The tan, sculpted muscles of his smooth chest and abs are sheer perfection. I'm startled by the speed at which a small heater turns on inside of me, the sudden warmth so intense that my stomach actually cramps with arousal. It only takes a second for the scene around Kohen to douse the flames of desire. He's standing in a sea of bubbles that reach his shins, nearing the brace on his left leg; and he's clearly not happy about the foam party in his kitchen floor based on the cocoa-colored glare I meet when my eyes are finally able to lift to his.

"What the hell did you do, Roxanne?" he shouts at me, his fists gripping his crutches tightly.

"I...um, well, I clean when I get stressed out, so I did some dusting and started the dishwasher."

"Why does it look like a bubble bath in my kitchen?"

"I dunno. Must be something wrong with the washer," I tell him. He reaches over and turns the machine off and then picks up the mostly empty bottle of orange dish detergent from the sink. "Did you put this shit in there?"

"Well, yeah, of course," I answer.

"Oh my God," he grumbles. "The dishwasher uses its own detergent. You know, dishwasher detergent!"

"Wait, there's a special detergent for it?" I ask in confusion.

Kohen's growl of frustration is my answer.

"I-I didn't know! It's not like I've ever used a dishwasher before," I tell him.

The anger slides off his face as his jaw drops. "How is that possible? Were you raised with the Amish?"

"Ah, no, I was raised by a single father in Bumfuck, Tennessee," I reply. "Now where's your mop so I can start cleaning this mess up?" I ask, my face warming with a blush of embarrassment, both because of the stupid thing I've done and the fact that I was raised in a household that could barely afford the necessities, much less a freaking dishwasher. College was even worse since I lived in the dorm paid for by my scholarship with only a small microwave.

"Mop and bucket are in the closet at the end of the hall," he says tersely.

"Go sit down and I'll clean this up," I tell him on the short walk. "Don't want you falling and hurting your other leg!"

When I get back, Kohen's leaning his back against the counter between his propped up crutches. There's a roll of paper towels in his hands, and he's tearing a couple off like they'll be enough to wipe up all the million suds, despite my order to let me handle it. I set the mop and bucket down and try to wrestle the roll of towels from his hands.

"I've got this," I tell him.

"Clearly you don't," he replies, yanking the roll back.

"Why are you being such a dick about this?" I mutter, giving up on the paper towels and turning around to grab the mop. That's when I feel it, a cold, soggy towel slapping the skin of my lower back where my t-shirt was raised. At first, I think it must've been an accident since Kohen has such a stick up his ass that he wouldn't have done such a thing. But then I hear it, his snorts of laughter, and it's on.

Grabbing the handle of the mop, I soak the long threads in the suds and then lift it to paint Kohen's bare chest like the mop's a giant paintbrush and he's my canvas.

He knocks the mop away, but not before I douse him good, leaving behind a shirt made of suds behind.

"You little bitch," he mutters while ripping off more towels. "Is this how you treat cripples?"

"When the cripple's an asshole," I reply with a giggle before mopping up more suds and dumping them on top of Kohen's head.

He gasps at the coolness running down his face and neck before he reaches up and grabs the wooden handle of the mop, giving it a tug. I refuse to let go, so we play tug of war with it. When it becomes obvious that he's gonna win despite having just one good leg, I stoop down and gather suds in both my hands. Since he doesn't have anywhere to go without his crutches, he's unable to stop me from rubbing more foam into his face, leaving behind a full Santa beard dripping from his chin. It's the funniest shit I've ever seen, causing me to double over with laughter as he wipes his hands over his face trying to clear the bubbles away. It's an impossible feat, though. While I'm cackling, Kohen launches more damp rags at my face. At this rate, we're gonna be late for practice and never get the kitchen clean, but it's too much fun to stop. I pick up the rags that rain down on me and launch them back at Kohen.

"Good thing you're a kicker because you can't throw worth a shit," he remarks with a grin when I miss my target – his head – several times in a row.

"I know, right? How could anyone miss your big ole melon?" I tease, taking a step closer to throw my next sudsy ball.

I'm caught off guard, not realizing that I'm close enough to Kohen for him to reach me. He grabs both of my arms and pulls me to him where his back's still propped up against the counter. I slam against his bare, damp chest, the shock of which is short-lived when I get a face full of cold suds. Gasping, I wipe off what I can from my eyes so I can see. Without stopping to think about it, I keep hold of the handful of suds from my face and grab the elastic band of Kohen's shorts, my next intended target, getting ready to fill them with bubbles when I stupidly make the mistake of glancing down.

"Oh my God," I mutter, freezing in surprise, my eyes locked on this unexpected discovery. "You're not wearing any underwear."

"I'm...not wearing any underwear," Kohen confirms, our faces inches apart, both of us still panting, gazes lowered.

Deep in the back of my mind I know that I need to let go, to allow the elastic to pop back into place, concealing his private parts, yet I don't, out of curiosity or fascination. I'm not sure which. Feeling his hardness through layers of clothing weeks ago was one thing, but seeing it...wow.

He's so very neatly manscaped that there's absolutely nothing obstructing the clear view of his long, thick brick of a cock that's proudly pointing to the right like a directional arrow indicating the way to the bedrooms. For the past six years, I've had only a minimum of experience with this particular male appendage, never having been very impressed or really interested in sex. But at the moment, my mouth waters and core clenches with an unfamiliar hunger as my breathing becomes ragged and heavy. I realize my body's craving what lies beneath, wanting to touch it, taste it, and feel it moving inside of me...

"Ah!" I squeal like a little girl and jump backward, letting go of Kohen's waistband when his cock suddenly twitches upward as if sensing my wayward thoughts.

Kohen chuckles at my response, making me feel even more pathetic. "It's not a snake; it won't bite you," he says while I grab the mop and get to work so that I don't have to look at him. "Although, your *boyfriend* probably wouldn't appreciate you ogling another man's dick long enough to memorize every vein."

"Boyfriend?" I repeat in confusion. And then I realize that Kohen must think Paxton and I are together. Like a couple. The thought has me snorting as I start mopping up suds as far away from Kohen as I can get. "You're right. Sorry for looking at your...package," I say without correcting his wrong assumption. This is good. Let him think I have a boyfriend, and then there are even more reasons why I shouldn't touch him or vice versa.

I'm not emotionally equipped to deal with a sexual relationship with a teammate, and it wouldn't be fair to start something with Kohen or any other man and not be able to, well, finish it. My holdups are my own, but I can't expect a guy like him to understand that while I want more, like holding hands and waking up in each other's arms, I'm not sure it really exists. And I...I just can't see me being able to overcome the experiences of my past anytime soon, to actually be able to trust a man, especially a teammate.

Jeez, but now my living arrangement with Kohen is gonna be even more strained because every time I look at him here or on the field, anywhere really, I'm gonna be thinking about his impressive cock, trying to figure out what makes it so unique that at the sight of it I was hypnotized. For the first time in my life, I wanted to drop to my knees and taste him.

Chapter Nineteen

Kohen

Roxanne remains radio silent after she got a good, lonnng look at the Captain. That's right; I named my dick since he is, in fact, the Captain of the *Wet Dream*. He's giving a full salute too now thanks to her intense scrutiny and obvious appreciation. If I didn't know any better, I would say it's the first cock she's ever seen, but that's ridiculous. She's a gorgeous girl with a boyfriend. Sure, the boyfriend looks like a tool, but I'm sure she's seen his instrument more times than she can count. And, yeah, that's not the topic I want to be thinking about right now. Instead, I would rather go back to the alternate universe I was just thrown into where instead of just looking, Roxanne reached down and used the wet suds in her hand to jerk me off. Or even better, told me how huge I am. Or, in the best scenario ever, kneeled before me and wrapped her lips around the Captain, sucking him until I choked out "There she blows, matey!"

My dick jerks in agreement inside the thin nylon of my shorts with that pirate fantasy, and I know there's only one thing left to do.

Reaching for the stupid crutches, I shove them underneath my armpits and maneuver through the sea of foam down the hall to my bedroom. I barely shut the door before my hand dives into the front of my shorts and my fist starts pumping my hard shaft. Leaning my back against the door with all my weight on my uninjured right leg, I let go of the crutches, sending them tumbling in a clatter to the floor. I don't care, I'll find them later. Right now, the need to get off is almost overwhelming. Sure, I've been horny before, but never this desperate. I've got to release the Kraken, or I'm pretty sure I'm gonna die.

Leaning my head against the wooden door, my eyes shut; and then I imagine the alternative universe again in great detail. In this field goal fantasy, Roxanne's naked on my bed that's just a few feet away, her long, sexy legs raised like uprights resting on my shoulders, my dick buried deep inside her tight heat while she chants, "It's good! It's good! It's so fucking good!" as my balls slap her ass.

With a twist of my wrist, I brush my thumb over my sensitive cockhead that's already damp from pre-cum, causing all the muscles in my body to seize at once. Then, I'm coming so hard in my hand that I nearly topple over. I grab the dresser for balance with my left hand while my right squeezes every drop of cum it can out of my shaft.

Wow.

What the hell's wrong with me? I ask my bedroom ceiling.

It's got to be that, with the injury and training camp, I was too backed up and needed to get off. Now that I've taken care of the problem, I'm sure it won't happen again. Roxanne's not only my teammate now but also my roommate. Coach asked me to look out for her after that fucker Dane made a move on her, and I refuse to stoop so low. Besides, she has a boyfriend, so she's completely off limits anyway.

Now, if I can just stop replaying the way her grassy green eyes widened and jaw fell open looking at my cock, everything will be under control. But, see, there's just one little problem.

I don't want to forget how she looked.

Even if I'm only lying to myself, I'm gonna hold on tight to the notion that boyfriend or not, Roxanne liked what she saw, and for one small moment, the most gorgeous woman I've ever seen wanted me too.

Early Thursday morning, Roxanne and I are all packed up for the trip to New Orleans to play the Knights in our first preseason game. She's nervous, as evidenced by her inability to sit still for more than two seconds and the way she tugs on her ladybug bracelet. Last night I heard her vacuuming the floors at midnight, which didn't bother me except for the fact that only the bedrooms have carpet, and the rest are hardwoods. She avoided my room, which was disappointing, but probably for the best. Seeing her in the shorts and tight-fitting tank she sleeps in so close to my bed would've only added fuel to the fire simmering in my boxer briefs.

Today, I am wearing underwear. I usually do when I leave the house. It was also a necessity since my current outfit is so minuscule I would be flashing the world without them.

Roxanne and I decide to ride to the airport together since I still can't drive and all. Of course, I was a little terrified to be in the same Jeep with the woman who ran into me, but Roxy is driving like a granny, even on the highway, probably because of the recent accident. Or because she's laughing so hard at me she's afraid she'll run us off the road.

Today, I'm unfortunately dressed in the outfit she picked out for me to wear on the plane as part of the hands-on-the-steering-wheel bet I lost. Although, seeing Roxanne come apart still goes down as a win in my book.

"Well, I've gotta say that you have hands down picked the most embarrassing outfit ever," I tell her, gesturing down to the red and black polka dot leotard. The tight material is only covered with a tiny matching tutu followed up by red garters attached to black fishnet stockings on my good leg and the top of the brace on my bad one. Oh, and how could I possibly forget about the antenna headband that keeps hitting the top of the SUV and the wings. "This is gonna be a hard one for the guys to top."

Roxy snickers before holding her palm up between our faces. "Stop talking to me before I wreck," she says. "I should've made you ride in the back. It's too fuckin' funny…"

I roll my eyes when she starts into another fit of laughter.

"So what's with you and ladybugs?" I ask her while she drives, holding the wheel at ten and two, noticing a ladybug charm hanging from her rearview mirror. "And where the fuck were you planning to wear this to? A strip club?"

"It's a Halloween costume, jackass! And as far as the ladybugs go, well, it's just what my dad started buying me after my mom left," she says sobering up. "He didn't know what to buy me for my birthday or Christmas. Girly stuff was all foreign to him. All he knew was that I liked ladybugs, so that's what he always bought."

Fuck, that's sad.

"He didn't buy that costume, though. That was all me," she adds.

"So you still like them?" I ask. "The ladybugs?"

"Yeah, sure. I mean they're cute and are supposed to be lucky. My dad is superstitious and gives them as lucky charms. Maybe they worked, because I'm the first woman to play professional football."

"I'm sure hard work and dedication also helped," I offer.

"Yeah, but it doesn't hurt to have a little luck on your side either," she says, her smile returning.

I've never been one of those superstitious guys who wears the same socks or doesn't shave while on a winning streak. Those things are what people who want to feel in control of something do, but I know that without training and effort, none of those lucky charms will work, and fuck if it's worth stinking to high hell like some of my teammates.

A few minutes later we're at the airport and loading up. Some of my teammates double over laughing at my getup before someone starts blasting Aerosmith's "Dude Looks Like a Lady" on their cell phone. I look ridiculous, I know, but I have to remind myself that it was totally worth it.

By the time I hop on one foot up the steps of the team's private plane, I'm annoyed to see Roxanne sitting next to Quinton.

"Yo, Kohen, man?" Quinton says with a smirk. "Your pantyhose are showing."

"Fuck you," I tell him.

"So what bet did you lose this time?" he asks.

Now it's my turn to grin when Roxanne's face turns the shade of red on my tutu.

"I'll let you do the honors, Roxanne," I say, taking the empty seat across the aisle from them. I tell myself that it's to do the job Coach gave me, keep an eye out for Roxy. Quinton and I have been cordial at practice since the ride back from training camp, but that's about it. Not that we were good friends before that.

"Oh, um, on the way to camp, Kohen just bet me I couldn't keep my hands on the wheel the entire trip."

"Sounds easy," Quinton says with a shrug. "Kohen's losing his touch."

"Obviously," I mutter sarcastically. The truth is, I would lose that bet over and over again every single time.

Lathan comes aboard the plane a little later, looking like complete shit. His blond Mohawk is disheveled like he's been tugging on his hair in frustration, and the bags under his eyes are heavier than my luggage.

Shit.

I'm a selfish bastard because I completely forgot that his mom had an appointment yesterday.

"Hey, bro, you okay?" I ask him when he slips into my row and takes the window seat next to me without even a hint of a smile at seeing my embarrassing ladybug costume.

He shakes his head, slumping further into the leather cushions. "I need alcohol and lots of it."

"The news that bad?" I ask since it's not like him to drink on game day, even if it is just preseason and he'll only be on the field for a few plays.

"Yep," he mutters, taking a deep breath. "Cancer's back."

"Fuck, I'm sorry. How bad this time?" I ask.

"Bad. It's in her pancreas now."

"Shit. That means more chemo?"

"Uh-huh and radiation. Without it...without it the doctor said she's only got a few months, but there are no guarantees with all that torture either..."

"God, I'm sorry," I tell him, giving his shoulder a squeeze. "Is she up for all that again?"

"Yeah, said she was. I just hope it works," he replies while looking out the window of the unmoving plane. "It has to."

I can't imagine what my best friend is going through. Sure, my mother is still around, but it's not like we've ever been close. Chase and I were nothing more than living, breathing ornaments to her and our father. Pawns to further his political career since our state still elects sheriffs. Mom and Dad put on a front that we were the typical American family. Chase and I were really nothing more than a fake front. Our parents were wax figures who were either unable or unwilling to show emotion toward us, unless it was disappointment. If Chase or I stepped a toe out of the strict line that could cost a dip in the polls that election year, we received frowns and sharp words to straighten up and stop embarrassing them.

So, no, I can't even contemplate what Lathan's going through, caring about someone who's always been there for you and loving them so much that it hurts to imagine losing them. He stays quiet even after we take off, but my neighbors on the other side of me are anything but soft spoken.

Roxanne and Quinton joke and laugh with each other like old buddies, and it irks me. The sound of her laughter coerced by him is like nails on a fucking chalkboard. Not only are they being inconsiderate to Lathan, who Quinton hasn't bothered to speak to, but how dare Roxanne flirt with a teammate when she already has a man? I didn't take her for the slutty type, but maybe I was wrong.

"Your boyfriend coming to the game?" I ask Roxanne when there's a pause in what is evidently Quinton's stand-up act.

Her head whips around in my direction, sending her ponytail swishing in Quinton's face.

"You talking to me, Ladybug?" she asks with both of her blonde eyebrows raised, lips quirked up.

"Yeah, since Quinton doesn't have any boyfriends. At least none that I know of," I state, causing our quarterback to flip me off from the other side of her

"Not that it's any of your business, but Paxton's my best friend, not my boyfriend," Roxanne says.

"Oh, really?" I ask skeptically, remembering the protective way he acted toward her and the threat on my good knee. "Then you might want to tell him that."

Roxy snorts and then covers her mouth as she continues to laugh. "Believe me, there's no doubt that Paxton *knows* we're only friends. I'm not exactly his type."

"Uh-huh, sure," I mutter. "What man in his right mind doesn't want a tall, beautiful, blonde woman?" The words leave my mouth before I even realize what I've said. It's the truth, but I didn't mean to blurt out that she's beautiful in front of our teammates.

"How about a gay man?" she answers with a smug smile.

"Oh," I reply as I chew on that tidbit. Didn't see that one coming.

So does that mean Roxy's not currently dating anyone? Because that's not good, not at all. I was banking on another dude in her life to make sure I didn't make a move on her. There are still other hurdles, like her being my roommate and teammate, but none of those were as big as the boyfriend one. Or maybe now that I know she's not seeing anyone, I can't stand the thought of her falling for someone else, someone like Quinton, the notorious heartbreaker. There are too many thoughts swirling around my head, and there's only one thing I'm certain of when it comes to Roxanne.

I'm so fucked.

Chapter Twenty

Roxy

After getting dressed in a small, private room at the stadium, I line up in my full pads and wait in the hot, stuffy tunnel with the rest of my teammates. Hearing the crowd roaring just beyond, even if they are booing us since we're the visiting team, is still one of the proudest moments of my life.

For years I've dreamed of being on this field, while I was told over and over again that the only way to make it would be to trade in my cleats for pompoms. Fuck that, I told them all. And now, here I am.

When the announcer introduces us over the PA, I run out behind a few of my teammates; and instead of boos, the sound of the crowd flips like the coin about to be tossed in the center of the field, changing to clapping and cheers.

Glancing around the Knights' massive dome, I realize that the camera is broadcasting me on the jumbotrons, and the crowd's actually on their feet...for me, the first woman to ever play professional football, despite all the negative press I've received about the accident and the fact that I play for the visiting team.

They understand and appreciate that this moment is a historical event, not just for me, but for an entire half of the population that's been a long time coming. I never had any feminist agendas when I started playing flag football. Football is the sport I've always loved like it's the most natural thing in the world, ever since my dad taught me how to throw a football when I was four years old. And while the boys and men who I've played with haven't made it easy for me, I stuck through the tough times and never gave up, overcoming enormous obstacles to be right here on the green turf with spotlights shining down on me.

Oh shit.

The weight of everyone's expectations is suddenly a pressure on my shoulders so intense that I can't seem to move or get any air.

While I never intended to be a role model, I have to accept the fact that I'm here representing women all over the world and that there are probably young girls watching me right now, looking up to me, wishing me success.

Oh God. What if I screw up and can't hack it with the big boys? Then I'll go down in history as the first failed woman in football. That's not the legacy I wanted to have. I wanted to be the best damn kicker in the league so that no one even gives a shit about my gender.

"Don't do that," a voice on the sideline calls out to me, reeling me in from the rising panic from staring at all the people in the noisy stands. Down here on the field, I suddenly feel like an insignificant ant that's about to get trampled.

"Roxanne?"

Hearing my name, I turn in the direction and find Kohen propped up on his crutches on the sidelines. And just like every other time I see him, I feel guilty that he's not dressed in his pads and uniform ready to play. Seeing him also triggers a few other types of emotions, ones that are new and becoming addictive. Kohen's beautiful and…mesmerizing, making me desperate for a taste of him. Only I already know that one taste wouldn't ever be enough. If I let myself indulge in him, it could possibly turn into a lifelong dependency that I'm not sure if I could handle.

"Don't you dare do that," he says as if reading my mind. Hobbling over closer, his chiseled jaw with a hint of dark stubble is clenched tight either in annoyance or pain.

"Don't do what?" I ask, peeling my helmet off to try and suck in more oxygen. Is there enough for all of us in this freaking dome? Then I get a whiff of Kohen's scent that's masculine and delicious like hazelnut, matching his melted candy bar eyes.

"Don't doubt yourself. Or panic. You've got this, Roxanne. Your leg is one of the best in the league."

His comforting words reel me in, centering me, calming me, and right now that's what I need.

"What if I fuck up?" I ask him seriously. Speaking the words aloud has my heart beating triple time in my chest.

"You're not gonna fuck up. Just pretend that we're on the practice field and nail the ball whenever they need you to through the uprights like you always do."

"I don't want to let everyone down," I say, meaning my teammates and all the little girls who look up to me.

"No one's perfect, not on this team or in the world. If you make a mistake, learn from it, and don't do it again," he says with a slap to my shoulder pads as if it's that simple. "Okay?"

"Okay," I repeat with a nod.

After we all stand for the national anthem, our team captains win the coin toss and defer until the second half. Thankfully, Warren is kicking off and doing the punting tonight. All I have to worry about is field goals and extra points.

It doesn't take long before my number is called. In the first quarter, our defense gets the Knights' offense off the field with three and out, then Quinton easily moves the ball right on down the field to score a touchdown. I can't even celebrate the points on the board knowing that this is it. I'm no longer just a woman in pads wearing a Wildcats jersey. It's finally time for me to jog out onto the field and do my job.

My teammates shout encouragement as I set up for the extra point. Warren's holding for me, and I've done this hundreds of times in practice. In college, I made every single extra point. Now's not the time to break that streak.

Waiting for my signal as the seconds on the play clock tick down, I give a nod and then Warren calls for the ball. I drown out everything else, focusing only on the familiar pigskin as Warren stands it up underneath his finger, laces out just like they're supposed to be. Moving forward, my foot connects with the seam of the ball at full speed; and then it's sailing through the air and dead center between the uprights.

Thank fuck!

My breath rushes out in relief as the guys congratulate me with pats on the back and on my helmet.

In an elated daze, I follow my teammates back over to the sidelines, getting more congratulations on my very first point before I end up in front of Kohen, who is smiling like a proud father. There's not a trace of jealousy or anger that it was me on the field and not him.

"Easy, right?" he asks.

"Easy," I agree with my own grin, wanting to hug him but refraining as I take my helmet off and go over to the practice net to try a few kicks just in case. Now, let's hope our offense scores on every drive so I don't have to try to make any field goals.

The game clock ticks faster than I expected, and I end up kicking just one more extra point before halftime. When we retake the field, the Knights decide to stage a comeback with a vengeance. Hugh Vincent, our second string quarterback, goes into the game for the second half to get in a few reps; but unfortunately, his first throw is picked off and run back for a touchdown.

The score is tied twenty-one to twenty-one, and the clock is running out, which means I'm facing my worst nightmare. We get the ball back, but Hugh is out of timeouts and Coach doesn't want to risk a turnover, so they send me in to try and nail a fifty-two yard field goal to win the game. We're indoors with no wind gusts to worry about, and I've made a sixty yarder in practice several times. Should be easy, right?

As I take the field, over the PA system blares a new song they haven't played all night, "Roxanne" by The Police. Great, nothing instills confidence like a song with my name in it about prostitution.

Then, when I line up on the right hash mark, the uprights look like they're miles away rather than just fifty-two yards. Telling myself I can do this, I try to block all the other noises out. But as soon as I raise my leg, I know the ball's not gonna make it. I hold my breath as it flies end over end too fast through the air and then breezes past the left goal post by inches.

Fuck.

"It's all right."

"Good try, Roxy."

"We'll get them in overtime."

My teammates try to sound upbeat, but I know they're disappointed in me. I can't even look at Kohen, because I'm certain he would've easily made that field goal, but he's not playing because of me.

Our defense is obviously tired from enduring a full game, and most are inexperienced second and third string players that are vying for a roster spot during these preseason games. So it's no big surprise when, on the first play of overtime, the Knights' quarterback launches the ball forty yards down the field, and their wide receiver catches it and runs it into the end zone with not a single touch from our corners.

Game fucking over.

Chapter Twenty-One

Kohen

I knock softly on Roxanne's hotel door and prop my shoulder against the wall to help keep the crutches steady. Shit, I know she's kicking herself in the ass, and she shouldn't be. After we had lost in overtime, Roxanne shook hands with the other team and then headed for her changing room since they don't have locker room facilities to accommodate her. When I asked the guys, none of them saw her on any of the team's buses, so I'm not even sure if she came back to the hotel yet.

"Roxanne, if you're in there, please open up," I say through the door while knocking again.

"Go away," it sounds like she replies. Good, she did make it back okay; only, she's not getting rid of me that easily.

"I'm gonna keep banging on the door, then your neighbor's gonna call and report you for noise if you don't let me in," I warn her with another loud knock.

I hear the chain on the other side being undone, and then she cracks the door open about three inches.

Fresh from a shower I assume she took in her room, Roxanne's blonde hair is damp and piled up on top of her head. She's wearing black cotton shorts and a thin, white Wildcats tee. Did I mention her shirt is see-through and she's not wearing a bra? Yeahhhh.

Swallowing and lifting my eyes to hers, I say, "I, um, just wanted to make sure you're okay. We've all been there."

"The mighty Kohen Hendricks has lost a game? I find that hard to believe," she says with a shake of her head. "I choked. I fucking choked." Her voice breaks on the last word as she turns away and her shoulders shake as she starts to cry. I know that's just one more thing she's gonna hate about herself in the morning --- crying in front of me. And fuck if I don't hate seeing her upset, doubting herself when she shouldn't.

"Come here," I say as I hobble further into the room, letting the door shut behind me. Once I've hopped over to her, I let go of my crutches to reach for her shoulders, turning her around and pulling her into my arms.

"That was a long ass field goal, and Coach just wanted to give you some practice," I tell her, wobbling to keep my balance on one leg. "He didn't actually expect you to make it." Roxanne scoffs at that last comment and tries to pull away from my arms, which I don't allow. Only, the push and shove motions throw me more off balance. I try to throw my palm out to grab the wall, but Roxanne shifts her weight, and then we're both going down to the floor with her on top of me. Air rushes out of my lungs with the force of impact.

"Shit, sorry," Roxanne says as she sits up, straddling my waist with her palms pressed against my chest to push herself up. "I swear I'm not always trying to hurt you; it just seems to happen."

From this new position of hers, the see-through t-shirt falls forward, giving me an unobstructed view of her bare tits. Jesus, they're mouthwatering perfection with rosy pink nipples.

Roxanne wiggling to get off me only makes the proof of my physical attraction to her more obvious. And when she gasps and freezes above me, her water-filled green eyes widening, I know she's felt my cock hardening through the thin layer of my nylon pants. Tonight I may be wearing boxer briefs, but there's no containing the Kraken when it decides to rise.

"Um, is that a dildo in your pocket or are you just happy to see me?" Roxanne asks with a giggle, pressing her ass down harder onto my erection and making me groan.

"It's a dildo," I tell her, sitting up on my elbows. "You know, for when you tell me to go fuck myself."

"I haven't said that all day," she replies innocently, not so subtly rocking her hips.

"A new record," I mutter, my fists tightening by my sides with the urge to grab her hips and press her down or reach up and squeeze a handful of her tits while she continues to look so fucking tempting sitting on me. "Now stop riding my dick unless you're gonna get naked."

Roxanne's big, surprised eyes meet mine, and then time seems to stand still. Seconds tick by, each one pushing me deeper into that alternate reality, the one where this gorgeous woman is as desperate for me as I am for her. My words may have come out casually, but I don't want her to move off of me. No, I want her to pull my pants down and sink her pussy that's so hot I can feel the heat through our clothes, right down on my cock.

When Roxanne doesn't move off of me, I start to think that maybe it's possible that she actually does want me. Is she waiting for me to cave and make the first move?

Unwilling to let this moment pass without finding out, I sit up at the same time Roxy leans forward until our lips meet. This is no soft, sweet kiss either. Our tongues anxiously stroke against each other for the first time in two weeks, and then it's game over.

The intensity of the kiss forces me to my back; and with my hands gripping her face, Roxy has no choice but to ride me down, our tongues still fighting for dominance. I'm losing, and it's so goddamn good that I let her take control. Panting breaths are exchanged into each other's mouths while we only pause long enough to jerk Roxy's shirt over her head. Her smooth hands slip underneath my tee, caressing my skin while pushing the material up as she goes until it's coming off. Cold chill bumps erupt and every muscle in my body tenses when her fingernails brush over my abs and spread up and over my pecs. My hands are jealous and want to feel more of her. I shove them both down the back of her shorts, underneath her panties. After sneaking a quick squeeze of her ass cheeks, I shove them down her legs, eager to get them out of the fucking way. Roxanne lifts up long enough to remove them and then returns her lips to mine.

My nylon pants and boxer briefs are the only remaining pieces of clothing between us. But not for long. Roxanne jerks just the waistbands to my thighs. And the next second I groan against her lips, trying not to shoot my load when she starts working her wet pussy down my shaft. She tortures me with one tight little inch at a time. And by the time she hits rock bottom, I can't take anymore.

I want to roll us over so that she's on her back underneath me and I can pump my hips, fucking her hard and fast; but in the shape my knee's in, I know that's not gonna happen for a few more weeks.

Wait, that's assuming we're gonna still be doing this in a few weeks. I already know I would move mountains to be able to get inside of her again.

"Ah fuck," I groan against her lips when Roxy sets the pace with slow rolls of her hips that are definitely gonna drive me fucking insane. My hands circle her narrow waist, wanting to slam her harder and faster on my cock. But then she sits up, breaking our kiss. Arching her back, she moans in pleasure. She's so fucking beautiful riding me, and the sounds she's making are so sexy that I decide she can take me any way she wants.

"Right there! Oh, God, Kohen!" Roxy cries out, her eyes shut, lips parted as her pussy clamps down on me, and I can't complain anymore. Now she's grinding on my cock frantically like her life depends on it, and I've got a front row seat as her tits bounce in front of my face, even more spectacular than I imagined. I'm almost scared to touch them, afraid they'll disappear like a mirage. Oh, but I have to risk it, reaching up to cup them both. So soft and full in my palms. Perfect.

There's no hope for me to last any longer when Roxy's pulsating pussy milks me dry in record-breaking time. Too short but too fucking amazing to stop, I come with a growl of insane pleasure as my cock erupts deep inside of her.

Roxy collapses on my damp chest after that, resting her face in the crook of my neck as we both try and catch our breath. That's when reality all starts coming back into focus, reminding me that I'm on the floor of my teammate's room, taking advantage of her when I knew she was emotional. Dammit. I was supposed to be watching out for her, not fucking her!

"Oh my God," Roxy mumbles softly, the least favorable way possible that those words can ever be spoken. The translation of which is, *What the fuck did we just do?*

Yep, less than five seconds later she's peeling herself off my sweaty chest and standing up quickly to pull her clothes back on. Her face is flushed, loose pieces of her wet hair falling down from her topknot, her eyes wide in horror. And I don't think she's ever been more gorgeous.

"That was...stupid," she says before she slumps down on the foot of the mattress with her face buried in her hands.

Wow. She didn't waste any time going into full regret mode.

"No, please don't hold back. Tell me how you *really* feel," I grumble sarcastically as I sit up and pull my pants and boxer briefs back up over my hips.

"What were we thinking?" she mutters.

"That it would feel really good to have your pussy slamming down on my cock?" I offer. "And what do you know; it was a perfect fit, like they were made for each other."

"Kohen!" she yells, finally looking up at me indignantly.

"We fucked. It's no big deal, Roxy," I tell her even if that's only mostly true.

"Why didn't you use a condom?" she hisses at me, making my jaw drop open in disbelief. Now she's gonna try and pin that shit on me?

"Oh, I'm sorry. Was I supposed to put a rubber on *before* I came up to your room to check on you? Because you really didn't give me time to hop back on the elevator. I mean, I'm not complaining, but you literally went from zero to fucking in less than sixty seconds."

"Look, I'm on the pill and have never done...*that* before," she says, her hand gesturing to where I'm still sitting on the floor.

"You've never had floor sex before?" I ask just because I like flustering her. She's a knockout who I'm certain has been with plenty of men, so I'm not sure why she's acting all shy and inexperienced. It's cute.

"Just tell me you're clean, asshole," Roxy huffs in exasperation.

"If I weren't, do you think now would be the ideal time to bring that shit up?" I ask.

Reaching behind her, Roxy grabs a hotel pillow and chucks it at me as she starts to laugh. And just like that, the crisis is thankfully averted.

Using the wall to pull my gimpy self up off the floor, I hop on one leg the three feet distance to the bed and tackle Roxy down flat to the mattress with me.

"Don't freak out," I tell her when her face is inches from mine. "I came to see how you were doing and cheer you up. I didn't plan on feeling you up, but did it help?"

"Yes, although, it could've lasted a little longer," she says with a grin.

"God, you're a ballbuster! You didn't even let me work my way up with foreplay before you started riding me."

Covering my lips with hers, she makes my exasperation disappear with a single stroke of her tongue against mine. There's also relief that since she's kissing me after freaking out that maybe she wants a repeat, that it wasn't just a one and done. At least that's what I was hoping before she suddenly pulls away.

"Aren't you worried, you know, about someone finding out?" she asks, searching my eyes while nervously biting her bottom lip.

"Who?" I ask, the mixture of lust and tingling, happy endorphins still making my thought process slow. "The media? How would they find out we fucked on your hotel floor?"

"No, I meant the team. You know, because you signed the addendum and all..." She looks at me expectantly, and I don't even consider lying to her.

"Oh, so, um, about that... Well, believe it or not, I never signed a copy."

"How...I mean, how is that possible?" she asks with cute creases stretching across her forehead. "I thought everyone had to turn them in at training camp. That's what management told me when the whole Dane shitstorm went down."

"Funny story," I start. "We were the last ones to training camp, so they had run out of forms and were supposed to be getting me one but never did. I don't know if it was because I'm on the injured reserve list for now or what..."

For some reason, Roxy doesn't seem nearly as amused as I am about the very convenient little oversight. In fact, she pulls away from me before I can protest; and then she's on her feet, pacing in front of the bed.

"What's wrong?" I sit up and ask since I'm fucking clueless. "Isn't this a good thing, seeing as how we would have just violated the hell out of it?"

"For you maybe," she mutters before she packs up her things as I watch in stunned disbelief. While I may have never intended to sleep with Roxy when I came to check on her, it happened. What I don't understand is why she's pissed or upset with me for not signing a piece of paper when she clearly wanted me. Words fail me, and then I'm out of time when Roxy opens the door and walks out of the hotel room without a backward glance.

Chapter Twenty-Two

Roxy

What the hell did I just do?

One minute I'm sulking alone in my room embarrassed that I let my team down, and the next I was naked, unable to get Kohen inside of me fast enough.

For the past six years I can count on one hand how many men I've had sex with, and without a thought I fucked him. On the floor. In a hotel room. A room in which the walls felt like they were closing in on me and Kohen's arms around my waist were smothering me.

After easing out of his grip, I gathered my things and left. Now I'm trying to figure out what the hell I'm gonna do. Which is becoming an all-too-familiar theme for my life lately.

The plane home doesn't leave until noon tomorrow, but there's no way I'm gonna be able to stay here, in the hotel or that room. I don't want to even be in this town right now. My mind's racing a mile a minute, and I need time to just think.

That's why I decide to rent a car and drive home. All thirteen hours. I'll pull over and sleep at a hotel when I get about halfway, but right now I need to be doing something, anything.

After I plug Wilmington into my phone's GPS, I follow the directions to the highway. From there, it's nothing but the dark, empty road in front of me. Well, doesn't that feel symbolic of my life?

Jeez, why did I have to go and ruin everything by sleeping with Kohen? The first thing I need to do when I get back to Wilmington is find somewhere else to stay. Being in Kohen's house will only make things more complicated.

What we did…it can't happen again. Not that I don't want it to. While it was short, it was…incredible. The pleasure I felt with him inside me was like nothing I've ever experienced before. Everything else, all the worry and disappointment disappeared.

My body reacted to him like it was the most natural thing in the world. That must be what sex for normal people is like --- an urge that they carry through with. In the past, for me, it's just usually been *Why the hell not?* after a few dates since I know guys expect it.

Stupidly, I didn't even think about needing protection and had sex without a condom. The football league checks all the players for everything under the sun, even STDs, so I'm pretty sure I don't have anything to worry about there with Kohen. The problem is I didn't even stop to think about it before I jerked his pants down and sank down on his cock.

Just the thought of being with him is enough to cause a pulsing between my legs. My body's already yearning to have him inside me again despite the chaos of my mind. This is precisely the reason why I shouldn't be sharing the same living space with him.

So why exactly did I get so upset when I found out he hadn't signed the same no contact agreement as the rest of the team? I'm not entirely sure. Maybe because I thought that if he had something to lose, like his contract, he would be less inclined to tell anyone, especially our teammates, that we slept together. Crazy, I know, but trust is earned and all that. How do I know for sure that he won't run his mouth? I don't. And that is the problem. Trusting him will only end badly. Sleeping with him is bound to end badly. I knew that, and yet I caved to the stupid desire.

I crashed and burned on the field when my team needed me the most, which is depressing as hell. And then Kohen was there, worried about me and being nice…

That should've been my first warning. When it comes to Kohen and me, we're rarely ever nice to each other.

Now, there's only one thing to do. I'll find an apartment in Wilmington, and I'll get Kohen to sign the contract addendum. That way, I won't have to worry about anything else happening between us. It sucks, and I hate it; but at the same time, I can't afford to be distracted when the whole country is watching, waiting for me to fail.

Well, that clarity took all of fifteen minutes. Now, what am I gonna do for the next twelve hours and forty-five minutes?

"I'm so sorry, Miss Benson, but you were not approved for an apartment," the young woman with her brown hair slicked back in a tight chignon tells me as I blink at her from across her desk.

"What do you mean I wasn't approved?" I ask, trying not to get snippy. "I brought in my paystub. As you can see, I'll easily be able to pay rent based on what they pay me, you know, as a professional football player for the Wildcats."

"Yes, but we ran your credit, and since you don't have an employment history of more than six months or any sort of credit history, no credit cards or loans you've paid back, we can't lease you an apartment. Do you have someone who can come in and co-sign for you?" she asks.

"My dad's in Tennessee, so I'm not sure when he could come in..."

"That's too bad. But good luck with the season," she says, cutting me off and getting up from behind her desk to show me out the door. Just like that and I'm no longer being wooed as a potential customer, but I'm being shooed.

Fuck.

Since I'm making bank now, I thought finding a place to live would be easy. I give them money for rent, and they let me live there. Apparently, that's not how it works. I have to have a job *history*. While I was in college, I had a football scholarship, and it paid the bills so I wouldn't have to juggle work and studying too.

Annoyed, I do the only thing I can. I get into my Jeep and head back to Kohen's. There's no point in going by another apartment complex since they're all probably gonna tell me the same thing. I guess that means my only options are finding a shady place to live from the classifieds that doesn't require a credit check or...staying with Kohen. At least until my dad comes down and can sign a rental agreement for me.

It's already dark when I finally take the turn for the marina because I spent hours after practice being shown around an apartment complex and filling out paperwork. Then it took them all of two seconds to kick me out.

For some reason, the marina parking lot is slammed full tonight, so I end up several rows back from my usual spot up front. Throwing my purse over my shoulder, I make my way back to the dock, and that's when I realize exactly what's going on.

Apparently, Kohen is throwing a party.

Even though we haven't spoken except when absolutely necessary at practice the last two days, he could've asked me before inviting people over since I live here too. At least for the time being.

The thumping bass from the stereo is so loud I can hear it before I see all the people standing on the deck, some splashing around, swimming below in the marina despite the signs saying not to do that. It doesn't take long to realize that the majority of the guests are women. Pretty ones in skimpy bikinis.

Kohen and I are gonna have words.

Although, this is *his* boat. Logically, I know he should be able to have a party whenever he wants without my permission, so why am I so damn angry?

"Excuse me," I say to a group of bottle blondes so I can get through the sliding glass door that's standing wide open. I pretend to ignore their hisses, talking shit about me as soon as I pass.

"Hey, Roxy," Lathan calls out from the kitchen where he's grabbing a bottle of water from the fridge.

"Hey. Have you seen Kohen?" I ask as I glance around the crowded room, recognizing some of the male faces from the team, but all the females are strangers.

"Ah, yeah, I think he's in the hot tub," Lathan answers, a blush coloring his cheeks, which I take to mean Kohen is currently out on the deck, soaking in bubbles surrounded by girls in bikinis.

"Oh," I reply, not sure how else to react to that lovely piece of news other than to toss my cookies. Maybe that's just the boat rocking more than usual with all the people moving around on it. Yeah, I'm sure it's sea sickness and not jealousy. Why would I care if Kohen screws one or ten of the attractive young women he invited over? It's not like I'll ever sleep with him again.

142

Yesterday, I left a copy of the addendum on the kitchen counter. Kohen signed it and turned it in at practice. Therefore, we absolutely cannot mess around again. Ever. Even if I've wanted to crawl into his bed the last two nights or tackle him down on the field to kiss his irritating face when he yelled at me for not following through on my kicks or for taking too long to line up...

"You okay?" Lathan asks. "You look a little, um, green."

"I'm fine," I tell him, grabbing my own bottle of water. Resting with my back against the counter next to Lathan just because I don't want to go hide in my room all alone, I unscrew the lid on the bottle and ask him, "So, who are all these...people?" I barely caught myself before I said sluts.

"Oh, ah, well, most are Lady Cats."

"Pfft," I laugh before I slap the back of my hand still clutching the bottle lid over my mouth. "Cheerleaders? Seriously? How...cliché, right?"

"Yeah," he mumbles in agreement.

Glancing over, I realize Lathan's eyes are downcast, studying the tops of his sneakers instead of any of the half-naked women wandering around us. "This isn't your sort of scene, is it?" I ask him.

"No," he answers, raising his eyes to mine. "I never even got invited to parties until I got signed with the Wildcats."

"Really?" I ask.

"Yeah. Ugly duckling, remember?" he says, patting his chest with a grin.

"Sure. Right," I say, taking a sip of my water. "I don't buy it." Even if Lathan weren't over six feet tall and buff, he would still have his adorable baby face with stormy gray eyes and thick, sandy blond hair.

"It's true," he says. "Yours truly was nicknamed Porky or Pork Sausage, you know, because my last name is Savage."

"Kids are mean," I mutter. "And not very creative."

"Everything they said was the truth. I was obese, like three-fifty until my senior year of college."

"Wow," I say in surprise. "You turned out okay, though. Playing football?"

"Yeah. I played linebacker my first three years at State. During the summer breaks, I started working out a lot. By my senior year, I was this size and playing tight end."

"Good for you," I tell him honestly. "But that doesn't explain why you're standing here, instead of talking to one of these bikini-clad floozies that are currently checking you out."

Her turns around, putting his back to the room. "I'm just busy, you know, so I don't have time for dating. And I don't want to lead anyone on."

"Well, that's...refreshing," I say since he's such a contradiction to the typical playboy professional athlete. "Someday you're gonna make some girl a lucky lady."

"That's not fair," he says, blowing out a breath as he looks at the ceiling. "You're pretty and play football, so you're not supposed to be nice too."

I laugh before I can help myself. "Sorry. I'll try to do better," I tease. "Just ask Kohen. Usually, I'm a raging bitch."

Chapter Twenty-Three

Kohen

A beautiful woman is, at this very moment, easing her hand up my thigh not so subtly underneath the Jacuzzi bubbles, but the Captain could care less. I blame my cock's disinterest entirely on Roxy.

For the last two hours, maybe three now, I've been thinking about her, wondering where the hell she is. After practice, she didn't come home like usual, which worries me.

Other than the occasionally required word here or there during practice, she's been avoiding me since the night we slept together and she ran. I still have no idea what the fuck that was about, and it's driving me fucking insane.

Now that I know how amazing it is to be with Roxy, I want her again. But no. She had to go and make me sign that shit saying I won't lay a finger on her. Frustrating woman.

I stupidly thought that if I threw a party, I could spend some time with a nice girl, preferably in my bed, to get Roxy off my mind. No such luck. My cock's staging a mutiny because of her. Janna, one of the very beautiful Lady Cats, wants me and is down to fuck, but I can't get out of my own damn head.

"It sucks you won't get to play in Thursday night's first home game," Janna says, pouting her Botox inflated lip while pressing her implants that are about to float out of her tiny, triangle top against my upper arm.

"Yeah," I agree as her fake nails continue to creep up my board shorts toward my cock. Her long dark waves are probably extensions too. I'm not sure if there's an inch left of her that's authentic, unlike Roxy who is naturally gorgeous from head to toe...

Fuck.

Where the hell is she, anyway?

I have her phone number, but I didn't want to call her up, sounding like her father. But enough is enough.

Grabbing the side of the tub, I heft myself up from the bubbles, balancing on my good foot and trying to figure out how the hell to climb out. Since I can't step out one foot at a time, I have to sit on the edge to throw both legs over so I can put my weight down on my right one. Jon took me off the crutches, so I can walk on the left one, but I'm still supposed to avoid putting all my weight on it at first.

"Where are you going?" Pouty asks.

Grabbing a towel, I say, "inside," without further explanation or invitation as I dry off.

Once I'm no longer dripping wet, I wrap the towel around my hips and walk through the open sliding glass door. And there Roxy is, standing next to Lathan, laughing. Fuck, now I'm jealous of my own best friend. Again, it's one woman's fault. She's done nothing but give me hell since the second she ran me over! If she's not causing me physical pain, she's making me a headcase!

"Where have you been?" I storm over and ask her.

Roxy blinks at me before she clenches her jaw and narrows her eyes in anger. I also notice she's making a concentrated effort to not lower her eyes and ogle me below the neck.

"That's none of your business," she replies and then takes a sip from her water bottle. I give Lathan a look that says get lost, and my friend quickly obeys, heading to the living room. "Where are your crutches?" she asks without lowering her eyes. Yep, she wants to look at my bare chest and stomach but refuses to give in.

"Don't need them anymore," I say.

"Good for you," she says flatly.

"Yeah, good for me."

"Is this a special occasion?" she asks, her green eyes skating around the room full of people before returning to mine.

"Yeah," I say and wait to finish my statement, watching as her eyebrows arch in surprise and curiosity. Anything's better than anger. "I don't need crutches anymore."

"That's not exactly a cause for this type of celebration," she mutters. "Looks like a plastic surgery convention."

My lips quirk up without my permission.

"Then I guess you've never been on crutches," I say, ignoring her insult of the women.

"Nope," she replies, sipping from her bottle again and drawing my eyes to her lips. I still remember how soft they are and how they taste. I'm not sure I'll ever forget either of those things.

"Makes it easier to go up steps," I say just because she's talking to me and I don't want her to stop.

"I bet," she agrees.

"No more sore armpits."

"Hmm."

"I'm not nearly as clumsy, either. You know, falling down or whatever," I say and wait for her response. Dammit, I want her to talk to me about what the fuck happened the other night!

"That's…good," she eventually says with her eyes lowered to the ground. "I mean, no one wants to fuck a klutz."

Her cheeks turn pink, and I know she's thinking about the other night when we were fucking on the floor in the hotel room.

"Nope, definitely not. Unless it's a pity fuck?" I ask, wanting her to give me something to explain what happened between us.

"Uh-uh," she says. "Maybe a pity blowjob, but a pity fuck is out of the question, you know, because it might make the injury worse."

"Well, damn. I think I want the crutches back now since I apparently missed out on any pity blowjobs."

"Ah. Too late now," Roxy says as she moves away from the kitchen counter and starts down the hall. "Everyone's already seen you without them."

"Wait, Roxy," I call out to her. "Where were you tonight?" I ask again, hoping she'll tell me.

"Apartment hunting," she says. And before I can formulate a response to that kick in the balls, she's disappeared into her room.

Goddamn it. I don't want her to move out. It's nice actually having someone else around, even if all we do is sleep in different rooms. And even if I would prefer that we were sleeping together, which is an unbreakable rule from my current playbook. Although, the last rule doesn't apply to Roxy since she is a teammate, and does calling her honey count as a pet name? Whatever, I don't want to lose her as my roommate.

Roxy's been keeping my house spotless, except for dishes. After the day she flooded the kitchen with bubbles, she's refused to touch them. She cooks too, although she burns everything. At first, I thought she just hadn't figured out the timing for the oven, you know, because it's new and super quick. But she stills burns shit, so maybe it's just her. Whenever it happens, she'll light this green Yankee Candle in a jar that smells just like freshly mowed grass. It's comforting and warm, maybe because it reminds me of being on the field. Or her.

So while Roxy hasn't lived here long, I'm already attached to having her around. I know her sudden desire to move probably has to do with us fucking. I'll just have to convince her that it won't happen again, even if that's the opposite of what I want.

Roxy

Once I'm able to make my escape to my room, I get comfortable, changing into my Wildcats blue tank and yellow pajama shorts. Nothing better to do, I pull out one of the footballs from the cardboard box on the bedroom floor. I'm not sure how many balls I've accumulated now, but it's quite the collection. All of them are abused and filled up with words written in black permanent marker, except for this one.

Grabbing the silver sharpie from the dresser, I sit cross-legged in the middle of the bed, the ball in my lap to add a few things to it. This particular one is sparsely written on and has more air inflating it since I haven't kicked the shit out of it over and over again like all the others. This one is special.

A knock sounds quietly on my door over the music of the party, but I ignore it, figuring it's one of the guests looking for a room to screw in. Which reminds me of how odd it is that Kohen turned the master bedroom into his weight room and took one of the smaller rooms to sleep in. Maybe it's because it just had more space for all the exercise equipment.

When my bedroom door suddenly flies wide open, I startle in surprise before shouting, "Get out of my room!" and throwing the football at whoever the hell broke in. Only after the leather leaves my hand do I realize it's Kohen. And based on the fact that he's now hunched over with his hands on his crotch, my short pass apparently hit him square in the nuts.

Fuck.

He reaches out a hand, grabbing hold of the door before he goes to his knees, likely remembering that one of them is already fucked up at the last minute. I scramble off the bed to help him straighten all the way up as he continues to grimace in pain.

"Shit. I'm sorry, Kohen. I didn't know it was you," I tell him, leading him over to the edge of the bed for him to sit down.

"You're trying…to kill me," he groans, still practically doubled over.

"No, I'm not. You just keep catching me off guard!" I exclaim taking a seat next to him. "Can I do anything or get you anything?" I ask.

"Ice," he says, so I hop up and scurry to the kitchen, searching several drawers before I find a plastic baggie to fill with ice from the front dispenser on the refrigerator. Back in my room, I shut the door to drown out the noise of the music and chatter before taking the bag to Kohen.

He's laid out on his back now, legs still hanging over the side.

"Here," I tell him, sitting on the bed beside him and offering him the ice pack. Kohen takes it and raises a knee in the air before tucking the bag against his crotch.

"Fuck, that's cold," he says, shivering since he's still wearing his soaking wet board shorts.

"Do you, um, do you want to take the wet shorts off and I can give you a towel or something?" I ask him.

"Yeah," he answers with a nod. Lifting the ice in one hand, he starts tugging his bottoms down his hips until they hit they floor. I try to look away, I swear I do, but after his cock is set free, it's impossible. My mouth goes dry at the sight of not only his impressive length but massive girth even though his shaft is only semi-hard, resting against his thigh that's now also bare. I've been unable to forget the way he felt moving inside me, not only filling every inch, but stretching me so I could take all of him.

The sound of crunching finally draws my eyes upward, and I realize that while I had been staring at his junk, Kohen had opened the bag of ice and started popping pieces into his mouth, chomping down on them.

"Want some?" he asks, holding up the bag.

"No, thanks," I say in confusion at his calm tone. I thought he was in excruciating pain...

And then I see it, the red, circular welt on his lower abdomen.

"I didn't hit you in the balls, did I?" I ask him.

Chomp. Chomp. "Nope," Kohen answer with a smirk.

"You jerk!" I shout, slapping him on the chest. "Then why the hell are you naked on my bed?"

"We need to talk," he says. "I just took advantage of your wrong assumption."

Scoffing, I stand up to leave, but Kohen grabs my arm and tugs me back down to the bed, millimeters away from his nakedness.

"We haven't talked yet," he says.

"Then put some clothes on!" I tell him, trying to pull my arm out of his grip.

"Hey, you're the one who suggested I take my shorts off."

"Oh my God, you're a juvenile boy trapped in the body of a man."

"Why do you want to move out?" he asks, and the change of topic has me deflating, my shoulders slumping.

"I don't know. Maybe because my roommate doesn't respect my privacy and is currently naked in my bed. That's just one of many reasons," I tell him.

"Why did you run?"

"What?" I ask in confusion.

"After the game the other night."

"Oh," I mutter, my eyes lowered to his chest and abs that I can't seem to stop looking at. "Because I don't sleep with teammates."

"Then shouldn't you have left *before* you fucked me?"

I try to get up again, but not only does Kohen win the tug of war, but after my ass hits the mattress, he throws his left leg over me to hold me down. It's his injured left leg, so I can't move it away without hurting him, and he knows I won't.

"You don't fight fair," I tell him with a sigh of defeat, relaxing against the comforter.

"What's going on, Roxy?" he asks, his face inches away from mine, but I look at the ceiling instead of his warm, melted dark chocolate and caramel colored eyes. "You obviously wanted me at the time, so what changed afterward?"

"I don't know," I mutter.

"I'm not buying that," Kohen says, grabbing my chin to turn my face to his. "So tell me the truth. Why did you bolt after I told you I hadn't signed the paperwork?"

I blow a breath out and focus again on Kohen's chest while I try to think of a response. Should I tell him the truth? Would he understand? Guess there's no harm in him knowing now.

"If you didn't sign it, then there was nothing to keep you from running your mouth," I finally admit to him.

"So you were all bent out of shape worried that I would tell someone we slept together?" he asks.

"Without the threat of losing your contract hanging over your head, there was nothing keeping you from telling everyone what we did."

"Do you want to know how many people I've told?" Kohen asks, causing my eyes to snap back to his and my heart to stutter in my chest. Fuck. Does everyone on the team think I'm a slut now?

"How many?" I ask, needing to know.

"Zero," he says, causing all the air to whoosh out of my lungs in relief.

"So no one knows?" I ask. "Not even Lathan or Quinton?"

"No one. After you had left, I went back to my room, and Lathan thought I had just gone to get dinner. I didn't correct him," he says. "Which really sucked, because then I couldn't order room service, so I went to bed hungry. And worried all night about where you had run off to."

"Oh," I mutter, unsure of what else to say.

"All you had to do was ask, and I would've told you that I had no plans to spread our business around."

"And how would I have known if I could trust you?" I ask.

Kohen sighs before he answers. "I guess you wouldn't know that until I proved it."

"Yeah."

"So why is it so important that no one finds out?" he asks. Still holding my chin in his grip, he rubs his thumb back and forth underneath.

"Because I want to be the first woman of football, not the first floozy of football," I tell him honestly.

"You're worried about what everyone would think about you sleeping with a teammate?" he asks.

I nod.

"You shouldn't give a shit what anyone thinks. I don't. But I know that you don't have it as easy as the other guys and me."

"Nope. I sleep with one person on the team, and I'm a slut. You could sleep with all the Lady Cats at the same time, and you would get nothing but kudos."

"You ever slept with a teammate before?" he asks.

"Not since high school," I answer.

"Bad experience?"

"Ha!" I bark out a non-humorous laugh. "My dad and I had to move afterward."

Kohen's forehead wrinkles in confusion. "Tell me, Roxy."

Since I've told him everything else, I take a shaky breath and then let it go. "When I was a sophomore, I made varsity. I was even the starter. All of the guys on the team were so nice to me, flirting, buying me shit, inviting me out to dinner and parties. It was nice to feel popular. I thought it was because I was proving myself on the field…"

"It wasn't?" Kohen asks when I hesitate.

"One guy in particular, Tommy, a senior, one of the team captains, an all-state wide receiver, homecoming king, the works, put in an extra effort, and I…I fell for it. He was my first, and that same night I found out the whole team had a bet going, you know, for whoever could pop my cherry first."

"Those callous assholes," Kohen growls. "Did you report them?"

"No. But I got revenge on Tommy, rupturing one of his testicles."

"Holy shit. *That's* how you got the Ballbuster nickname?" he asks.

"Yeah. I hated it at the time, but none of the guys tried to touch me again afterward. They were jerks, making my life miserable in school. So, my Dad quit his job and we moved so I could keep playing football."

"Wow."

"Yeah."

"I'm rethinking having your knee between my legs now," Kohen says, making me laugh. "If you had been about four inches lower with your throw, I would be in some serious pain right now."

"You shouldn't have busted in my room," I tell him. "How did you get in? The door was locked."

"Yeah, but I have the key," he says with a grin.

I scoff. "What if I had been naked?"

"That's why I had to get in here so fast."

"Bastard," I tell him, lifting my knee until it brushes him between the legs. Kohen closes his eyes and sucks in a breath, definitely not because he's in pain. I repeat the motion, and he groans and thrusts his hips forward seeking more contact with my skin.

I'm not sure who moves first. Almost simultaneously, Kohen and I both have our fingers threaded through each other's hair, lips crashing, tongues seeking entrance. It's a frenzy as our bodies try to get closer with one goal in mind. The pulse between my thighs is desperate, needing to be impaled on his thickness that's pressing against my thigh. His deep, penetrating tongue chases every thought but that one from my head and liquefies my bones as they try to melt through my clothing to find the warmth of his naked skin.

Kohen lowers his hand from my hair to grab my ass and roll me on top of him, both of us moaning into each other's mouths the moment our lower bodies perfectly align with only my shorts and panties keeping us from joining in what I know from experience will be ecstasy.

"Off," Kohen orders against my lips as he yanks my tank top up and over my head before going to work on my bottoms, shoving my shorts and panties down my legs as far as he can go. I kick them off the rest of the way and then straddle his hips, positioning my opening on the tip of his cock.

"No, not yet," he says, finally pulling his mouth away from mine. Both of us are breathing heavy as I look down at his face and try to figure out why he put on the brakes. Oh right! We need a condom.

Instead of mentioning the necessary prophylactics, though, Kohen grins up at me and reaches for my hips as he says, "You're not rushing me this time."

With a sudden, insistent tug, I find myself moving up Kohen's body until I'm straddling his face. I don't even know what hit me when his tongue begins lapping at my center. My muscles tense and hips jerk automatically, trying to get away, but Kohen has a tight grip on my thighs, pulling me back down to his hot mouth.

"*Oooh,*" I moan as my body turns limp, surrendering to the sweet torture of my pussy getting fucked by his slick tongue.

"Mmm," Kohen groans against my flesh, making me shudder. "There's that sweet honey I've been craving." He kisses, licks, sucks and I don't even know what else between my legs. No longer trying to get away, Kohen's at risk of suffocating when my hips start slamming down on his talented tongue, begging him for more as I get closer and closer to my release. My limited experience with sex before always felt like getting off a roller coaster at the highest point. Instead of teetering at the top, Kohen takes me right over the edge screaming, giving me the push I needed to ride it all the way through. I had no idea an orgasm could be so intense since he's the first man who's ever put his mouth between my legs.

My eyes are still closed when Kohen eases me down his body and fills me with his cock.

"*Oooh, God,*" I moan, falling forward on his chest as he takes me on the next amusement ride. This one is the mechanical bull, bouncing me up and down on his cock as I try to hang on and not fall off. My fingernails dig into his shoulders, and I bury my face in his neck, gasping with each thrust as he fucks me deep from the bottom. It's so different from when I was in control, riding him on the hotel floor. The fullness is almost overwhelming, but oh so good.

It doesn't take long before I'm climbing up to the top of the roller coaster again, light-headed and dizzy, muscles clenching. My body shakes on top of Kohen's as I ride the waves of every drop and upside down loop, coming on his cock this time while he fucks me through the tremors.

"Fuck, Roxy," Kohen groans. He slams my hips down on his one last time before he grunts and erupts inside me. Once he's finished, he relaxes his hold, soothing his hands up and down my back and over my ass as we both continue to pant, trying to catch our breath.

"Goddamn, that was good," he says, and I nod my agreement against his neck. So good that neither he nor I were quiet about how much we were enjoying it.

"Aren't you worried about someone finding out?" I ask, and Kohen tenses up underneath me.

"What is this? Déjà vu?" he asks. "No one is gonna find out!"

"There are a lot of people right outside the door," I remind him.

"Fuck them," he says dismissively. "If you and I don't tell anyone, then no one will know for sure. Rumors are just that, rumors."

I push myself up on shaky arms to find my clothes, but Kohen pulls me back down on top of him.

"Nuh-uh. You're not gonna run off this time. Besides, I want an encore," he says, grabbing the back of my head to bring my lips down to his, kissing me softly. "Stay with me all night."

"What? No," I answer with a shake of my head. "And you've got all those people here…"

"I don't care about any of them," he says, kissing me again. "They'll all leave eventually."

"If you say so," I tell him. Since I don't want him to leave right now, I relax against him, enjoying the warmth of his body against mine, our tongues casually getting familiar with each other.

"See, this is nice," Kohen says against my lips. "We could've done this if you hadn't run from me last time."

"Sorry," I say, placing a kiss on his chest. "You taste like chlorine."

"Well, you know what that means, right?" Kohen asks.

"What?"

"We need a shower."

"We?" I ask.

"Yeah, because now you've got my chlorine and…various other substances on you."

"Why didn't you use a condom?" I ask him.

"Jesus Christ! This argument again?" He laughs with a shake of his head. "I guess I need to start wrapping my dick up whenever I'm around you in case the mood suddenly strikes."

"Who says it's gonna happen again?" I ask with an arched eyebrow.

"I do," he answers with a slap to my ass. "Tonight. In the next few minutes. I would bet my boat on it."

"Hmm," I reply. "I think I could hold out on you tonight if this boat is at stake."

"No way," he says, pulling my lips down to his again. Forcing his tongue into my mouth, he proves me wrong. There's no way I'm walking away from him tonight. For the last few days, I've regretted walking away from the hotel room. Now that I know it wasn't a fluke and our second time was just as good if not better than the first time together, I want more. Especially more of the magic he works with his tongue between my legs. Feeling his cock hardening underneath me again, I suddenly have the urge to pay him back for his incredible oral skills.

Reluctantly, I finally pull my mouth from his and climb off of him, standing up beside the bed. "Let's go shower," I tell Kohen, reaching for his hand to pull him up. He doesn't resist.

Chapter Twenty-Four

Kohen

Lord help me.

I'm in a steaming hot shower with the most gorgeous woman in the world, and bless her heart, she's in the best position known to man.

On.

Her.

Knees.

Did I mention my cock is in her mouth getting the shit sucked out of it? Hell yeah.

Roxy's blowjob technique is nearly as perfect as her kicking. Whether her mouth is working me deep or shallow, she follows through with her tight fist, and my balls are receiving plenty of attention.

"Fucking…goddamn, Roxy," I grunt between pants, slapping my palms against the shower wall in her guest bathroom to hold me up as my eyes roll back in my head.

In my alternate universe, I've imagined nearly this exact scenario a time or ten, but the reality feels so much better. All I can think about at the moment is, *please don't let her stop* and *how the fuck can I make sure this happens again? And again. And then a few more blissful times before I leave this world for good.*

Holy shit!

Is this how men find themselves in tuxes standing at an altar? They meet a woman who they would gladly die for if it meant being with her just one more time, but pray it turns out to be a few more than that? 'Cause, yeah, I could actually see myself giving up the single life and maybe even my soul to be with Roxy again.

Her beautiful bobbing head, unfortunately, comes to a stop before she lets my dick slip from her mouth, looking up at me with those big, green eyes, droplets of water scattered across her all-natural face. I know it's makeup-free because there are no dark smears around her eyes. She doesn't need any special enhancement to make her more breathtaking.

"Do you want me to keep going or do you want me to stand up against the wall so you can fuck me from behind?" she asks.

Jesus.

The final Jeopardy song plays in my mind as I quickly weigh the pros and cons of those two choices. Actually, there are no cons for either, just pros, so how the fuck am I supposed to decide between those two incredible choices? I can't. It's impossible. Roxy's short-circuited my brain, and I can't think anymore.

"You decide," I tell her, and she nods seriously as if she understands the conundrum she's presented me with.

"I don't want to chance hurting your knee even more," Roxy says before her lips eagerly seal around my cock again and suck my brains out. "And I want to taste you," she quickly adds before going back to work.

I love this woman. Not just because she's giving me a-fucking-mazing head at the moment, but because she chose option A to go easy on my sore knee. She obviously wanted me to fuck her from behind. Otherwise, she wouldn't have brought it up. But she's selflessly finishing me off with her mouth. Which makes me want to lick her pussy again in appreciation. Do you see the vicious cycle being created?

Roxy sucks hard on the head of my cock while squeezing my shaft tightly, and I come with what can only be described as a battle cry.

This is it. She's killed me. My soul leaves my body, floating high above us on a rush of endorphins from an orgasm so intense I think it may have exorcised demons.

I stand there and recover while Roxy finishes washing. When she turns the water off, I still haven't moved, and it has nothing to do with my knee.

"You coming back to bed?" she asks over her shoulder before grabbing a towel and drying off.

"Yeah, definitely." There's nothing I want more than to curl up underneath the sheets with Roxy and stay there the rest of the night. Hopefully, I can ravage her again, but after those two amazing rounds, it may not be right away.

Once I'm dry, I join Roxy, who is already cuddled down in bed like she's cold. I'm looking forward to warming her up. I slip under the sheets and reach for her, bringing her closer until her toned body with perfect curves in all the right places is pressing against me from our chests to our feet tangled together.

"Ow, fuck," I groan when her knee rams mine.

"Shit, sorry," Roxy mutters, quickly rolling away. "Let's just spoon, so I don't hurt you."

"Won't argue with that," I tell her, fitting my hips against her ass.

"Aren't you worried about them trashing your boat?" she asks.

"No," I tell her truthfully. The party-goers could do anything but sink this bitch, and I wouldn't care. It would be worth it to get to stay in this bed with Roxy for a few more hours, her soft skin against mine. I rub my hand over her hip, up the dip in her hourglass figure before cupping her breast, making her giggle.

"So how nervous are you about the game this week?" I ask her.

"Don't remind me," she groans.

"Hey, at least we're at home, and you won't have to worry about any booing or shitty songs," I tell her, thinking about how the Knights played "Roxanne" to throw her off right before the field goal she missed last week.

"That's true," she says.

"Your dad coming to the game?" I ask.

"Nah. He would have to leave tomorrow to drive all the way here and back, which would mean missing several days of practice. I know he wants to, but I told him to wait until they have a break later in the season."

"Why doesn't he just fly? He could leave Thursday afternoon and be here in a few hours; then go back Thursday night after the game or Friday morning."

"Too expensive," she says with a shake of her head.

"Oh."

"I told him I would buy the tickets, but he told me to save my money and not spend it on him. He's stubborn like that."

"Sounds like it," I reply. "At least he wants to come. My parents only use the tickets I send them to wine and dine some high society member so they can convince them to support my dad's election campaign."

"That sucks," Roxy says, grabbing my hand from her breast and intertwining our fingers.

"Yeah," I agree. "Chase comes to home games whenever he can, usually decked out in face paint or with a big sign and shit just to embarrass the hell out of my parents on television. It's hilarious."

"He sounds funny. You'll have to introduce us some time," she says.

"I will. He'll probably be at this week's preseason home opener even if I'm not playing."

"That's sweet."

"Nah, he just loves football and being a part of the excitement in the stadium."

"I can't wait to take the home field for the first time, although I'll probably throw up the first time I have to kick a field goal or extra point.

"You'll be fine," I assure her. "Besides, these games don't even count. They're just to give everyone a few games to work out the kinks and help coaches decide who to cut before the season starts."

"I want to go practice in the stadium tomorrow."

"Good idea," I reply.

"Will you come with me?"

"Yeah, sure. I'll ask Coach Sigmon to make the arrangements in the morning."

"Thanks."

"No problem," I tell her, thrusting my cock into the crease of her ass. "Anything you want, it's yours right now while I'm still buzzing from that double dose of orgasms. Better hurry before the offer expires."

"In that case, I'll take your boat with a side of your Audi."

"Give me a few more nights like this, and that could probably be arranged," I tease.

"Kohen..." Roxy starts, and I can tell by the tone of her voice that I'm not gonna like what she's about to say. "Maybe we shouldn't..."

"Oh, we definitely should," I disagree. To distract her from her argument, I release her hand to slip my fingers down her stomach while placing open mouth kisses on her neck. Roxy gasps when I rub two fingertips over her clit, and it doesn't take long for her ass to start grinding against my hard cock.

Tonight I'm gonna rock her world so many times that she won't be able to even fathom the idea of sleeping alone in her bed without me. I want her desperate for me. Addicted. Then she'll finally know exactly how I'm starting to feel about her.

Sometime around two o'clock in the morning I wake up thirsty and dehydrated from the amount of sweat and other bodily fluids I've lost over the past few hours. The boat finally sounds quiet, like all the party-goers are gone, so I decide to go grab a bottle of water from the fridge and lock up.

I get up still naked from the bed and stumble my way over to the door in the dark. As soon as I turn the knob, I realize how stupid we were to leave it unlocked the whole time. Thankfully we weren't disturbed at least.

Right as I step into the hall, my foot hits something on the floor, nearly making me break my neck. My arms shoot out, and I catch myself on either side of the hallway. The lights still on in the living room show me that the near fall was all thanks to the football on the floor, the one Roxy nailed me in the stomach with hours earlier. I pick it up so I won't trip on it again and neither will Roxy, placing it on the kitchen counter. That's why I see them ---the letters written in a silver marker all over it. Some are full sentences while others are just one word: *honey, beautiful woman, looking gorgeous, tall, beautiful blonde, your leg is one of the best in the league.*

They're compliments, I realize. Not only that, but they're all my words. Well, all but "looking gorgeous" that I recognize as Quinton's words, making me wish they were mine. Strange that she would write all those things on a football.

I grab my bottle of water, lock the sliding glass doors, and then return to Roxy's room to use the john before climbing back in bed with her. There are still several cardboard boxes taking up space on the floor, and I have to maneuver my way through the maze to and from the bathroom. From the dim light coming through the windows, I notice that a box beside her bed is full of more footballs. Grabbing one, I realize that it's softer than the other, like it's losing its air. Recognizing more markings, I carry it into the hallway, using the light from the living room to read it. On this one, there are various words written in black; and, unfortunately, I also remember that some came out of my mouth: *conniving little bitch, Tonya Harding, maneater, manipulative bitch, fucking bitch.*

Why would she write all those horrible things down? And, God, I feel like shit for saying them. When we first met in the parking lot that day, I never gave Roxy the benefit of the doubt. I was wrong, which I realized as soon as I calmed down, remembering that I was distracted. That was all on her too, not that she knew it at the time. It's not her fault that after I saw the photo of her for the first time I was awestruck and needed to see her again.

I wish I could take some soap to my words written on the football and scrub them away, making them disappear from her memory too. But since I'm pretty certain she used a black permanent marker, I doubt that's possible. Maybe from now on I can start giving her more compliments to write instead of hateful comments. There's several I could think of off the tip of my tongue ---fucking gorgeous, breathtaking, best sex I've ever had, blowjob champion of the world, just to name a few.

Chapter Twenty-Five

Roxy

I'm so nervous that my hands are shaking and my teeth are chattering. This is even worse than the game last week, because now I know exactly how much pressure will be on me once I run out of the tunnel with my teammates. Sure, Kohen's right about how preseason wins and losses don't count in the league, but to me, they matter. I've missed a field goal once, and I refuse to do it again.

"Miss Benson, you have a visitor," Melinda, the lady the team hired to be the locker room attendant for the sole female, tells me from the other side of the wall. She's giving me privacy, which I appreciate even though I'm already dressed and ready in my pads.

"I'll be right out," I tell her, figuring it's someone else from the press wanting to do an interview. Like my stomach isn't in enough knots without having to actually talk about being nervous with a microphone and camera shoved in my face.

Grabbing my helmet from the bench, I decide to face the music and get it over with. Maybe it'll be good to have something to keep my mind busy until kickoff.

Only, when I step out into the hallway, there are no reporters. It's just one tall, lanky fan wearing my number three jersey with pale blond hair peeking out from underneath his Wildcats hat.

"Daddy!" I exclaim before throwing my arms around his neck, nearly knocking him out with the helmet still clutched in my hand.

"Good to see you, Ladybug," he says when he gives me a crushing bear hug.

"I'm so glad you came!" I tell him as I pull away to see his face. "But you shouldn't have missed practice. The team needs you."

"So do you. And I only missed this afternoon. I'll even be back sleeping in my bed tonight."

"How is that possible?" I ask him.

"Well, you see, there's this crazy invention with wings and an engine that helps it fly through the air," he answers with a grin.

"You flew? But I bet last-minute tickets were outrageous! I would've paid for them, you stubborn man!" I tell him with a poke to his chest.

"Quit fussing. I didn't pay for them either."

"Did you hitch a ride in the cargo hold?" I tease.

"Nope. Thanks to a friend of yours, I received plane tickets to and from all of the home games."

"A friend of mine?" I repeat.

"Yeah, kind of crazy that he would do something so nice for you after you ran him over with your Jeep..."

"Oh my God. *Kohen* bought the tickets?" I ask in amazement, my jaw falling open.

"Sure did. There was also a note that said they were non-refundable, so I had no choice but to use them."

"Wow," I say with a shake of my head. "I can't believe he did that."

"Paxton is here too, but he pretended to get lost so he could linger around the guy's locker room," my dad tells me, making me laugh.

"That does sound like something Pax would do," I admit with a smile. "Well, tell him he better find me after the game instead of ogling the players."

"Will do," he assures me. "Oh, and I brought you a little something. Thought you might need a good luck charm."

"Daddy, you didn't have to do that. Knowing you're here in the stands cheering for me is all I need for luck," I tell him while he reaches into his pocket and pulls out a tiny white jewelry box.

"You can never have too much luck, Ladybug," he says, lifting the top to reveal a red and black beaded ankle bracelet with the occasional silver ladybug charm mixed in.

"Thank you," I tell my dad, removing the jewelry from the box before wrapping him in another hug. "Now I'll have a lucky leg."

"You're welcome. Now go kick the shit out of some balls for your old man," he says with a slap to my shoulder pads.

"See you after the game?" I ask.

"Of course. Love you, Ladybug."

"Love you too," I tell him with a kiss on his cheek before I bend down to hook the anklet around my right leg and start toward the tunnel to wait for the rest of the team.

The nerves are still there but now subdued thanks to being surprised by my dad and Paxton coming to cheer me on. And then there's the warmth in my chest because Kohen did this for me. He'll be on the field waiting on the sidelines when we run out, and it's gonna be hard not to kiss him when I see his sweet, gorgeous face. There will be plenty of time for that later tonight once we win this first home game.

Kohen

As soon as Roxy jogs out through the smoke when the announcer calls her name to deafening cheers for the first time on the home field, I know from the smile on her face that she's feeling more confident and that she's gonna kick ass tonight. Or more specifically some balls.

Removing her helmet, she jogs over to the sidelines, and I nearly lose my balance from how beautiful she is up close, her long, light blonde hair falling around her shoulders, exuding radiance. This is maybe the first time I've ever seen her look so happy, the love of football obvious in her expression, the worry and hesitation absent.

"Thank you," she says when she's in front of me. "I just saw my dad. You didn't have to do that, but I'm really glad you did."

"You're welcome," I tell her. "It seemed important to you..."

"It was. It is," she agrees, blinking back tears. "Damn you for making me break Roxy Rules one and two." She fans her face subtly.

"Roxy Rules?" I ask with a grin since I have my own rules, ones she has all but demolished.

"Yeah, no sleeping with teammates is number one, and no crying is number two."

"Oh, well I think you need new rules. Or an amendment," I tell her quietly. "Like no sleeping with teammates, except for Kohen."

"Right," she says with an eye roll. "Well, now you know one way to keep getting an invite into my bed."

I run my finger and thumb over my mouth in case any cameras or observers are around before I say my next words. "Lick your pussy until you melt into the sheets?"

"Ah, no. But that may work too," she says, laughing as her cheeks turn red. "I meant surprising me with visits from my dad."

"I'm a little concerned about the oddness of that correlation, but damn if it'll stop me from doing it again," I tell her.

"Having him here just makes me happy," she says. "It's nice to know that no matter how many people are waiting for me to fail, he's cheering for me to succeed."

"He's not the only one," I say. "This whole crowd is cheering for you. Now, aren't you supposed to be doing kickoff today?"

"Oh shit!" Roxy says, spinning around and watching as our other team captains, Quinton, Nixon and Lathan, walk back to the sidelines after the coin toss.

"You're up," Quinton tells Roxy with a grin.

"Shit, shit, shit," she mutters as she tugs her helmet back on.

"You've got this," I tell her. "Just kick it through the back of the end zone, and then you won't have to even worry about possibly being the only person who can stop a run back for a touchdown."

She scoffs and then starts to jog out onto the field with the rest of our special team line.

"Roxy!" I call out.

She stops and turns around.

"Forgetting something?" I ask.

Her eyes widen before she runs back over and grabs the tee from one of the equipment managers, then gives me a thumbs up.

After she takes the football from the referee and stands it up on the tee, I hold my breath, waiting for her kick. I know she can do this, as long as she doesn't panic.

With a raise of her right arm, she leads the charge down the field. Her foot connects with the ball, and not only does she send it sailing through the end zone, but she also puts it dead center through the uprights. Of course, we won't get points for it, but it's still a high note on which to start the game.

Our defensive line gives her high fives as they take the field, and the rest of our teammates pat her on her shoulder pads in congratulations as she comes back to the sidelines.

"Easy, right?" I ask her when she's next to me.

"Yeah, easy," she agrees with a grin. "I just imagined the ball was super light, filled with hot air, you know, sort of like you're head."

I chuckle at her insult. "Always busting my balls."

"I'll kiss them better tonight," she whispers before walking away and leaving me standing there with an ache behind the fly of my khaki shorts.

Chapter Twenty-Six

Roxy

After celebrating the preseason win at a late dinner with my teammates, Dad and Paxton, I take my two favorite people in the world to the airport and say goodbye.

While I'll miss them of course, on the ride home I can't help but smile. Our team won, and I was a part of that win with three extra points and two field goals. I also punted and did all of the kickoffs. Coach Griffin said he was impressed with how good I was helping with field position and that I might have the starting job over Warren.

Parking at the dock, Kohen's car is already back in the lot since he drove separately now that he no longer needs the crutches. I use my key to let myself inside the houseboat; and then once I take a quick shower, I don't even consider climbing into my bed alone. Instead, I tiptoe naked down the hall to Kohen's room, figuring he's asleep but ready to surprise him by slipping under his sheets.

When I open his bedroom door, I realize that he's definitely still awake. Not only that, but there are candles lit up all around the room. And since his room has a sliding glass door that leads to the deck, he has it open, allowing the gentle breeze smelling of the ocean to fill the room.

"This is...wow, Kohen," I tell him, my eyes finally finding the incredible man in bed with his hands propped behind his head on the pillow, a scorching hot grin on his face.

I'm climbing on the bed kissing him before he can open his mouth to respond. He didn't go to all this trouble to try and convince me to fuck him. He did it because he wanted to impress me, show me that he's trying to be more. It's sweet, just like sending my dad and Paxton plane tickets to the home games.

As soon as my tongue slips into Kohen's mouth, he's no longer laid back, relaxing. He becomes an active participant, shoving down the blankets covering him and separating us. Squeezing my ass cheeks in both of his palms, he pulls me against him so that we're skin to skin, not even a thin sheet of paper could fit between us.

"I missed you," he says against my lips, making me smile.

"I just saw you half an hour or so ago," I remind him.

"I've missed touching you. Kissing you. Being inside you," he replies, pressing me down so that my wet pussy slips along the length of his hard cock.

"Me too," I tell him honestly.

When I first came out on the field tonight, I wanted to jump in his arms so badly I couldn't stand it. That also reminds me of the promise I made him earlier, so I move my mouth down to his chest and stomach, kissing and licking his incredible body as I slide lower.

"I'm the luckiest man ever," Kohen says when I place my lips on the tip of his cock.

"Must be all my ladybugs," I tell him with a smile.

Wrapping my fist around the base of his shaft to hold it up, I run the flat of my tongue down the underside of his thickness until my mouth finds the thin skin of his sac. Kohen gasps for air when I roll my tongue around one of his balls and then the other before sucking it into my mouth.

"Fuck, Roxy," he groans, squirming on the mattress. "Get my dick wet and then ride me, baby."

Hearing the need in his voice, I move my mouth back up to his cock, stretching my lips around his girth to suck him deep over and over again until he's nice and slick. I don't stop until Kohen grabs my hair to pull me off of him and up his body. He brings my lips crashing down to his with one hand while the other reaches between us to shove his dick inside me. I'm so ready for him that he slides right in without any resistance. My body greedily takes him deep inside me, and I moan in pleasure while bearing down on his fullness.

"God, I need you to move," Kohen groans, but I shake my head.

"Can't. Feels too good." Rocking forward on him, my clit hits the base of his cock, and I nearly combust. I vaguely hear Kohen grumble before I find myself on my back, him above me for the first time ever.

"Wait. Your knee," I warn him, afraid he'll hurt himself.

"Worth it," he says as he begins to pound into me, fast and hard.

"Deeper," I urge him, digging my fingernails into his tight ass to try and keep him inside. I love having his big body above me, on me, dominating me as he fucks me.

Kohen slips a hand between us, pressing it down on my pelvis and slamming his hips into me, making me cry out from the amazing pressure.

"That's all your sweet pussy can take, baby," he tells me. "A shame because I've got more dick for you. My balls aren't even slapping your ass."

"*Uhh, Kohen,*" I cry out, my back arching in need as the pressure in my core starts to build. When Kohen suddenly pulls out, I whimper in protest right before I'm flipped over, face down on the pillow.

"I need it deeper too," Kohen says. Kneeing my thighs wider apart, he grasps my hips, lifting them while shoving forward.

"*Ughhh, God!*" I moan when he hits the spot inside me that's never been touched before.

"Fuck, that's good," Kohen grunts between pumps of his hips, each thrust knocking the head of his cock against the ballooning pressure growing inside me, his balls slapping rapidly against my sensitive clit until I combust while screaming his name.

The explosion is so intense that I blackout for some length of time. When I come to again, blinking my eyes open, the first thing I notice is that I'm sprawled over Kohen's chest, and his lips are moving along the side of my face. Then I hear his soft words.

"*It's believed that she first came to Earth by lightning, sent by the goddess of love and beauty.*"

"The legend of ladybugs?" I ask him with a euphoric smile, having read something about the Nordic belief before.

"The legend of Roxy," he says before his lips cover mine.

When we break apart minutes or hours later, I ask Kohen, "Is your knee okay?"

"Never better," he answers, bending it, raising it in the air.

"Good," I say, swirling my fingertips over the smooth skin of his abdomen.

"Next week I may be able to start practicing again," he tells me.

"Really?" I ask, lifting my head to see his face. "That's great!"

"Jon said we'll start slowly at first."

"Yeah, but that's a good sign that you're doing so well," I reply.

"Don't worry; your job's still safe for the next few weeks."

"I don't care if I ride the bench," I tell him honestly. "Just being part of the team is the biggest accomplishment of my life. One that so many people told me would never happen."

"Yeah," he says, placing a kiss on the top of my head. "I know. It's just...I wish we could both start, because I see how much you love the game."

"You're better than me," I tell him. "Less likely to miss."

"Maybe. Maybe not," he says with a sigh. "But the difference in us is that I've never really loved football."

"Seriously?" I ask in shock. "What's not to love?"

"Soccer was my passion. Football was just a way to earn a scholarship in college, and a big payday in the professional league."

"So, you do it for the money? Really?" I ask in surprise.

"Don't forget the women," he adds with a wink.

"Whatever," I grumble.

"I would never have had all this if I were still playing soccer. Instead, I'd be living in a tiny apartment, probably working a part-time job just so I could pay the bills and play."

"That sucks," I say, thinking about what I would be doing if I hadn't gotten the call from the Wildcats. Well, I would've been miserable. Is that how Kohen feels about not playing soccer?

"Everything will work out," he eventually says with a squeeze to my shoulder. "Let's try and get some sleep. I bet you're exhausted from the game and all."

"Yeah," I mumble into his chest. "Should we blow out the candles before we pass out?"

"Nah. They're LEDs," he says, followed by a chuckle. "You think I would risk a candle catching fire on my boat if I'm out at sea? No way."

"Smart," I agree. "Oh, and I've been wondering, why did you decide to turn the master bedroom into a gym and sleep in a guest room?"

"Long story for another day," he replies sadly, followed by a kiss on the top of my head. "Good night, baby."

"Night, Kohen," I reply before drifting off to sleep.

Chapter Twenty-Seven

Kohen

When my brother Chase texts me he's in the stadium half an hour before the last preseason game kickoff, I head up to the family suites to find him.

Unfortunately, a conniving bitch from my past finds me first.

"Kohen!" Lola exclaims overly sweetly from behind me.

Before I turn around, I pray that during the past offseason her physical appearance has finally morphed to match the evil inside. Turning to face her, I'm disappointed to see that she's just as stunning as ever, and motherhood agrees with her. Her raven hair is now a pixie cut, but she's pretty enough to pull off the short hair. Wearing what's probably a yellow designer dress made to look casual, her charcoal eyes glow with glee since she's probably counting all the dollars her husband is making down on the field.

"How you doing, Lola?" I ask with a heavy sigh. It's not as if I can be an asshole to her like I really want. There are too many people wandering around us in the family suites, most of who know the two of us not only dated but were engaged before she started screwing Coach Powell. Yet another thing about her I hate besides the heartache, insecurities and loss of self-esteem she single-handedly caused. She also made everyone on the team and most of their family members feel sorry for me, the pathetic kicker who got the boot from the woman he loved.

"I'm wonderful, as always, but I was sorry to hear about your accident. Such a shame that little twit hit you and took your starting spot," she says, instantly causing a surge in my blood pressure.

"Roxanne's not a twit, and she didn't take my spot," I correct, the words mumbled since they have to try and force their way through my clenched teeth.

"Yes, that's right. Her name's Roxanne, like that old song about a whore," she replies with a fake smile, her insult so fucking hypocritical it's laughable.

How I not only managed to tolerate this woman for a year but actually considered marrying her is beyond me. Was I simply so stupid and naïve that I was blinded by her looks? Lola's still undeniably a very attractive woman. Any man would agree. But seeing her here now, after falling asleep with Roxy in bed beside me every night for the past two weeks, and waking up to not only her breathtaking physical beauty but the gorgeous, sweet woman I'm learning she is on the inside, well, Roxy makes Lola look like a hag.

"You know, in that *whore* song," I start, "maybe Sting was actually just begging for a woman he couldn't afford. And maybe the real problem he didn't understand about Roxanne was that unlike most other women, she simply couldn't be bought by anyone."

Lola's evil, manipulative brain is still trying to figure out what the hell I was talking about when my brother finds us.

"Excuse me, ma'am, do you happen to have any more trays of those spicy, hot wings?" Chase asks Lola with a fake uppity accent before feigning recognition. "Oh, shit. Sorry, Lola. I thought you were one of the food service staff."

With an indignant scoff, she storms away, and I offer him a subtle fist bump behind her back.

"Nice," I tell him. "She'll probably have nightmares about having to work in a kitchen."

"Thank fuck you didn't marry her and spawn tiny, money-grubbing panhandlers," he replies softly so only I can hear.

"Wow, that's sort of sad. Now I'm picturing dirty little people holding up cardboard signs," I tell him.

"Yeah, ones that say *My mom will suck your dick for a dollar*," he whispers.

"You're horrible," I say, unable to hold back my bark of laughter. A second later I hear a familiar voice across the room say, "*Could we get two more of these? Thanks, hon!*"

Spinning around, I find the source just in time. Roxy's friend, Paxton, holds up his bottle of beer to Lola, who vanishes from the suite. The man pulls off uppity a little better than my casually dressed brother since he's wearing another suit like the last time I saw him. Next to him is a tall, blond man, Roxy's father, wearing a Wildcats jersey with his daughter's number on the front. "Let me go introduce you to Roxanne's people," I tell my brother, leading him over to the two men.

"I overheard your whole exchange, her basically calling Roxy a whore and couldn't resist," Paxton says when we're next to him.

"Thanks. She deserved it," I say not bothering to fill him in on my and Lola's past. "Paxton and Mr. Benson, this is my younger brother Chase. Chase, this is Roxanne's best friend and dad."

"Nice to meet you," Chase says as they all shake hands. "I bet you're proud. Your daughter's giving my brother a run for his money."

"Hey now!" I speak up. "She has been under my tutelage for the past few weeks, so I have to take a little credit for her success."

"I know Roxy appreciates your help and letting her stay with you. She loves the boat, and I hope I get an invite one of these days," her dad says with a grin.

"She's staying with you?" Chase turns to me and asks, making me cringe since I haven't told him about that.

"Coach just wanted to keep her out of the press and make sure assholes stay away from her," I explain to Chase, avoiding his dark eyes.

"And they leave her security in the care of a cripple?" he teases, gesturing to my knee brace.

"Only a few teammates know about my houseboat, so she's safe there," I say while heat warms my face, remembering all the ways I've been *taking care of her* the last few weeks. "Well, I better get back down to the field," I tell them. "You guys have fun, and we'll see you after the game."

"See ya, Kohen, and thanks again for the plane tickets," her dad says before I can make my escape.

"I'll walk you down," Chase tells me, following along.

"Don't start –" I warn him after we leave the family suite.

"Did you, the man who swore he would never ever buy a woman anything again, give them plane tickets?" he asks as we walk past the concession stands and navigate through the crowd of people starting to fill the stadium.

"None of your business," I tell him softly.

"You did! Why? Oh my God. Are you fucking her?" he whispers, making my feet come to a stop to face him.

"Keep your mouth shut," I mutter under my breath.

"Have you lost your mind? What about the rules? Your play-it-safe playbook or whatever?" he asks.

"Roxy's...different," I say.

"You're blind because you're in love with her!" he exclaims.

"No, I'm not blind," I quickly rebuff. "And I've only known Roxy a few weeks so I'm not –"

"I thought you didn't trust her, but even though you've only known her a few weeks, you're letting her live with you, buying her family plane tickets. What the fuck are you thinking?"

"It's not like that, and I do trust her," I say. "Mostly."

"And what happens when you're ready to play, and you have to take back your starting spot from her? She's gonna be pissed, right?"

"No. Yes." I tug down the collar of my gray Wildcats tee since thinking about Roxy on the bench while I play makes me feel like I'm being strangled. Will she be upset and kick me out of her bed? I don't want to hurt her or lose her and what we have. It may be new, but it's amazing, and I'm not just referring to the sex. Knowing she's under the same roof with me is enough to make me so fucking happy.

"Look, yes, I wish we could both play," I tell my brother. "But it's not up to me. Coach will decide, and I'm fine with that. Hopefully, she will be too."

"Yeah. Hopefully," Chase mutters.

Between my brother's doubts and having all the shit from my past resurfacing after seeing Lola, I just want to have this game over with so Roxy and I can climb under the sheets tonight and make the rest of the world disappear. When I'm with her, everything is perfect and makes sense. The doubts and worries fade with the slightest brush of her lips or touch of her fingertips on my skin.

Sure, I may not be able to trust her one hundred percent yet, but I'm getting there. She has her own hang-ups about us too, worried our teammates will find out we're sleeping together and think she's a slut. Not that she has to worry about me running my mouth. We absolutely cannot let anyone know we're together now that I've signed the contract addendum, or I'll be out of a job.

"Kohen! How's rehab going?" Coach Griffin asks as the offensive line finishes warming up on the field.

"Great. Jon says there's a fifty percent chance I'll be ready next Sunday," I tell him. With everything that's been going on today I haven't even had a chance to tell Roxy. Or maybe I just didn't want to find the time to tell her she might be sitting on the bench as soon as next week since it's the first game of the season where it matters if we win or lose.

"Wow, that's sooner than we expected," Coach replies. "I don't want you to rush, but we sure could use you to start the season off right as soon as you feel up to it."

"You'll be the first to know if I'm ready," I tell him.

"And if not, you'll be the one to decide who we should put in, Roxanne or Warren."

"I decide?" I repeat for clarification.

"Yeah, Robert's orders," he explains. "We want you in when you're ready, but until then, Roxanne and Warren are aware that it's your call. I'm gonna let Warren give a field goal try a go tonight, but I already have my doubts that he can hack it."

Hold on a minute.

"You've already told her --- I mean, Roxy and Warren that I'll be making the call on who plays?" I ask with a nagging suspicion.

"Yeah," he answers with a nod.

"When?"

"Huh?" he asks, his brows drawing together.

"When did you tell Roxy that?" I ask.

Coach takes his hat off and scratches his head. "Well, I remember Robert giving her a heads up the day she signed her contract."

Motherfucker.

Has she been playing me so I would, in turn, play her?

Is this why Roxy hasn't been able to keep her hands off of me? Not out of guilt or genuine attraction? Was she trying to seduce me to secure the starting spot? God, I'm not sure if I'll ever be able to stop wondering if every single thing she does is a manipulation.

It sucks that I can't trust her, but Roxy hasn't exactly made it easy for me.

Chapter Twenty-Eight

Roxy

Tonight, Kohen was quiet on the sidelines, and I'm not sure what's going on with him. Our team won, despite the field goal Warren missed. Coach Griffin wanted to try him out in a game before the season starts, and now we know that he's not ready for punting or placekicking. I, on the other hand, not only punted well but made a fifty-yard field goal and two extra-point kicks.

At dinner, I got to meet Chase, Kohen's cute younger brother. While he acted pleasant enough, for some reason, I got the feeling he was giving me the cold shoulder or evil eye most of the meal. Either way, we made it through dinner; then I took my dad and Pax to the airport while Kohen said goodbye to Chase. His brother insisted on driving the three hours or so back home instead of staying with us.

When I step onto the dark boat, illuminated only by the dock lamps, I notice Kohen is sitting on the deck, looking out into the still marina water like he's deep in thought.

"Hey, you okay?" I ask as I approach.

"Hey," he replies quietly. When he doesn't say anything more, I take the seat next to him, ready to wait him out.

It's so beautiful out here in the marina, away from most of civilization, the water calm and relaxing. Yet, there's still a knot of worry in my belly, wondering what's been going on with Kohen all day. Finally, he speaks.

"I might be ready to play Sunday."

"That's great, Kohen!" I tell him, scooting to the edge of my seat because I want to jump up and hug him, but I don't since he's putting off *leave me alone* vibes. "Why don't you sound happy about that?" I ask.

"Because if I start, you won't."

"Yeah, so? You're the better kicker. Don't feel bad about that. Remember my Jeep and I are partially responsible for why you've missed the preseason games."

"If I can't play, who should start, you or Warren?" he asks, finally turning his head to look at me, his eyes darker, mostly melted chocolate without the caramel in the glow of the lamps.

"Is that a trick question?" I ask him, but he doesn't respond or crack a smile, just silently looks at me, waiting for me to answer. "Okay, let's see, I've made all but my first field goal in the preseason games and haven't missed any extra points. Warren's only had one try, but it was an easy, thirty-yard field goal, about the same distance as the standard extra point, and he missed."

I stop and wait for Kohen to agree or comment. He doesn't.

"If you're not sure, then we can have a kickoff next week in practice," I offer seriously. "I'll even break out the blindfold again because Dane was better than Warren."

That finally gets a reaction out of Kohen. He smiles, and my entire body warms and relaxes at the sight. "That was pretty funny to watch," he says.

"Yeah, it was hilarious when he was hauling bags of balls around the field as the Wildcat mascot too," I mutter. "Guess I embarrassed him so badly he felt he had to threaten and assault me..."

"Fuck, I'm sorry," Kohen says, reaching for my hand. When I accept, he pulls me to my feet and then down onto his lap, wrapping me in his arms. "I'm sorry," he says again into my hair. "You're right. You were so much better than Dane, and you're a helluva lot better than Warren. You'll start if I don't."

"Let's not worry or think about any of that right now," I tell him, winding my arms around his neck and placing a wet, open-mouthed kiss on his throat. "Tonight, I just want to think about you and me."

"Deal," Kohen agrees. He threads his fingers through my hair, bringing my mouth to his; and by the time our tongues meet, everything else around us has already disappeared. This kiss is different from all the others before it, and there have been a lot of kisses over the last few weeks. No, tonight, our kiss is not frantic and desperate. It's slow and sweet, while still sensual with the promise of more to come. There's no rush to get undressed, although Kohen does position my legs on either side of his waist so that I'm straddling him, my mound rubbing over his hard cock underneath his zipper with every slight movement. Only a few layers of clothing separate us.

The two of us kiss for what feels like hours, dry humping each other slowly, deliberately. Unlike most other times we've made out, Kohen's not caressing my breasts or grabbing my ass. He's just holding me to him, as tight as he can.

At some point, by mutual agreement with no words spoken, I stand up and slip off my shoes and clothes while Kohen pulls his shirt over his head and undoes his jeans, shoving them down without removing them. Once he's ready, I climb back on his lap; and then we make love in the same, slow, easy motion of my hips with his, our mouths staying connected, sharing breaths while we share our bodies outside on his boat. It's the most intimate I've ever been with anyone, and I never want it to end.

Chapter Twenty-Nine

Kohen

I wake up Friday morning to find Roxy's side of my bed empty. It still smells like her melon daiquiri shampoo, but I want the real thing, her, naked, so I can spoon against the warmth of her incredible backside.

A few weeks ago, if given a choice, I would have rather swam with sharks than slept in the same bed with a woman. Waking up with someone means you see them as more than a good time, a quick fuck. That shit is serious. Not a night has gone by that Roxy and I haven't shared a bed, whether it's hers or mine; it doesn't seem to matter. There's an unspoken rule that every night we have wild monkey sex before falling asleep together. Except for last night.

Last night on the deck was something entirely different. After I had realized what an idiot I was being for thinking she was using me to get the starting position when she's just, in reality, the best for the job, I wanted to apologize for all the horrible, unfair shit I thought about her. More than that, I wanted inside of her heart and soul.

I'm falling in love with Roxy, and that scares the fuck out of me. It means letting down my walls, overcoming insecurities and trusting her completely. The last time I let someone in, they took advantage of my blind love and devotion. Lola used me as a stepping stone on the team to get what she really wanted, and I fell for it. She made me think I wasn't good enough for her, and I hated how much that hurt. I never wanted to go down heartbreak road again, and maybe that makes me too cautious with Roxy. If I want her in my life, though, I need to man up and stop thinking she's out to screw me over like Lola.

The smell of cinnamon and maple syrup pull me out of my thoughts. The scent of food burning is oddly absent. Rolling out of bed, I pull on a pair of boxer briefs and head to the kitchen to investigate.

"Morning!" Roxy says when she sees me. "I made French toast. Hungry?"

"Ah, yeah," I answer, working the stiffness out of my knee as I move close enough to kiss her cheek, inspecting the two plates of food. "Huh. Not a speck of black on them."

"Hush," she says, turning around to face me with a smile and swatting my bare chest. "I only burn things in the oven, not on the stove."

"Good to know," I tease.

"It's a beautiful morning. You wanna eat out on the deck?" she asks, reaching up to rake her fingernails suggestively down the center of my chest and stomach, coming unfortunately to a stop at the top of my waistband. Now that I know she's thinking about what we did out there last night, I am too.

"After breakfast, I want dessert," I tell her, grabbing her hips to pull her closer.

"Deal," Roxy says, meeting my eyes with her heated ones. "We've got the whole day off, weekend too…"

"You're still gonna get in a few good workouts," I warn her.

"Coach Dildo gonna whip me into shape?" she teases.

"On the boat it's the Captain you need to worry about," I tell her, grabbing her hand and pressing it against the growing bulge protruding from my boxer briefs.

She squeezes me through the fabric, making my eyes nearly roll back in my head. "The Captain?" she asks, and I nod, unable to form words at the moment with all the blood rushing to her fist. "Feels like he could use some help with his…seamen."

I chuckle at her ridiculous joke right up until my boxer briefs pool around my ankles, and Roxy goes down to her knees on the kitchen floor. Holding my cock, she opens her mouth and looks up at me before she starts greedily sucking.

And that is how one of the best weekends of my life started.

Roxy

Friday morning after Kohen and I have breakfast, he decides to take the boat out to sea. I'm not sure how far he drives; but when we come to a stop, only the Atlantic Ocean surrounds us. It's like we're alone on our own private island.

"I love this," I tell Kohen while snuggling up against him where we're stretched out on the round, white chaise lounge, pillows propped up behind our backs. Out on the deck, the sun is warming us from above while the calm waves below rock us gently. "I didn't know something so peaceful existed."

"Me either," he says, pressing a kiss to the top of my head. "And out here we don't have to hide from anyone."

Knowing we can't be seen together like this out in public makes me sad. I wish we could enjoy this type of happiness everywhere, not just when we're alone at night. But the risks are too great for my reputation and Kohen's career, so we'll just have to make it work. It's a small sacrifice to have something so wonderful.

"Thanks to you, I've been thinking more about soccer recently," Kohen says.

"Oh yeah?" I look up at his face to ask him. "Is that a good thing?"

"Over the last few years, everything's been about football. I've forgotten how much I missed playing."

"If you wanted, you could join a community team during the offseason, right?" I ask.

"It all depends on if I get a contract extension and, if so, whether or not the team will approve me to play another competitive sport. I mean, I know it would be a huge liability if I were to hurt my knee again or receive any other type of injury and couldn't kick," he explains, his desire to play his favorite sport again obvious.

"But it's worth it to you?"

"Maybe," he answers with a shrug. "The boat's paid for, and I have some money in savings. I would just have to figure out how to afford the rest of my bills."

"I could help," I offer. "I mean, if I'm still staying here, it's only fair for me to pay for rent or at least the marina fees."

"Yeah, that could be a short-term solution, if necessary," he says, making it clear he wouldn't be comfortable with me helping him financially, but I'm glad to hear that it sounds like he wants me to stick around.

"Do you want me to keep staying with you?" I ask for clarity. "Just because we're together now, I don't want you to think I have to live with you so soon."

"No, I like having you here," he says with a kiss to my cheek. "And it's the easiest way for us to keep this a secret."

"That's true," I admit. "And I like having someone to share my days and nights with."

"Yeah," he answers with a chuckle. "Even though it's only been a few weeks, I've already forgotten what it was like to live alone. All I know is that it sucked."

"Being with you is different from having roommates. Definitely better since I don't have to listen to anyone having sex a few feet away from me," I tell him with a smile.

"And how often were *you* the one having sex a few feet away from your roommate?" he asks gruffly, sounding jealous.

"Never," I answer.

"Good."

"I slept with guys in *their* dorms or apartments."

"Fuck. I could've lived forever without that information," Kohen grumbles.

"There were only four guys in college and the one asshole in high school," I tell him honestly. "I'm guessing you had a quite a few more hookups than I did."

"A few," he answers with a grin. "But I already feel more for you than all of them combined."

Hearing that makes my heart swell even more for this man. Kohen already owns my body that constantly craves his touch, and now I'm pretty sure he possesses the missing piece of my soul.

Chapter Thirty

Kohen

On Monday, I'm back on the field first thing. No rehab, just practice for the first time all season.

Instead of sitting idly by while watching Roxy, I'm right there with her, warming up with a quick jog, stretching out on the ground beside her. And then, we're lining up at the thirty-three-yard line to practice extra-point kicks.

She nails her first one, and I...miss, the ball going wide left. Huh.

Maybe I just haven't warmed up enough. It was my left knee that was fucked up, so I didn't expect to have any real problems making it through the uprights using my kicking leg, the right one, once I was cleared for play.

I lay down while Jon comes over and stretches me out a little more, watching as Roxy moves back five yards at a time, making every ball our equipment guys give her.

"How did your left leg feel?" Jon asks while pushing my left knee to my chest.

"Fine," I tell him.

"You work your leg over the summer?"

"Of course," I tell him. Not only did I run a few miles almost every day, but I spent at least an hour in my home gym doing leg lifts, squats and the whole drill. At least twice a week I went out to the local college field and practiced kicking from near and far. Just a few days before the accident I made a sixty-five yarder, so my leg was in perfect condition.

Once I'm back on my feet, I practice a few air kicks and then set up the metal tripod holder to try once more from the thirty-three. Again, the ball careens to the left, but thankfully slips through the goal post.

I make the forty-yard try but miss again at the forty-five.

"Are you planting your left leg enough when you kick?" Roxy comes over and asks.

"Yes," I mutter in frustration.

"Well, you've got all week, so don't rush and overdo it today," she says. "Maybe you just need a little more time to recover."

"I'll be ready on Sunday," I tell her, even if there is a shred of doubt that five days isn't enough time to get back to where I was before she hit me. And, yeah, the accident is still a nagging thought I can't seem to get rid of.

Chapter Thirty-One

Kohen

We've just finished dinner Friday night when my cell phone suddenly starts pinging with new messages. I haven't looked at it in a few hours, so I grab it off the kitchen counter to check emails and shit while Roxy does the dishes --- manually, since she's still not confident enough to use the dishwasher.

As soon as I open up my text messages from Lathan, I see a photo of Roxy and me kissing on the front deck of the boat. It had to have been from just the other morning when she made me breakfast and right after she gave me a blowjob in the kitchen.

It takes a few seconds before the panic sets in.

Someone took our photo.

Who the hell was it? And how the fuck did Lathan get a copy?

I scroll back up to the beginning of his messages to read through them. I see "holy shit" and "gossip rag" before "Kohen, you are so fucked."

Just when I was about to get back on the field, this shit comes out? Ruining me. It's only a matter of time before the team's management calls and tells me I've been cut for violating that fucking contract about not touching Roxy.

"You okay?" Roxy asks, glancing at me over her shoulder.

That's when everything starts making sense. Since the very first day I met her…

"Did you do this?" I ask.

"Do what?" she asks, grabbing the dish towel to dry her hands before turning around to face me. God, with her hair up in her pajamas, she's so damn beautiful. Even now. And I'm a fucking idiot. All over again.

"You fucked me over, that's what!" I exclaim, barely refraining from throwing my phone that's clutched in my fist.

Roxy reels back from my harsh words. "Kohen, what's going on?"

"Did you hire a photographer? Is that why you insisted we have breakfast outside that day?"

"A photographer?" she repeats with a scrunched forehead. "I have no clue what you're talking about, so please just calm down–"

"Bullshit!" I yell. "That's why you freaked out. In the hotel room, after you fucked me the first time and then found out I hadn't signed the contract. You were planning to screw me over the whole time! And like a complete dumbass, I signed that shit and then fucked you again anyway!"

"No, I didn't –" she starts, but I interrupt.

"Shut up, get your shit, and get the fuck out of my house!" I tell her.

Roxy gasps before her shoulders slump forward and big green eyes glisten, breaking out her killer acting skills.

"Kohen, wait. Just talk to me! You-you can't mean that –" she says as she starts to come closer to me.

"Yes, I do," I assure her, holding my hands up to ward her off while seeing red. "You better stay the fuck away from me," I warn.

Chest heaving, I find my keys and get the hell off the boat, so angry I don't even trust myself around her, another woman I thought I loved, but she was only playing me.

Now, because of her, I've lost everything.

Chapter Thirty-Two

Roxy

After kicking every black marked football in my box through the uprights, I slump onto the grass at the twenty-yard line, not caring if it's wet. My face is too, so now my ass can match.

Hugging my knees to my chest, I can't stop thinking about the photos of Kohen and me. The ones that have been popping up all over the Internet. Who the fuck took them? Sure, the marina isn't private property, but only Kohen's teammates and family know his houseboat is there.

"Room for one more in your pity party?"

I squint into the early morning sun up at Quinton, wondering what he's doing out here so early.

"Yeah, sure. But you better have brought your own tissues. I'm all out."

Chuckling softly, Quinton takes a seat next to me on the grass. "So you and Kohen are more than roommates? I had wondered…"

I stay silent, figuring there's no reason to spread more rumors.

"You worried they're gonna boot him?" he asks.

"Yep," I answer. That's why I didn't sleep at all in the hotel room bed last night. "And Kohen, of course, thinks this was all part of my evil plan to screw him over."

"Fuck."

"Ditto," I agree with a sniffle.

"So then just talk to management and try to convince them to keep him. And find out who the fuck took the photos to clear things up with Kohen."

"Sounds easy," I mutter sarcastically. "I'll get right on that."

"You won't know unless you try, right?" he asks.

"He signed the contract," I tell him. "Actually, he didn't. Not at first. After we started…being more than roommates, he told me that by some oversight he never signed one. So, the bitch that I am, I got another copy and forced his signature on it."

"Hmm. That's not good," Quinton offers helpfully, stretching his long legs out in front of him.

"No, it's not."

"So, why would you have him sign it if you two were more than roommates?" he asks.

"I was...it's stupid," I admit, pulling up a blade of grass and sniffing it. The oniony smell has always comforted me, reminded me of home and made me happy. "I didn't want Kohen to tell anyone about us. With the contract hanging over his head..."

"He would have an incentive to keep his mouth shut," Quinton finishes.

"Yeah. But now Kohen thinks it was just me plotting to bring him down, like Dane. Like when I ran him over."

"One of those was an accident, and the other was completely different. Dane threatened you and tried to force himself on you. He had to go. Maybe they won't kick Kohen off the team."

"I never wanted to take his job from him," I say. "When I came here, I thought I would sit on the bench and learn from him until he decided to retire or go to another team. He should have the starting spot because he's better. That's the truth, but he'll never believe me."

"He doesn't trust you."

"Definitely not," I agree, tossing the blade of grass and plucking a new one.

"You ever wonder why that is?" Quinton asks.

"Because I ran him over the first day we met?" I offer.

"No, maybe his trust issue doesn't have anything to do with you. What if that's been his hold up for a while now?"

"What do you mean?" I ask, turning to face him. His jet-black hair is growing out but still taking the shape of a rooster's comb.

"Kohen ever tell you about Lola?"

"Ah, no. Lola? Why? Who the fuck is she?" I ask, unable to help the surge of jealousy at the unknown woman.

"Kohen's ex-fiancée."

Oh my God. He was engaged to marry some woman?

"When was that?"

"A few years ago," Quinton answers. "They broke up my first season actually. Because of me."

"What do you mean?"

"I was new to the team, didn't even know all my teammates' names yet. Kohen threw a party to celebrate buying his new houseboat. That night I met a beautiful woman, one who flirted with me, and things got heated pretty quickly. We fucked, and then I found out she was Kohen's fiancée."

"Holy shit!" I exclaim.

"Yeah. Kohen went apeshit on me, thought I knew about them and screwed her anyway. I may be a player, but I also have morals and had no fucking idea they were seeing each other. Of course, I wouldn't have touched her if I had known..."

"Wow."

"I felt bad and never even thought about her again. But she didn't disappear after stomping on Kohen's heart."

"What do you mean?" I ask.

"She married Coach Powers a few months later."

"No shit? The team's defensive coordinator?"

"Yep. They just had a baby together, a girl, I think. So, now can you see why Kohen may have trouble trusting women?"

"After that sort of past, yeah," I agree. "Poor Kohen. What a bitch!"

Quinton reaches over and grabs one of the discarded balls. "Manipulative bitch," he reads from it. "Bingo. We have a match."

Kohen and I both have been screwed over by people we cared about and who were supposed to give a shit about us. But this time, he's wrong about me. I just have to figure out a way to show him that I care about him.

Pulling out my phone from my coat's zipper pocket, I call up Winona. "Hey, girl. How are you holding up?" she answers.

"I need your help," I tell her.

"Anything."

"Can you find out who took the photos? And, more importantly, how they knew which one out of all the dozen or so marinas in town was Kohen's?"

"I'll try my best," she says. "You still laying low?"

"As low as I can go," I assure her.

"Good. I'll call if I have any updates."

"Thanks, Winona," I tell her before ending the call. "Will you go with me to try and meet with management?" I ask Quinton.

"Lead the way," he says, getting to his feet.

Luckily, the owner, manager, coaches and PR team were already gathered in a conference room discussing the situation when I showed up. I went in and stood before them as confidently as possible even though most of them were in expensive suits and I was in a ragged pair of shorts and pink jacket with grass all over me. Had I even showered before I left the hotel room? Nope, don't believe so.

"Thanks for giving me a moment of your time," I tell them. Someone offers me their chair, but I decline, wanting to stand up, take responsibility and get this over with. "I'm sure you've all seen the photos of Kohen and me together. And I know he signed the same agreement as everyone else, but he shouldn't have. He and I have been...romantically involved for several weeks. I should've brought it to the team's attention or quit or something, I'm not sure what. Well, I shouldn't have started anything with another teammate..."

"Miss Benson –" one of the men start, but I interrupt him, knowing he's going to say it's too late. That I can't change their minds.

"Please don't punish Kohen for something that was entirely my fault. I-I'm the one who made the first move on him. It was stupid, I know. But have you ever just cared about someone so much that nothing else mattered? I guess what I'm trying to say is that he was more important to me than this chance of a lifetime. So, I'm the one who should be released from the team, not him..."

"Miss Benson –"

"No, please," I beg, blinking back tears. "He's much better than I am, and maybe he's not back to where he was last season, but he will be. And again, it's my fault for hitting him with my Jeep. I have done *nothing* but hurt him since I got here, and I'll do anything it takes to keep him from losing his job as the team's starting kicker."

"Miss Benson?"

"Yes?" I ask, sighing in defeat.

"Could you please sign a written statement declaring that you and Mr. Hendricks were having a consensual relationship?" one of the lawyers asks.

"No!" I exclaim, gritting my teeth in anger and crossing my arms over my chest. "I won't sign anything for you to use to get rid of him. Did you hear anything I said?"

"Miss Benson," the owner, Mr. Wright, starts. "As long as you and Mr. Hendricks were having a consensual relationship, he won't be going anywhere. This document is just to protect him and the team from possible future lawsuits if the relationship were to…end badly."

"Huh?" I mutter in confusion.

"No part of your contract or his says that romantic relationships between teammates are not allowed. The same would have applied even if you had been male," Mr. Wright clarifies.

"But the contract addendum…"

"Was for *your* protection in cases of unwanted misconduct like that of Dane Adams."

"Oh."

"So will you wait in the lobby until the document is drafted to go ahead and sign it today?" one of the lawyers asks. "You can call in your manager too since she'll need to sign off on it as well."

"Sure. Absolutely," I say. "I'll get her in here right now."

"Great, so glad that's settled," Mr. Wright says. "Now if you'll excuse us, we have to make plans for our first home game of the regular season."

"Oh, right. Sorry for all the trouble," I tell them, quickly slipping out the door.

"So?" Quinton asks when he stands up from the waiting room chair.

"There's no problem," I tell him with a smile. "Kohen gets to stay, and everything is fine. I just need to sign a statement assuring everyone that it's consensual."

"Wow, that's great. See, I told you everything would work out," he says, offering me a hug.

"Yeah," I agree. "Now if I can just figure out a way to convince Kohen to trust me."

Chapter Thirty-Three

Kohen

The end is upon me.

Saturday afternoon, I'm sitting in the team's administrative office lobby, waiting for them to give me the axe.

This moment is a long time coming. It's almost as if I knew from the second I saw Roxy's face on the projector screen that first day that she was gonna be my downfall. Even knowing that I couldn't resist her. Sure, I'm angry at her for screwing me over, breaking my heart and taking away my career, but it's my own damn fault.

"Come on in, Mr. Hendricks," a guy in a suit I don't recognize says to me when he opens the conference room door.

I get to my feet, aware that my left knee seems to shift a little to the right under my weight before I walk into the room, a death march of sorts.

"Have a seat," the same guy says, motioning to an empty chair. I glance around as I lower myself down, seeing the team's manager, owner, Coach Griffin, Coach Bradley and two men in suits are present.

"I'm sure you know why you're here," the owner, Mr. Wright, starts.

"Yes, sir."

"So, the only question we have for you is whether or not you were in a consensual, romantic relationship with Miss Benson."

"I know what it looks like," I tell them, remembering every single last detail from the four photos that the press got their hands on thanks to Roxy. One was of me leaning down to kiss her in her chair on the deck, one of the two of us standing while lip-locked, and two dark photos from the night we had sex outside on the deck. In the first of those, Roxy is still dressed, in another, her naked skin glows in the darkness, her breasts and ass blurred out. Knowing someone was watching such a private, intimate moment makes me want to break shit. And then thinking that the moment wasn't even real makes me want to destroy everything in my sight. "I know what it looks like," I say again. "But honestly I don't know what we were. It wasn't a relationship…"

"It wasn't?" Mr. Wright asked, confusion wrinkling his brow.

"No. It was a lie. She made me sign the contract addendum, and then she...coerced me outside so that someone she set up could photograph us, making it look like we were together."

"Huh. That's not what Miss Benson said," Mr. Wright replies, leaning back thoughtfully in his leather chair.

"Then she's lying. And it's complete bullshit that none of you can see the manipulator she is. She wanted me gone so she could have my spot, and it worked! That's why I'm here, right? For you to give me my walking papers?" I ask in annoyance, fists clenched so tightly my fingers may break.

"You think Miss Benson wants you kicked off the team? That she set you up trying to get rid of you?" Mr. Wright asks calmly, which irritates the fuck out of me even more.

"Yes! That's exactly what she did!" I assure him.

"Then why do you think she came to us earlier today and begged us to keep you and release her from the team instead?"

"Because that's what she does! She manipulates...Wait, what?" I ask, my words drying up as his statement begins to sink in. Was that a trick question?

"This morning, Miss Benson came storming in here, without an appointment, and said you two were in a relationship and that she's the one who pursued you so you shouldn't be punished."

"Really?" I ask in shock. She tried to save my job? Was that an act too, trying to save face with management?

"Really," Mr. Wright says. "She signed a statement assuring us that not only was the relationship with you consensual but one, and I quote, 'based on mutual respect and great fondness.' Is that not correct? Because there's no provision in your contract regarding relationships with fellow teammates."

"There's not?" I ask.

"No. The contract addendum was to protect Miss Benson from men like Dane Adams."

"Oh."

"So, we need you to read over the same statement with your manager and sign it as soon as possible, unless you still contend Miss Benson was manipulating you?" he asks, arching an eyebrow to show his opinion on the issue.

"No, sir. I'll sign it," I tell him, swallowing past the football size knot in my throat. All the horrible shit I said about Roxy...this whole time I didn't want to believe her or trust her...

"Good," Mr. Wright says with a nod. "So, now we need to decide who will be starting in tomorrow's game. It's your decision. Will it be you or Miss Benson?"

Holy shit. Is he serious? I'm really not fired. Roxy stepped up to try and protect me, throwing herself under the bus to do so, only to find out we weren't even doing anything wrong. Now, her worst nightmare has come true. The photos of us hurt her more than me. They undermine her as a serious athlete, making everyone think she's just screwing around with a teammate. But we are more, *were* more, before I ruined the good thing we had by accusing her of being behind the photos.

"Mr. Hendricks?" the owner asks again to get my attention. "Who is going to be starting?"

"Oh, well, that's easy," I tell him. "You've gotta go with the best."

Chapter Thirty-Four

Roxy

I'm dragging ass when Winona and I walk out of the stadium. After we had grabbed a bite to eat to try and come up with a statement to release about the photos, I made a tough decision. There wasn't much to tell any more about Kohen and me. Now, it was nothing more than I fucked a player a few times and then he kicked me out of his house. But Winona was able to get the photographer to give her the name of the person who sold us out to try and catch us together --- Dane fucking Adams.

That's when I made a tough decision. One I should've pursued weeks ago but didn't want to draw more bad press. The thing is, assholes like Dane need to be punished by the criminal justice system, or else other women could become his victims, especially if they don't have a Quinton nearby to call for help.

So, I told the team's management my decision, and they agreed to do whatever it takes to help me pursue the communicating threats and sexual assault charges against Dane in court. Their PR team and Winona worked on a collaborative statement to release about what happened. Earlier tonight I showered, put on a dress and went before the cameras. Sure, this is only gonna make the media circus worse, but I owe it to all the other female athletes to do the right thing --- standing up to assholes like Dane instead of letting him get away with what he did.

"You good?" Winona asks when we walk up to my Jeep in the dark, mostly empty parking lot.

"Yeah," I tell her, digging my keys from my purse. "Thanks for all your help today."

"No problem. Anything you need –" she starts to say when I open my driver side door and then we're standing in the midst of a football avalanche as dozens of them come pouring out from my driver seat.

"What the hell?" I ask, jumping back in surprise as all the pigskins bounce and roll around our feet.

Since the dome light is now on inside the Jeep, I can see that every inch of the interior is filled with balls, which is why so many came pouring out when I opened the door.

"That's a lot of balls," Winona says from beside me. She picks one up from the ground and hands it to me, showing me the writing on it. Just three words written in silver marker stops my broken heart...

"*I'm an asshole,*" Winona reads over my shoulder.

I throw the ball down and pick up another one that says, "*You're breathtakingly beautiful.*"

"*I'm sorry,*" Winona reads aloud from another ball. "*Please forgive me.*"

"Wow," I say, feeling my broken heart mending a little more with each word, knowing they're from Kohen.

"Very sweet," Winona says, glancing around the puddle of pigskins. "Not very convenient, but sweet."

Then I pick up the football sitting in my seat with the most powerful message of them all.

"*I'm falling in love with you.*"

I reread the sentence over and over again, running my fingertips over the words, not quite believing they're real.

"Can you give me a ride?" I ask Winona since I'll have to figure out what to do with all the balls before I can drive my Jeep again.

"Sure," she says.

I shut the door of my SUV, leaving the balls on the ground since it's an impossible feat to stuff them all back inside. Still holding the last football, I climb into the passenger's seat of Winona's car and give her directions to the marina.

Chapter Thirty-Five

Kohen

The boat is quiet and lonely without Roxy. In just a few shorts weeks I got used to having her around, and it was nice. Really nice. But I fucked it up.

I hate seeing her empty bedroom. I can't even sit on the deck without thinking about her. The kitchen reminds me of all the food she burnt and, of course, the day she flooded it with dishwasher bubbles. In the workout room, I try to blast loud rock music and sweat her out of my system, but it's no use. She's gotten under my skin, wiggled her beautiful way into my heart, and seared her goodness within my soul.

Why I ever thought she was anything like Lola, I'm not sure. Lola was only looking for the easy way out, a free ride, a life of luxury, uncaring about who she hurt or anything else to get there. Roxy has worked her ass off on the field to be able to compete at the level of all the men in this sport. She doesn't ask for anything from anyone, preferring to go at it alone, probably because the teammates, who were supposed to support her when she was a teenager, let her down. Now, I've let her down too, and I'm not sure if she'll ever forgive me. That doesn't mean I won't stop trying, though.

Imagine my surprise when she knocks on my sliding glass door a little after ten that night. I nearly break my neck in my rush to get to it before she leaves. Although I assume she still has her key, so I'm not sure why she didn't let herself in. Maybe because the last time she was here I told her to get her shit and get the fuck out.

"Hey," I say after I unlock the door and slide it open.

"Hey," she says shyly. I'm not sure if she's ever been more gorgeous than she is right now, standing before me in a sleeveless, knee-length evergreen dress with a conservative V down the front. The color makes her grassy green eyes shine like a lighthouse in the darkest night until they lower to the football in her hands.

"You found my balls?" I ask, the phrasing instantly causing a smile to spread across her face.

"I found your balls," she repeats, looking back up at me. "Thank you."

"I thought you could use some new ones that say all the right things I should've said to you."

"Dane sent someone to take the photos," she blurts out. "It wasn't me."

"I know, and I'm sorry I accused you. I should've known you never wanted that sort of image out there in the media."

"Right. Well, the team's actually fine with everything. I was surprised, but they are. They'll probably ask you to sign a statement..."

"I already did," I tell her. "They said you came in and stood up for me. Thank you."

"And thanks again for the balls," she says, taking a step backward as if to leave instead of coming inside.

"You're starting tomorrow," I tell her to stop her from leaving.

"Why?" she asks, forehead crinkled. "You're ready. It's fine; I can sit the bench, Kohen."

"No, it's not fine. You're better than me," I tell her. "At least for right now."

"I don't know –"

"It's already been decided. You're the best kicker for the team."

"Really?" she asks with a grin.

"Really," I assure her. "I'm not sure what will happen once my knee heals, if it ever fully heals, but we'll figure it out. Okay?"

"Okay," she agrees with a nod. "I wouldn't mind just being the punter once you take over placekicking. I'm pretty damn good at it."

"Yeah, you are," I tell her with a smile. "So, can I convince you to come back? Stay with me again?" I ask.

"I don't know," she replies, biting her bottom lip.

"I miss you," I tell her. "So damn much. Who's gonna burn my food and flood my kitchen if you're not here?"

"Hush," she says with a laugh, slapping me in the chest. I grab her arm and pull her to me, covering her lips with mine. We kiss softly at first, and I wait patiently until she opens for me, allowing my tongue to slip inside, teasing hers. Her watermelon scent floods my senses, and like a Pavlov response, my mouth waters and I need her so much I can't stand it.

"Give me another chance," I say when we both come up for air. My forehead rests against hers while holding her in my arms, and she's still gripping the football between us. "It won't happen overnight, but I want to trust you with my heart."

"Quinton told me about Lola," she says, and hearing that name is like nails on a chalkboard.

"Why?" I ask. "To brag about how she wanted him instead of me?"

"No, he told me what a bitch she was. How she screwed you over when you trusted her. Loved her."

"Oh," I mutter.

"But I'm not her, and I would never hurt you," she says, kissing me again. "At least not on purpose. Just don't walk out in front of my Jeep again."

"Deal," I tell her.

"So, um, did you mean this?" she asks, holding up the football and spinning it around to the writing above the seam.

"Yes," I tell her with a grin.

"Good," she replies. "Because I've been falling in love with you too."

"Good," I respond, taking the ball from her and tossing it over my shoulder. Hands now free, Roxy wraps them around my neck; and just as our lips are about to meet again, my cell phone starts vibrating in my front pocket. "Ignore it," I say.

"Kind of hard to," she says with a grin, grinding the front of her body against the same pocket. It stops vibrating and then starts again.

"Fuck," I grumble, finally letting her go with one hand to pull it out. "Lathan," I inform Roxy when I see his name on the screen. "Let me just make sure nothing's happened to his mom."

"Yeah, sure, answer it," Roxy urges.

"What's up?" I say into the phone, but quickly have to pull it away from my ear when I hear a baby screeching like a banshee on the other end. "Lathan?" I ask, looking at the screen again to make sure it really was his name showing up.

"Yo, Kohen! Do you know where Roxy is?" he shouts over the screaming in the background.

"Ah, yeah. Why?" I ask in confusion. "And is that a baby?"

"Yeah, does Roxy know anything about making them, like, stop crying? Can you and her come over to Quinton's? There a...situation."

"A situation?" I repeat, looking at Roxy, who I'm sure can hear every yelled word he says.

"Yeah, you won't believe this, but someone dumped a freaking baby on Quinton's doorstep with a note saying it's his."

"Holy shit," I mutter.

"Tiny little guy. We were just watching it sleep in its plastic seat thing, and then all of a sudden it woke up and started wailing. Now it won't stop."

"We're on the way," Roxy shouts, which causes me to frown.

"Really?" I ask her, covering up the microphone. "We were about to have really hot makeup sex, weren't we?"

"Yeah, but all the baby crying has sort of killed the mood," she says with a wince. "Come on, they need our help."

"Fine," I grumble into the phone. "We're on the way. Tell Quinton we're even now."

"Thanks, Kohen!" Lathan says before hanging up.

"I'll make it up to you later," Roxy says with a poke to my chest before running her fingernail down to the waistband of my jeans.

"Promise?" I ask.

"Promise," she says, stealing a quick kiss.

Chapter Thirty-Six

Roxy

"Wow. Quinton's house is huge," I say to Kohen when he pulls into the oceanfront mansion's driveway. We're in Kohen's Audi since mine is still slam packed, literally balls to every wall.

"No shit. It's almost as big as Quinton's ego," he answers with a laugh.

Illuminated only by the porch lights over the double staircase leading up the front of the stone fortress, it's impossible for me to count the number of windows that make up the sprawling Mediterranean style home.

After we both climb out of the car, Kohen comes around to my side and grabs my hand, weaving our fingers together.

"No more hiding," he says, bringing my knuckles up to his lips to brush a kiss over them.

God, this man...

"And I want everyone to know you're mine," he adds as we walk up the steps together to the front door.

"I'm yours," I assure him with a face-splitting smile, glad to have all the horrible drama behind us.

Before we even press the button to ring the doorbell, the sounds of a screeching baby can already be heard.

While we wait, a thought occurs to me.

"Oh, so I want to keep all of your balls, but I'm not sure how to get them home. How the hell did you cram them in there anyway?" I ask Kohen while we wait for the door to open.

"You really should lock your car, by the way," he says with a grin before ringing the doorbell again, since they apparently can't hear it over the noise. "I had help. Paid Ryan, one of the equipment guys, for the cost of the balls plus his time and assistance. Tomorrow we can see if he has a truck or something to unload them into."

Lathan finally opens the massive door with Quinton standing behind him, now quadrupling the sounds of the crying baby. Both of their heads of hair are messy and disheveled, a pair of blond and black Mohawks gone off the rails as they look back and forth between Kohen and me in a panic.

"Help?" Quinton asks, directing the question at me.

"Why me? Do you just assume that I know what to do with a baby because I'm a woman?" I tease him, crossing my arms over my chest to look indignant while my ovaries are practically jumping up and down with the urge to run inside and wrap the little banshee in my arms to provide some comfort.

"No. Maybe. Yes!" Quinton shouts, covering both of his ears with his giant palms. "You're the only one I trust not to break my son. I mean, if he really is my son," he rambles with a wince. "Even if he's not, it wouldn't be cool to break someone else's baby, right?"

"Explanation accepted," I say as I push past them into the house. Kohen doesn't let go of my hand, which the guys immediately notice.

"Whoa. So this is, what, like official now?" Lathan asks Kohen while my ovaries lead the way to the living room.

"Official," Kohen yells to be heard.

"And Quinton said you both get to stay on the team?" Lathan asks.

"Yep. And Roxy's starting tomorrow," Kohen tells them as they follow behind us.

Jeez, this place is huge. But we're definitely getting closer.

"Congrats!" Lathan yells to me as we reach the epicenter of the crises.

"Thanks," I raise my voice to reply.

A gray baby car seat with blue trim is sitting alone in the middle of the fancy wooden floor.

"Has he been in that seat the whole time? That's at least one reason he's crying. He wants out; wants to be held."

When I step around in front of the car seat, I gasp and fall to my knees in my dress.

"Oh my goodness!" I say as I let go of Kohen's hand to start unbuckling the harness straps over the teeny, tiny baby boy. He's definitely a newborn, barely taking up any space in the seat, dressed in a blue and white striped beanie hat and a blue fleece outfit complete with adorable footies.

Once I pull his arms free, I scoop him up with a hand behind his back and the other cradling his delicate head. As soon as I get him settled, tucked in the crook of my arm, his cries lessen. When his head turns toward my breast with his open mouth leading the way, it's obvious the little guy is hungry.

"Did he come with a bottle by chance?" I look up to ask the guys and realize they've all taken a seat on the floor, Kohen on my left, Quinton to my right and Lathan behind the car seat.

"I think so," Lathan says. Getting to his feet, he goes and grabs a black diaper bag from the sofa and brings it over, retaking his seat on the floor.

"Wow, he's little," Kohen says. "No bigger than a football."

"Yeah, he's probably just a few days old," I tell him.

"That can't be my kid, right? I mean, my baby would be, like...ten times his size," Quinton says.

"Actually, genius, even big men start out as little babies, otherwise how would women push them out?" I explain to him.

"Got a bottle, but it's empty," Lathan says, holding one of the small four-ounce ones up in the air. "Can't you, like, you know, whip it out and let him eat?"

"Oh my God," I mutter, rolling my eyes in exasperation. *Men.* "My jugs are empty. Only having a baby fills them up. Jeez."

"Ohhh," they all mumble like this is breaking news.

"Okay, Lathan, look through the bag and see if there are any containers that say infant formula," I tell him, speaking slowly so that he can keep up.

"How do you know all this baby stuff?" Kohen asks.

"I babysat in the offseason around our neighborhood when I was a teenager," I tell them, looking down at the cute little guy rooting around on my dress. "Babies were my favorite," I say, then immediately worry that the mention of me loving children might freak Kohen out. "I mean, I don't want one. Well, not right now or anytime soon because my kicking career would be over, but someday..."

"Yeah, me too," Kohen says, his eyes warm with meaning behind them. Depending on how things go, he thankfully hasn't ruled out that sort of future for us someday.

"Found it!" Lathan shouts, holding up a small canister. His loud voice makes the baby start fussing again. "Shit, sorry."

"Okay, all we need now is water. Quinton, you got any filtered or purified water?" I ask him.

"Ah, yeah, the kitchen faucet has a purifier on it."

"Good. Why don't you do the honors since you'll be here alone with him tonight?" I suggest.

"What the fuck? No, you guys can't leave him here with me! I don't even know how to, like, pick him up or whatever. He'll just scream, and we've got our first game tomorrow! I need to be rested and ready!"

"Calm down," I tell him. I understand that he's nervous because he's never done this before, and also probably freaking out about the possibility that the baby is his. But if so, then he's gonna have to step up and figure out how to be a father. "I'll show you how to do everything you need to know before we leave. Then we'll come back over in the morning to check on things before we go to the stadium, okay?"

"Who's gonna watch him during the game?" Quinton asks me.

"Guess we've got a few calls to make tonight," I tell him. "First, take the bottle to the kitchen, put four ounces of water in it and then however many scoops the container says to add for four ounces. Easy, right?"

"Um, yeah," Quinton says as he gets to his feet and takes the bottle and canister down the hall.

A few minutes later he comes back with a bottle full of water and undissolved powder.

"Great, now shake it until you can't see the powder chunks floating around and have a seat on the sofa," I tell him.

Like a giant robot taking orders, he does as I asked with a blank expression on his face. Once he's settled against the armrest, I cradle the baby while pushing myself off the floor and take the bundle over to him.

"What are you doing?" Quinton asks as I start to lower the baby to his arms.

"Showing you how to hold a baby." I tuck the little guy in the crook of his right arm and slip mine out from underneath. "There, you're doing it."

"Wow. He's so…light and warm," Quinton mutters while he looks down at the baby boy, holding what could be his son for the very first time.

"Let me see your phone," I tell Kohen, who pulls the device out of his pocket and hands it to me, the crack still down the middle of the screen. I snap a few quick pictures before I lift Quinton's left hand still gripping the bottle and bring it to the baby's lips. He takes the nipple into his mouth with no hesitation and starts drinking it down.

"He was hungry. He's a growing boy," I say while snapping a few more photos. "Especially if he's gonna be six feet six like his daddy."

"He may not be mine," Quinton argues with a frown.

"If it turns out he is yours, do you have any idea who the mother may be?" I ask, taking a seat on the sofa next to Quinton. Kohen settles down on my other side, grasping my hand in his again.

"No. No name on the note," Quinton answers. "All it said was, *I can't do this anymore. He's yours, I'm certain of it. You would have known about him sooner if you read your mail.*"

"Wow. Okay. So first thing's first, let me call the local hospitals and police department just to make sure we don't have someone's stolen baby. Then, you'll need to go get a DNA test on Monday, probably take him to a pediatrician and get him checked out too."

"Yeah," Quinton says, his forehead creased in thought.

"In the meantime, try to think of who you may have slept with around nine months ago, so the end of December? If he was born a few weeks early, maybe the first of January?" I offer.

"Ugh, don't remind me," Lathan says when he slumps down into a brown leather recliner. "January second we lost big time in the first round of the playoffs."

"Aw, fuck," Quinton mutters, leaning his head back against the sofa. "That was a bad night. I got shitfaced doing a bar crawl with Cameron and Nixon. I made them both drink a shot for every dropped pass of mine, and I had to do a shot for every interception I threw. For the *entire* season. We all lost count around the tenth or eleventh one. I woke up the next morning naked except for my shoes in the back of a cop car with three different club wristbands on."

"Shit, dude. I didn't know that. Did you get arrested?" Lathan asks him.

"No, but only because the cops were apparently big fans. They said they picked me up on an indecent exposure call when I was wandering around Nixon's neighborhood. Since they recognized me, they drove me around until I woke up and gave them my address. When I got home, I signed some jerseys and shit to thank them for not throwing my sorry ass in jail or selling me out to the paparazzi."

"So you think the mother is someone you hooked up with that night?" I ask him.

"Maybe. That's the only night of my life that I don't remember all the shit I did."

"And since you didn't keep it in your pants, now you've got a baby on your doorstep," Lathan says.

"We still don't know for sure that he's mine," Quinton replies.

"In the meantime, though, he's your responsibility," I tell Quinton. "Once he finishes eating, I'll show you how to change him. Kohen, can you and Lathan go to Target and buy some newborn diapers and a pack and play?"

"A pack and what?" Kohen asks.

"I'll send you a text with pictures," I tell him with a kiss on his cheek.

"Okay, but when I get back, you and I are going home," he says when he stands up. "Sorry, Quinton."

"Yeah, yeah. I'll make Lathan stay to help out," the quarterback says.

"No way, bro," Lathan argues. "At least one of us needs to be fresh and ready tomorrow; and since my dick is free and clear in this situation, it's gonna be me."

Quinton snorts. "I'll take a crying baby any day over your long, miserable years of suffering with your virginity."

I gasp in shock at that surprising revelation the same time Kohen speaks up and says, "Amen."

"While I would rather you keep your big mouths shut about my personal shit, I'm not ashamed," Lathan says, his cheeks reddening despite his words. "If this baby is yours, you'll have to spend the rest of your *life* taking care of him," he tells Quinton, who blanches at the thought. "And, Kohen, you nearly lost your million-dollar career because of your dick. So, tell me again what I'm missing out on by *not* sleeping around?"

The guys remain silent.

"I approve, Lathan," I tell him. "One day, you're gonna make a woman fall in love with you even harder when she finds out that you waited your whole life just for her. She'll feel cherished and special."

"Thank you," Lathan says to me with a small smile.

"Hopefully she won't have already worked her way through an entire football team before she finds you," Kohen responds pessimistically, so I elbow him in the gut. "Ow."

"Don't you have some baby shopping to do?" I ask Kohen.

"The sooner we get this done the sooner we go home, so I can remind you how cherished and special you are," he says with a quick kiss that deepens.

"Don't forget the condoms," Quinton interrupts.

"Mood killer," Kohen says when he gives me a final kiss before leaving.

Kohen

Lathan and I get back to Quinton's house with the baby supplies. And while the three of us try to follow the directions for setting up the portable bed thing, Roxy holds the sleeping baby. I was amazed by how much she knew about taking care of kids and pretty damn impressed. One day she'll make a great mother, and I really hope it'll be with our babies.

"I can't believe someone could just leave their baby behind, especially one as adorable as he is," Roxy says after we set up the baby bed in Quinton's room and lay the little guy down to sleep.

"Yeah, and I'm clearly the wrong man to pick for the job," Quinton says, taking a seat on the foot of his king bed.

Roxy made a few calls, but no one has reported a missing baby. Thankfully Quinton's parents are coming to the game tomorrow and agreed to babysit their potential grandson. After that, who knows...

"You'll figure it out," Roxy assures him with a squeeze to his shoulder. "And who knows, maybe she'll show back up in a few days."

"Maybe," he says sadly.

"Well, I'm gonna head out," Lathan tells us. "See you all tomorrow. Good luck, Quinton."

"Thanks," Quinton replies.

"We better get going too," I tell Roxy.

"Yeah, it's getting late," she replies reluctantly, her green eyes locked on the sleeping baby. "But now you've got my number, so you can call if there's an emergency," she says to Quinton.

"Okay, thanks, Roxy," Quinton tells her before the two embrace. And, yeah, a few weeks ago I would've lost my shit in a jealous rage, but I trust Roxy and know her and Quinton are nothing more than friends.

"Thank you too, Kohen," Quinton then says to me, offering a fist bump, which I hit.

"No problem. See you in the morning," I tell him before leading Roxy into the hallway with a hand on her lower back.

"You're really good at this baby thing," I tell Roxy, who stops and turns around to flash me a smile.

"You think so?" she asks.

"Definitely. But how's your mood now? Still slaughtered thanks to the crying baby?" I ask her, sweeping a strand of her long, blonde hair behind her ear.

"I'm pretty sure you can revive it," she answers, reaching up to drape her arms around my neck.

"How about I start with mouth-to-mouth?" I ask, brushing my lips over hers several times in a row while flattening her against the wall with my body.

"Oh yeah, that's doing the trick," she whispers.

"Here?" I ask her against her lips, knowing she'll understand exactly what I'm asking.

"Here," she quickly agrees.

"Changed our minds. We're staying, Quinton," I yell out.

"Thank God," he replies in relief before I pull Roxy into one of the guest bedrooms and lock the door.

Yanking her emerald dress over her head, I tell her she can keep her matching heels on for now.

"I think it's time for the field goal fantasy," I tell her as she slips her lime green thong off and crawls up on the bed.

"Field goal fantasy?" she asks while I finish undressing. She stretches out on her side with her head propped up on her elbow to watch me. "Does this fantasy happen to involve my legs raised in the air while your balls slam into my...end zone?"

"Oh my God, yes," I groan when she nails it. "That's exactly the one."

Finally naked, I stroll to the end of the bed and pull Roxy by her foot until her ass is on the edge of the mattress. Lifting her high heels, I rest them both on my shoulders. My palms glide up and down her long, gorgeous limbs before I drag one finger through the center of her uprights, parting her wet folds.

"Important to...stretch and warm up first," I tell her, easing one finger in and out of her tight pussy before adding another finger to get her good and ready for me.

"Mmm, yeah," she moans, closing her eyes and biting down on her bottom lip. Her fists tightly clutch handfuls of the bedding on either side of her body.

"Fuck," I groan, withdrawing my fingers. "Time's running out. You're too fucking sexy for me to wait any longer," I tell her as I reach down and start to line my cock up.

"Don't miss," Roxy teases with a smile, still playing along with my fantasy.

"Never," I assure her as I press forward, filling her, stretching her to take all of me inside of her. When I can't possibly go any further, I wrap my fingers around her thighs, gripping them so I can pull out to slam home again until I'm balls deep.

"Ohmygod, yes!" she shouts, her back arching off the mattress.

"Is it good?" I ask when I pick up the pace and start pumping into her over and over again.

"Yes! It's good. *Sooo good!*" she moans. "*Harder! Ugh! Right there!*"

"God, I love makeup sex," I tell her, watching her tits bounce with each and every one of my powerful thrusts. She's so beautiful laid out before me, giving herself to me in every single way. Nothing has ever felt as perfect as being with Roxy, and to think that I almost fucked up and lost her for good is terrifying. "I'm so sorry I was a dick to you, baby."

"Don't stop! I'm...this close...to forgiving you," she gasps, holding up her finger and thumb to indicate an inch.

Reaching down, I work my thumb over her clit until she cries out with her release, her body bucking against mine as I finish inside of her.

Kissing one of her ankles that's still next to my face and then the other with the ladybug charms, I let her legs go so Roxy can lower them. She squirms back further up the bed, and I climb over beside her, holding her while we catch our breath.

"Forgiven," she says with a sweet kiss to my nose.

"Not yet," I say. "But I'll keep trying to make it up to you."

"Tell me what the rest of your balls say," she demands with a grin, and so I spend the next half hour telling her about all the messages written just for her.

Roxy is an amazing woman, and I don't deserve her. Even after I was such an asshole to her, she's given me another chance. And I know that this time I won't let her down.

Epilogue

Roxy

Today's the last game of the season, which is sort of sad. The Wildcats didn't make it to the playoffs this year, but there's always next year. Our star quarterback and tight end have both had a few life-changing distractions this season, but we also had a tough schedule.

Over the next few months of the offseason, I'll be organizing a new all-girl football camp sponsored by the Wildcats, which is so exciting, and Kohen also got his wish. Not only did he just sign a two-year contract extension, but he also has permission from the team to play soccer during the spring.

"I think you should kick this last one," Kohen says to me after Quinton throws a ten-yard pass for a touchdown with the game clock winding down.

"What?" I ask Kohen over the cheers since we're playing our last game at home. "Your knee hasn't bothered you in weeks, and this is a gimme kick."

Since the fourth game of the season, Kohen has been the team's starting placekicker, back to his normal ass-kicking self, and I've been punting, which is great because sometimes I even get a chance to tackle the returner. Kohen has made every kick this season except for a fifty-five yarder in a windy New England stadium, so I have no clue why he wants me kicking this extra point.

"Come on," he says, slapping my shoulder pads. "You started this season, so I think you should end it."

"You know I haven't kicked for a score in weeks," I remind him, poking with my finger in the center of the yellow six on his jersey.

"Like you said, it's a gimme. No point in arguing, I make the calls, remember? Let's go, and I'll hold for you," he says, grabbing me by the arm to pull me onto the field.

Fine, if he wants me to kick the last one, I'll kick the last one. We're up by thirteen with only a minute to go in the fourth quarter. Still, if I miss, though, I'm gonna kick his ass.

Pulling my helmet on, I line up and quickly count my steps backward and to the left. Kohen's kneeling in position, waiting for my signal, which I give him with a nod. The ball's snapped, and just as I start to take my steps, I see two words written in silver ink and realize Kohen's not holding the tip of the football with his index finger but some sort of tiny square box. Too late to stop my forward momentum, I haul back and kick the ball anyway, watching as it sails right through the middle of the goal posts. Fuck yes!

When I turn back around to Kohen, he's still kneeling, holding a ring box in his palm.

"Oh my God," I gasp as he opens the box, revealing a diamond ring. The entire stadium has gone silent, or maybe I've blocked the crowd out, focusing on one gorgeous man before me, on his knee...

"Roxanne Benson, I started falling in love with you the first moment I ever saw you. Literally," Kohen says with a wink and flashes me a smile. "Now, after how amazing the last few months have been, I can't imagine my life without you. You're sweet, driven, funny, and gorgeous. I know you can't cook worth a shit or operate kitchen appliances very well, but none of that matters to me. I love every single second I have with you. So, will you do me the honor of wearing my name on the back of your jersey? Will you marry me?"

Kohen

Forget days, hours, or even minutes. The defining moments of my life have always been measured in seconds. To most people, seconds are inconsequential, too small and insignificant to count. Yet, if you string a few together, it could be the difference in winning or losing, being the hero or a chump, starting a new life with someone or getting kicked in the nuts by the ballbusting woman you love.

Football stadiums aren't the only place where everything can change in a matter of seconds, but that's exactly where I was when my life was forever altered in one second with the uttering of one single word.

"Yes!" Roxy exclaims, tackling me down to the ground. Our stupid helmets and pads are in the way as I try to get closer to her. Remembering where we are with thousands of people watching, I get control of myself and only give her a quick kiss after we sit up and manage to get our helmets off.

"I knew you would say yes," I tell her as I pull the ring from the box and slip it on her finger.

"Oh really?" she asks with an uncontrollable grin as the crowd roars in celebration around us.

"Yeah, because I had a few lucky ladybugs backing me up."

Looking down at her finger, Roxy finally sees the ladybug and flowers accented with red rubies, intertwined on each side of the platinum band leading up to the diamond solitaire.

"It's perfect," she tells me. "I love you."

"I love you, too," I say with another kiss. "Now. Forever. Always, baby."

The End

You'll get to see more of Roxy and Kohen in Quinton's story!
Look for *Perfect Spiral* in 2017!

ABOUT THE AUTHOR

New York Times bestselling author Lane Hart lives in North Carolina with her husband, author D.B. West, their two daughters, a few lazy cats and a pair of rambunctious Pomeranians.

When Lane's not writing she spends her free time relaxing at the beach while looking for sea turtles in the summer months and cheering on the Carolina Panthers in the fall.

Connect with Lane:

Twitter: https://twitter.com/WritingfromHart
Facebook: http://www.facebook.com/lanehartbooks
Website: http://www.lanehartbooks.com
Email: lane.hart@hotmail.com

Find all of Lane's books on Amazon!

Made in the USA
Middletown, DE
26 April 2018